# AMONG THE STARS

## by
## G. David Nordley

Brief Candle Press titles
by G. David Nordley

TO CLIMB A FLAT MOUNTAIN

THE BLACK HOLE PROJECT
(with C. Sanford Lowe)

AFTER THE VIKINGS

PRELUDE TO STARS

# AMONG THE STARS

Brief Candle
Press

Publishing History
Previous versions of these stories were published as follows:
"Barriers" *The Magazine of Fantasy and Science Fiction*, October 1992
"In his Image" *Analog Science Fiction/Science Fact*, August 1992
"War, Ice, Egg, Universe" *Asimov's Science Fiction Magazine*, October 2002
"Hell Orbit" in *Visual Journeys,* Hadley Rille Books, 2007
"The Forest Between the Worlds" *Asimov's Science Fiction Magazine*, February 2000.
"The Fountain" *Asimov's Science Fiction Magazine*, June 2013
"The Touch" in *The Age of Reason,* SFF Net, 1999

All other material is original to this work and is printed with permission of the author and publisher.

First published in 2014 by Variations on a Theme

Cover design: Brief Candle Press

First Brief Candle Press edition published 2015
www.briefcandlepress.com

ISBN: 978-1-942319-04-7

# DEDICATION

To Gerald Perkins (1944-2007)

# ACKNOWLEDGMENTS

My thanks to Dawn Minette who was the first reader for Barriers and the second for In HIS Image (the late Algis Budrys was the first), and to the Whensday People writer's group for their gift of time as first readers on the rest of these stories. Thanks also go to Gardner Dozois, Sheila Williams, Stan Schmidt, Eric Reynolds and Kris Rusch for buying these stories, and to Deb Houdek of Variations on a Theme for buying them again for this collection.

G. David Nordley, February 2014.

# PREFACE

*Among the Stars* is the first of several new collections in Variations on a Theme's project to make my backlist available in modern print and electronic media. These stories comprise most of my interstellar short fiction as of 2013. Excluded are the Trimus Stories, which will get their own collection, "Fugue on a Sunken Continent" which may get its own book, and stories written with coauthors. They range from a story of the realities of family separation with the first interstellar colony to a very far future in which beings who are human only in their memories (but determinedly so) and who range across intergalactic space committing random acts of kindness. Following the stories are "Story Notes" with some background information on each story.

G. David Nordley, Feb. 2014

# TABLE OF CONTENTS

# BARRIERS

The tables didn't meet exactly that Thanksgiving. Not so bad, I grudgingly admitted, for a twelve-year-old script being acted out across four and a third light-years. There was just a little offset: Jenny's plate was a millimeter or two ahead of mine. That was all the difference that met the eye, just enough to notice the barrier if you knew what to look for.

Their side, as usual, was a mirror image of ours: Uncle Ted even had their turkey legs pointed to his left to match Dad's turkey with its legs to the right. The china, of course, was exactly the same, including the two pieces from Grandmother's collection that had gone with them when they left for Alpha Centauri. Just a traditional family get-together. Sure it was.

We all filed in together and waved at each other just like the script said. Aunt Lucy carried in a plate of dressing which was probably just as good as Mom's and looked exactly like it now. Last year she hadn't been able to get all the ingredients, but things had apparently gone better this year. A good harvest at the colony, I guessed. Cousins Billy and Linda were bigger and in school now, but otherwise hadn't changed much. They were still kids and we wouldn't get to see them in their teens for a few more years.

Traditions are nice, but they feel a little stultifying when they are so rigorously enforced. Of course there was no choice; if any of us failed to follow the script Dad and Uncle Ted had worked out ten years ago, it would ruin the illusion for everyone else. This was a once-a-year fantasy, of course, a charade put on by two stubborn men, twin brothers who needed to pretend they were still together. But we all went along with it for their sakes.

So we each followed our cues, walked up to the line that divided our families and said our hellos to our counterparts as if there were nothing between us, as if the family were whole again and all the space that had come between us were just a bad dream.

My sister Ellen walked up to little Cousin Linda on their side of the table and talked about the great time she was having as a sophomore at Rice. "The social life is on a beam line, like from here to there at double cee," she said with impossible hyperbole. "I've been seeing this guy in my vidlit class who's a real amphibian, takes me to all the dives..." and so on. I kind of smiled to myself wondering what kind of message she was sending about herself to the twenty-four-year-old woman who would actually be on the other side.

Cousin Linda just started speaking when her turn came, like it said on the script, and Ellen had to shut up in mid-sentence. Linda had made the ninth grade cheerleading squad and had been on her first date. She'd taken pictures of the sun through the school telescope and had her own vegetable garden taking up half the wall of her room.

Cousin Billy matched Bobby's height and interest in baseball. His big news was that they had an honest-to-god ball field now, under a dome where they could fit four little league games in at once. Bobby related his own junior high exploits and how he'd managed to get a seat in the sixth game of the World Series this year and watched the Twins win their thirteenth title against Caracas.

Then it was my turn to talk to Jenny. At thirteen, she was more beautiful than I remembered, and as I looked at the young teenager in front of me, slim and tan in a simple white shirt and skirt, I tried to think of what she'd look like at my age. That got my heart thumping and I almost forgot what I was going to say. But as soon as I started talking, the dam burst and the words poured out.

"...and it looks like I'll get a 3.0 grade point for my first semester, if I can just keep this up. If my Astro Engineering major holds up two more years," I laughed, "I'm going to come see you someday. I've gone to a few dances, but the women aren't as pretty as you. Got a friend named Mary that can really waltz though. We're going to try to get on Ball Time doing a classic J. S. Or maybe the new Merry Widow Fantasy by the Leher Layers. It's all a three hundred year retro time warp - you should see all the Maria Theresa hair on campus. Mary's just a friend, though. Fun in her own way, but she's an ultimate groundhog. Not someone I'd take to Miller's Pond."

That was our secret, what we did at Miller's pond at five in the morning that exciting, sad, last week before the split; it was the last day we were allowed to touch each other. A lot of people think you can't fall in love at eight, but I think we did. At least she said so. So we'd made a sort of comic attempt to do it, which amounted to nothing but a lot of bare-naked hugging that was kind of nice anyway. I'd been losing my best friend, who I'd explored all the woods with, made snow angels with, and created awful poison potions of mud and weeds to feed to Cousin Billy. I wish I could have held onto her forever. But we were scared to death of what our parents would do if they caught us, so we said good-by and got back to our respective homes before the adults woke up.

I told her some more stuff about winning a state fair prize and then it was her turn.

"I've got all my Girl Scout badges," she said. "Mom and I grew the biggest tomato in the community. I've read all the Nancy Drew on Mars books you sent me last Christmas. Linda wants me to try out for cheerleaders next year, but I'd rather play moonball - if we get enough kids for a team. Dad's trying to make a real violin out of fiberglass and glue. No electronics, just like they used to be. If it works, I'm going to learn how to play it."

She went on about classes, stupid boys, and neat teachers while I looked at her, a college junior eating my heart out. For the last couple of years the families were together, we'd just assumed we were going to get married when we grew up, first cousins or not. Maybe if we'd told someone... It probably wouldn't have made any difference.

"I really miss you," she finished, and there were tears in her eyes too.

Then we all sat down, said the family grace together right on cue and got down to the food, passing comments across the line about how good everything was. Jenny kept glancing at me and me at her while we ate. I knew that because I was doing some serious looking myself, imagining that she was five years older and not wearing anything under the white blouse.

When she wasn't eating, or looking at me, she was writing something on the palm of her hand. What happened next was kind of weird, like she was reading my mind retroactively. When Uncle Ted and Dad, at exactly the same time, started knocking their wine glasses with spoons, and she knew I'd be looking, she flashed me a note. Well, not flashed; she held it up for a whole minute, grinning, hoping no one would notice on her side. It didn't matter on our side, of course.

*Come to the corner with me after the plum pudding,* the note said, *and I'll show you something you didn't see at Miller's Pond.*

We all finished the plum pudding right on schedule as we had on the previous ten occasions, and then she got up from her chair and went over to the corner where the inviolable line met the wall of the room and stood with her back to her family, but turned toward the wall so her back was sort of turned to us too. I got up and followed her and did the same thing, mirror image, thinking she'd have to do that again ten years from now, or things would look pretty silly.

She stared at where my face would be before I got there and kept staring until I felt, ridiculous as it might seem, that we were communing somehow. Then she looked down and I saw that she had opened the front of her shirt so that I could clearly see the just thickened cone and budding nipple of her brand new right breast. I looked up again and saw her face with an expression of... what? Pride? Love? Naughtiness? Defiance? Then she grinned and blew me kisses across four light years.

Then she did the unthinkable, breaking all the rules, admitting that this was all an act, a charade. And yet at the same time making this Thanksgiving dinner the most memorable, before or since. She put her left hand, the one she had written on, and placed it right on the barrier, flush against the glass or whatever it was on her side, proving it existed, proving that our families were now utterly separated by a barrier of space and time that would have been inconceivable to anyone but astronomers in the previous century.

With this act she admitted that she was an image, transmitted four point three years ago from a moon of the second planet of Alpha Centauri B, held for another eight and a half months until Thanksgiving, that she was really an unknowable eighteen now, wondering if the twenty-year-old who received the message she sent five years earlier had thought she was mature enough. Written on the palm were the words: "I will wait twenty years."

I said out loud. "I'll do it, Jenny. Somehow. I'll really try." If at thirteen, she had the guts to defy space and time, so did I.

"You'll do what?" Bobby wanted to know.

"Stifle it. Kid. Later."

Jenny and I, appearing to move in unison despite the thirty trillion kilometers and five years between us, went back to our seats to listen to the after dinner speeches of our parents: the ones we loved out of duty - and secretly hated for tearing us apart when we were too young and too afraid to protest; the ones who carried on this annual tableau which mocked our need to interact, to touch, to feel each other in all voluptuous senses of that word. But we would rebel. Oh yes, we would rebel though it cost us half our lives.

Five years later I went to the corner again in synchronization with a very self-possessed young lady with a glint of laughter in her eye and perhaps a slight blush of embarrassment on her face. But the will was still there; she had written *fifteen years* on her palm this time.

*I've got my commission* I wrote on mine. *I'm coming.*

I knew that was my last Thanksgiving at home; my first billet would leave from Earthport in January, and astronauts aren't often home for holidays. The old high-resolution holoscreen worked as well as ever, but I could tell Mom and Dad were becoming a little blasé about things. Aunt Lucy had just gotten out of the hospital and served roast beef instead of turkey. In five years, the traditional comments about the traditional recipe wouldn't fit. Uncle Ted's hair didn't match Dad's; it wasn't white yet - it was like looking at Dad five years ago. You could see dad thinking about how much he'd aged.

Except for Jenny and me, the synchronization wasn't nearly as good, either, on Uncle Ted's end or on ours. Bob and Bill traded notes on twenty-second century chromaticists instead of baseball, talking right over each other. Ellen was on Mars and didn't make it, leaving Cousin Linda to talk to an empty spot on our side of the line. Of course Linda wouldn't know that until five years later when she probably wasn't there herself. We finished dessert early and had to wait ten minutes. But with four Thanksgivings in the pipeline, so to speak, no one quite had the heart to call it quits. I suppose they're still doing it after some fashion.

Fifteen years, I thought, as the *John Young* docked at *Caroline Herschel Station* — seventeen for her. After four maddening hours of shutdown chores, I was free and hustled to the arrival lounge, still in uniform, crew bag over my shoulder, on a fool's errand.

But she was there, traces of frost in her hair, if anything slimmer and more elegant than her last picture — a study in professorial dignity. There was no sign of a husband or boyfriend. She didn't recognize me at first — must have been the gray in my beard. But a supernova would have had a hard time competing with that grin when she caught on to who I was. Then it was all tears and embraces and to hell with dignity and whatever the bystanders thought.

Yeah, I was two years late. It had taken me five years of bouncing around the solar system to finally wrangle a billet on the *Young*. But I'd called ahead and asked for a little more time.

"What," she asked me, "is two more years in the face of eternity?" and she showed me the palm of her hand. I laughed because she had written there the same thing I'd written on mine: *I love you*.

# STORY NOTES:

I sold this Thanksgiving story to *Fantasy and Science Fiction* about twenty years ago. Thanksgiving will be next week, as I write. After Kris Rusch bought it, I continued sending stories to her, which she would reject, and then I would send them to Gardner Dozois at *Asimov's* and he would buy them. Obviously, my stuff fit better there. After a few years of this, I simply sent them to Gardner first. For a few years, Gardner, Stan Schmidt at *Analog*, or Algis Budrys at *Tomorrow*, bought everything and there weren't any stories left over for *F&SF*. Then I spent more and more time working on novels and there was hardly any short fiction to send anywhere. The little there was has gone mostly to anthologies by prior arrangement, and I don't have anything left over from those exercises either. So, this remains my only sale to *F&SF*.

It takes place in the early years of interstellar travel, before genetic engineering has indefinitely extended the human lifetime. I would not be totally astounded if things happen in the other order, but putting one's fingers to the keyboard collapses the wave function and a choice is made. It recalls, I hope, the poignancy of the European settlement of America or Australia, with families rent apart by distance; difficult enough for adults but particularly hard on very young adults of the Romeo and Juliet age.

I think about all the families that move apart due to job relocation distance, adventure, misadventure, spouses from different places and so on. Many cousins and even brothers and sisters never see each other again. The universe itself may suffer a similar fate. Many will try to resist this entropy, however, and sometimes small victories will be won. And maybe big ones as well.

—GDN, Nov. 2013

# IN HIS IMAGE

**B**ishop Dimitri Osarian stroked his long beard and looked gravely at the three red numbers displayed on the window of his four hundredth floor office suite in the Humani Interstellarum Society headquarters in Copernicus Dome.

The first number recorded the genetic difference between the Earth-Human mean and the most divergent of the human colonies from the terrestrial mean. That had been C. J. Station in the Ross 128 belt for the last dozen years. It was 1.42 on the Johnson-Wu scale. On the same scale, the difference between Human and Chimpanzee was ten. Were the Ceejays still human? Did they have souls? "Summon Brother Ignatius," he told his office.

The middle number gave the greatest difference between any pair of colonies. That was up to a chilling 2.4. Would a Ceejay even be fertile with a Mu Cassiopeian? And the last number measured the drift on Earth itself, compared to preserved DNA from three hundred fifty years ago. Even that was approaching 0.7. As he watched, the range increased by another tenth. That, he thought, must mean news from an outer colony, years old already, and bad news. The numbers grew with each new report as they had for thirty-six years.

Placing the transparent holoviewer screen to interrupt his view of the nuns in the gardens of the library convent was an act of discipline. Like the flames of St. Junipero's candle, this served to both punish and stimulate himself, should his effort ever slack.

Sister Annette had not been there for many years, anyway. He remembered how she had tried to get him to do something creative, spontaneous, or joyful in senior music. Only a few years older than himself, he idolized her. She was beauty incarnate, all lightness and air. But he couldn't give her what she asked – even then the problem weighed too heavily on him. He had been called, and so he had bitterly suppressed the temptations of his flesh.

Now the numbers told him a story of his failure. For, despite his best efforts at promulgating the most rigorous possible Humani Naturae doctrine for control of genetic engineering, for all his pleas and prayers to preserve the species, Homo Sapiens was dying.

True, there was nothing grotesque to grab onto, to exploit for propaganda. No third eyes, no deliberate hermaphrodites, or four breasted women yet. Just a little bit here, a little bit there: an improved memory for Tau Cetians, an end to acne and baldness for Epsilindians, better infrared vision for the Ceejays, life extension for everyone. It just added up. It was like watching the rain forests disappear.

His door hissed and Brother Ignatius interrupted Dimitri's self-indulgent funk.

"I have some good news for a change," he announced, ample form bouncing with his usual bubbling enthusiasm. "They've finally outlawed family shield birthmarks on New Anglia!"

"I thank God for taking the scales from those eyes," he sighed. "But we've a worse problem at Ross 128. They're planning a retrovirus to grow radio transceivers in people's heads so that everyone will be able to hear their station cybermind all the time. They're justifying it as a safety measure!"

"Oh." The jolly Jesuit was quickly serious. "More erosion of self-discipline, moral decay. If you can't remember to have your mobile with you at all times, well, think of what other moral disciplines and observances might slip away! We must realize however that our news is twelve years old."

"Just so. Msgr. O'Connor was fighting it by pointing out that parents won't be able to hear what sort of music their kids are receiving, but the wags were already saying they hope it means they won't *have* to. But that's not why. God created us in his image, but we're losing that image. We're wiping out his handiwork, not with destruction but with, with...dissipation."

There were tears in Brother Ignatius' eyes, so joyful but seconds ago. "Dinosaurs. If we can't stop it, they'll someday find they're about as close to their own descendants as dinosaurs are to birds! Your grace, I think we need the big guns on this."

"I fear you may be right. But after the fiasco on voluntary conception... Will they have the nerve to back us?"

*That* genetic atrocity had become a United Nations law in 2084, over the strident objections of the old church. No woman could become pregnant now unless she actively *wanted* to, and so the moral structure of centuries had collapsed. But the church had been reborn when the birthrate collapsed as well, and Pope Victoria I had convinced many believers that it was their *duty* to procreate. God's law of evolution had then insured that the population would become overwhelmingly of the church, and in sixty years, it had. He remembered the spiritual passion of his youth, and those unclean thoughts about St. Victoria, for which he still did penance.

Even so, HIS was nominally independent, a supplicant to, not an arm of, the church. Dimitri counted a sprinkling of Jews, Sikhs, and even Anglicans among his colleagues. "Vatican 4 convenes next year, and I know the Pope is with us. Will that be soon enough?"

"For an encyclical? Perhaps? What is another two years or so when just under a dozen years are needed for them to get the message? It will have to be soon enough... though we shall have to pray for the souls who die with abominations while the message is in transit, those who might have been saved if they had known the true word."

"Let me see if I can get it on the agenda."

On time as usual! At ninety-five, Bishop Emeritus Dimitri had to feel his way to the door, leaning on his cane even in lunar gravity. Balance, he thought, not strength, was the issue. His mind was still as sharp and inflexible as ever, and he looked forward to these Wednesday visits of Bishop Ignatius. His loyal told friend would read those hellish red numbers he could no longer see and listen to his advice about a world he no longer knew.

"We've done well considering," Ignatius observed. "Everything is still under 3.0 except for Ross 128. Of course the data from the furthest colonies is forty years old."

"Peace, brother, that cannot be helped. I'm afraid to ask, but have the statisticians agreed on what effect the encyclical, for which we worked so diligently, has had on *those* reprobates?"

"Very little, I'm afraid. Perhaps if Victoria III had been more telegenic..." The Pope's long face, wide mouth, stringy hair, and stubborn refusal to do anything about them hadn't made her a great saleswoman. "But God Himself intervened it would seem. The transceiver task was much more difficult, technically, than they thought." Ignatius chortled. "Electric eel genes did not fit well into human patterns."

Horrors! Dimitri crossed himself. "There were experiments?"

"Computer simulations, Father. They are very good about that, at least at Ross 128. The last paper cited numerous incompatibilities and unintended side effects."

"Oh? But such difficulties are always overcome. The point is that the church must continue. God does not act to save us from our own moral failings." He fell silent. The lesson was a hard one for the Churches, Dimitri thought, but one that was finally beginning to sink in.

"Would you guide me on a walk on the grounds?" he asked at last.

"Gladly, Father. Uh, we have much to talk about."

They were quiet during the long descent. They walked slowly through the ground floor and he followed the dark patch he knew to be Bishop Ignatius through the ground level with as much dignity as he could. Dim shadows went by, to be replaced by a green openness, which he felt as much as saw. His dying optic nerves let warmth and brightness through, at least. The smell of the green grass and open air wondered him like a new thing. How long had it been? Two decades since he had ventured out? He momentarily thought to ask about the world around him. What did people wear now? Who was president of the Interplanetary Association and why. But that was unworthy; he had one mission, one purpose, and God was apparently going to keep him alive until it reached an end.

A young woman greeted them as they walked, her voice soft, well rounded, and clear, bringing forth ancient memories of longing, which he had so victoriously resisted.

"Who was that?" he asked.

"Annette Seagull. I thought you knew her. She was once Sister Annette."

"I knew a Sister Annette once." That was an understatement, but this was not a time of confession. "An angel of a woman... but she would be over a hundred now." He took a few more painful paces. "Why, I wonder, did this Sister Annette leave the church?" Just then he heard a slow repetitive swish and a light breeze rustled his robes. His world dimmed briefly, and he heard the musical laughter of her voice again, from above. What was that? Oh no!

Ignatius was silent for a long while, then cleared his throat. "Her modification was not compatible with natural law doctrine, your grace, nor, she says, with any reasonable design of brassiere."

"You mean she was... and..." Had God taken his sight so that he would not see what he had fantasized about so many years? Lead me not into temptation, he recited to himself.

"I'm afraid so. Perhaps the exuberance of flight is incompatible with the discipline of modesty." his friend sighed. "Well, your grace, these large physical modifications are often less complex than the intricate biochemical ones, and contribute less to the Johnson-Wu score. In her case, the wings were probably budded and not inheritable. Fashions change, lunar gravity is forgiving, we've become used to casual dress on the ground as well, and... oh, there are so many other *worse* problems."

He could visualize the cherubic smile and worldly shrug Ignatius could effect at some harmless impropriety, so easy to forgive because of the cleric's basic goodness and loyalty. But this was not harmless.

"Worse? Oh, yes. Ross 128. Where were we? How close have they come? Uh, can you find a bench? I must rest for a while now." Even on the moon. The burdens of life should not be forever, and now, at times he could visualize the light of glory growing at the end of his tunnel.

"The report form C. J. Station says that reception is no problem: the ear itself provides the Fourier transform hardware for signal analysis, to understand a mix of frequencies as speech. It remains only to devise an analog to the inner ear, which would be stimulated by radio waves instead of sound. But to transmit... Human vocal apparatus is very complex..."

"Humph. I'm surprised they didn't simply reverse the process of the auditory circuits, less change that way." What was he saying! He berated himself. Blasphemy! His own mind was becoming inured to the sacrileges being committed against the human form as a matter of course. What will happen to the image of God? Forgive me, he prayed. "Ignatius, the day is coming when we may as soon labor to save the soul of a horse!"

"Or someone who looks like a horse will labor to save *our* souls."

"Ignatius!"

"Sorry." Can there be a naughty twinkle in a voice, Dimitri wondered. "Perhaps a compromise will be found..." Ignatius had become practical too, bearing the responsibilities of office. Once, he would have fulminated that *any* deviation was wrong; now, cooked for

decades in a brew of statistical figures until soft, his ethics became relative. Dimitri grunted a grudging assent.

"You needed to talk to me about a local issue?"

"Yes, Father. The standard deviation of our own group is up to 0.18," Ignatius hesitated. "And most of it traces to one individual. Even though his deviation is in the conservative direction, it is still a little unseemly. Without this outlier, our standard deviation would be back to .02, within an order of magnitude of what it was in the old days."

"And what modification might this person be guilty of? I shall pray for him!"

"Not a modification, your grace, but his reluctance to submit to long-blessed medical adjustments. Uh, he refuses the geriatric retrovirus, your grace."

He turned in sightless protest to his friend. So it had come to this, Dimitri thought. He, himself was the outlier. He could remove the outlier by ending his own existence, as he prayed God would do for him. But that would be unnatural and a sin. So, like Job, to fulfill his calling, he must submit to what he detests. Very well, but in compensation, he shall be allowed to view Sister Annette. No, not just view, but abandon everything, grow wings, fly to the top of the dome with her some night, and mate under the stars. There, *that* fantasy should earn him another year of purgatory.

"I will submit," he croaked. "Let us return now." He pushed it on the way back. His heart, already pounding, might still give God the opportunity to spare him the coming trial.

✦ ✧ ✦

Former Bishop Emeritus, now Dimitri Cardinal Osarian, slammed his hand on his polished moon rock desk. The abominations! Mu Cassiopeians with *gills*! The spirit of Carol Severance must be chortling. And his own appearance! Had he rejoined the battle only to be mocked and humiliated? He even had to shave his head and bleach his beard to preserve his identity. Vanity or humility? Why couldn't he tell the difference anymore?

He looked out window on the thousandth floor on the L1 tower at the pristine vacuum plain. He sighed. At least he was no longer distracted by nuns in a garden, flying or otherwise. The Copernicus crater rim was no longer visible, covered with buildings. Even Her Holiness was pushing for a modification in the fertility rate, and perhaps a strategic retreat in that direction was called for. But it must be the same for everyone. And at least it wouldn't show.

But some of these other blasphemies! Gradually the bizarre had crept in. Fertile hermaphrodites fifty light years away, some accursed place in Virgo had aroused the gay orders – the far-off modification had eliminated their cohorts by making it impossible to have an abnormal sexual preference to resist! But the scarlet numbers were still under three and a quarter, under two if you didn't include the old human baseline. And now, in the face of the thirty-year-old news of an alien contact, feelings of human community were popular again. Perhaps, the war could be won, at least in terms of conformity.

Perhaps it had been pride to oppose evolution of the species. But then, why did it feel so right at the time? And why did he feel doubts now that the counterattack was underway?

"Show me the status on Gabriel," he ordered. The red numbers were instantly replaced by graphs of genomes verified and simulations completed. Quietly, at his direction, in the most secret bowels of the building, a hundred and eighty floors below the surface, a retro-retrovirus was being prepared to reinsert *true* human genes, as defined by the now respectable mean of HIS headquarters. He felt better; the satisfaction of accomplishment.

Dimitri summoned Ignatius. No government would allow this attack, of course. But no government, except perhaps that of the Vatican, would be asked. And, like any modern virus, Gabriel would be carefully programmed to defend itself. But a trial was called for..

"I think I know where to test our little project," he began when his friend arrived.

Ignatius, less rotund now that his metabolism adjusted itself for the lower stress of lunar gravity, but still brimming with the joy of life, and a thirst to combat evil, chuckled. "Might you be thinking of those now-scarcely-human beings at Ceejay?"

The older man grinned. "Actually, Ross 128. What does 'lift up thy voice' mean if one doesn't use a voice?" He shook his head. "It's been a while since you've traveled, Brother Ignatius. Though I shall miss you, perhaps a pastoral visit is called for, and if you are carrying a little something else?" Would holes in hands and earlobes grow painfully closed on vain decorations? And those men with false vaginas, filled with nerves and having no reproductive purpose... no, the thought was too obscene. Forgive me, but those who had grown wings; would they fall from the sky as the unholy flesh sloughed from their backs? Yes, Father, I willingly sacrifice Annette to you.

"Ah," Ignatius shrugged, a twinkle in his eye. A friend with whom to share an unworthy thought, he imagined that Ignatius wanted nothing more than to be there as Gabriel took effect. "Do you still have some of that Tharsis brut? It may be my last taste of it in a while."

Dimitri nodded and produced a pair of glasses from the cooler in his great desk.

"I'll save some for when you return. In celebration."

In a life of two centuries, Dimitri thought, twenty-five years goes by in an instant. He was viewing his correspondence to answer file, low priority division, and there were several letters he had procrastinated about at least that long. The one he looked at now brought a private smile. The letter was sarcastic, from an Epsilindian monk who did not know his proper role; *of course* no one had done genetic analysis on the consecrated host to see if it was still compatible with the human digestive system! Was he serious? The arrogance!

The index was still under 3.8. Homo Sapiens were still closer to each other than to chimpanzees. He did his part, with reluctance submitting to the regular, approved updates needed to keep him from becoming an outlier again.

He longed for news of Ignatius' mission. For nearly a quarter century they had waited and worried; it is a long time to keep a secret. But they were not irresponsible. Nothing would be released without validation on a large, isolated population. The message confirming Ignatius' safe arrival at Ross 128 had reached them just last year. His guarded reports mentioned nothing, of course, of the HIS secret agenda, but the normal missionary work had gone well, he wrote. Pictures of Earth humans side by side with Ceejays, and especially the babies, had had an effect. Mechanical wings were back in style there; besides they performed so much better than the biological ones and, it was said, were less of a nuisance in bed.

That report had occasioned a visit to his former teacher, who had simply laughed and flitted away to her aerial ballet company. He had to pray to repress his tears.

But this last message, sent just before Ignatius' departure, had been cryptic. He spoke of a potential compromise regarding those obscene genetically engineered radios, something about natural wideband low frequency sensitivity being exploited to reduce the amount of change, but Dimitri didn't follow it. It wouldn't matter if their covert project had worked.

Security demanded that news of the effects of the retro-retrovirus await Ignatius' physical return. The secular governments now popular took a dim view of such church meddling, and only by avoiding all cybernetic networks had they kept the secret. There was little loss in time; in this age of near lightspeed beamrider spaceliners, this return was necessarily close on the heels of the last report. Indeed, Ignatius must already be in the solar system. Now they only awaited word of his landing.

Returning to his mail, Dimitri deadpanned an answer to the Epsilindian monk, citing the superlative 0.003 historical genetic variance they had achieved with the human digestive system. He did not mention that, if Christ were to walk into a twenty-third century hospital, He could not give or receive a blood transfusion. Without divine intervention, of course.

He had gotten down to the twenty-three year old letters when the door hissed, and Ignatius walked into Dimitri's office, smiling and bubbly, looking little the worse for wear.

"Welcome, welcome," Dimitri chattered, reaching for the sparkling wine he had always kept ready in the cabinet behind him. "I see they didn't make you grow horns! Ha, ha. A little crowded, here, I know, but fertility is down again. It's just that there was a lot of inertia in the form of youngsters ready to have families. Oh, things were tense on Earth, but New Saint Peter's should be finished in only a couple of years. They already have the rubble cleared. But what of you? And what of our experiment?"

"I'm afraid it was detected," Ignatius told him, "and I was given quite a lecture. The good news is that there's growing serious concern about what it means to be human, there as well. I had to make some compromises to keep our project quiet, but they agreed. We'll just have to shove it under the rug for a few more years, I'm afraid. And I see that you have adjusted to the inevitability."

The disappointment hit him like a blow. Then, as he sadly turned back to Ignatius, Dimitri's world came to an end, his hopes shattered, the illusions of a lifetime evaporated like mist. Why not fly with you now Annette? Nothing else matters, he thought, as he looked with speechless wide-eyed horror at his friend, his protégé. Ignatius continued as if his old friend were unaffected.

"Not you, Ignatius! Oh why?" he finally cried out.

"But the mission went well," Ignatius insisted. "We got a net reduction in their Johnson-Wu. Would you believe that! A net reduction! What it comes down to is that people still want to look like people. And be people, when it's not inconvenient. The compromise, which *you* suggested in principle, if you remember, was quite successful.

"You see, we already contained, in our auditory system, the latent ability to receive electromagnetic waves. Nerves can act like antennae when exposed to electromagnetic radiation of the right frequency, in fact some cases of tinnitus in which there is no apparent pathology have been explained in this manner. Now, each hair cell in the Organ of Corti is connected to a nerve of unique length. All that was needed was the right transmitter and a mapping function from intended vocal sound to the transmit frequency mix. They found it in the visual cortex, only slightly modified of course. Isn't that a miracle?"

Dimitri clasped his hands to his head, grimacing in spiritual agony, as if he were trying to squeeze the abomination from it.

"Oh, Lord," he cried, "first Annette and now Ignatius. How have I failed you? Leave me, Devil, leave me forever." He shouted at Ignatius.

He did not know Ignatius. He *never* knew Ignatius! Ignatius was dead! This... this pseudo-Human he had become, except to drink champagne without even pausing in his conversation, had... not... once... moved... his... lips.

# STORY NOTES:

I wrote this story in less than a day while attending the week-long Silicon Valley Writer's Workshop with Algis Budrys in 1990. I was visiting Silicon Valley from Boron California, where I still lived while trying to sell our house while Gayle was becoming established at Apple Computer. Our workshop task was to outline and write a story during the workshop. Taking full advantage of Algis, I wrote two: the official one which was critiqued by the group, and this one, for which Algis and then Dawn Minette were the only readers. He made a few marks, told me to send it off, and Stan Schmidt bought it.

It was written well before I had any idea of a formal future history, but it is more-or-less consistent, though sharp-eyed readers with good memories will find the interstellar settlement scenario perhaps a little accelerated and missing some aspects. It was written, of course, well before anyone had confirmed discovery of any extrasolar planetary systems and the distant colonies are O'Neill-type space colonies rather than planets.

It was an effort to treat with gentle humor a very real future subject that might otherwise cause considerable difficulty for some people. The future rapid speciation of humanity with interstellar settlement and genetic engineering is something that in all likelihood cannot be prevented, the distances are just too great to allow any kind of control. But I think that a sense of nostalgia and the conservatism of most masses of people will result in at least some of our progeny continuing to look like us, no matter how different they may be inside. But, to paraphrase Niebuhr, morphological conservatives shall have to strive to hold on to what they can, have the serenity to let go of what they must, and have the wisdom to know the difference. Or things could get very messy.

—GDN, Nov. 2013

# WAR, EGG, ICE, UNIVERSE

I shall start four cycles before the Westerian invasion, the threat of which I then appreciated only as a source of support for my research into the source of lightstone.

My third-molting-father, Professor Colonel Threeclickson, had come to express his worries about my slow field work in the deepest part of the long valley that gave our land its name, some eight-to-the-fourth body lengths from the University. His fronds drooped toward the ice and he glowed with white noise as all the hairs on his four long legs vibrated in disharmony. Reaching over with a long arm, he lifted up my head.

"Up there," he said, waving his three remaining arms upward. "The answers lie above."

I could not nod agreement with his pincer under my mandible like that, but managed a polite "Yes, sir," from my spiracles.

He let go and I brought my head down again, but only to the level of my upper thorax.

Threeclickson's spiracle covers clapped. "You are always staring at the ice, Loudpincers. Elevate your ambitions."

I bent my neck up again so my head was at the level of his. "Sir. The ice is where we find the lightstone that takes our instruments up there. If we knew where lightstone came from, we might be able to find more of it, and, perhaps, even ascend ourselves, without dying first."

Threeclickson seemed mollified; the hair on his legs settled down and assumed its normal texture. "Your logic is right, but be wary of becoming too indirect. You know that Professor General Icescriber has proposed building an ascent sphere of ice?"

I shivered with the thought of such an adventure as well as from lingering fears from larvahood, myths about the eater of disobedient souls in the land of the dead. "Yes... uh, sir... I've seen drawings of it. It's one arm thick all around with polished areas to see through; it should resist crushing and let us get really high – if we can find or make enough lightstone to lift it."

Threeclickson laughed with staccato slaps of his spiracle valves, which made his upper thorax sparkle. "I rather supposed that would appeal to you. At my third molting, I shared that ambition. There is some promising related research that, however, must be held among the staff for now..." He trailed off. "But the water above is not friendly to life. As a body goes up, its heavy parts are compressed and we cannot breathe easily above eight to the fifth body-lengths. It is, after all, the realm of the dead.... Well, Loudpincers, have you looked at the latest lightstone research?"

"Goodphaser thinks it works its way up from further below."

The professor huffed currents out of his spiracles. "So much is obvious."

"Softtipspawn has a theory that lightstone might be connected with the periodicity of icecover plant growth," I ventured.

"Pure speculation. I know she is a friend of yours, but biology isn't Softtipspawn's field. Major Lecturer Tightpincers *is* a zoologist, however, and she is pretty sure that lightstone is excreted by an unknown species of giant iceworm—little iceworms have long been known to feed on concentrated minerals released from warmfall water as it freezes."

I tried to imaging a huge worm tunneling through solid ice and couldn't, so I maintained a respectful silence. Threeclickson and Tightpincers were thick, and if rumors were to be believed, might spawn together next feasting season.

"I can tell you don't think much of that one," Threeclickson said, accusingly.

"Sir... it's very difficult to observe anything in a warmfall," I said. "The warm water makes one slow or even unconscious."

"She surrounds herself with ice before going in and is usually conscious for long enough to note what happens. I must admit there has been a problem getting others to replicate this. Well, what else have you found out?"

I recited my research. "Lightstone comes in many varieties and varies in lifting power per unit volume, though it takes a sensitive balance to see the difference. Lightstone with the most inertia lifts most strongly. Some people have timed the rise of lightstone through the ice to the surface by protecting the surface over them from variations and taking measurements every feast cycle. They drift upward at varying rates, usually less than one over eight-to-the-fourth body lengths in a cycle."

"Brightpincers and Loudlegs," Threeclickson replied. "They're visiting from Great Warmfall. And they've also shown that solutions of ground lightstone are the same as found in iceworm excrement, by the way. Well, what conclusion do you draw from all of this?"

I hesitated, not sure I should tell Threeclickson all my cosmo-logical speculations, but vanity spoke. "I think they might be concentrated by living things, not living *in* the ice, but rather on the other side of the ice. There could be another shell of water beyond this one, further out from the center. Like an egg of ice with many shells. But that's just speculation," I hurried to add.

"And not original. There is a long history of stories about beings from the underworld. Unfortunately, they are tales to make larva more attentive."

I opened my pincers. I could not help that. "I need more data. Since I've covered almost all of the base's allocated research area, the only way to get more is to go, well, deeper. Lightstone comes from somewhere."

Another spiracle flap. "Well, I haven't seen any giant iceworms either, so maybe. But be careful who you say that to; I would not want to see my molt-son ridiculed." He waved his fronds. "Going down to go up! The Mystical Church would love it. But your logic seems unassailable."

He waved an arm toward the west; a dim glow of noise marked the direction of our neighbors in Crossvalleys. "I wish our Long Valley were likewise unassailable. But Highfronds' Westerian Empire draws nearer. They are absorbing Crossvalleys – see the glow of their war machines? We are getting refugees daily."

I shivered. Crossvalleys was but a thirty-cycle hike from Long Valley, and only Lushole lay between them and us. "We are no match for the empire in population," I said.

"Aye, but do we just allow ourselves to be eaten or enslaved? Our one hope lies in better weapons, and that means better research. So, do your research, but keep in mind the needs of defense; the research must pay off soon, Loudpincers. There is not much time. Goodcycle."

"Goodcycle, sir."

He scrabbled off among the hillocks and ridges of the research field, lit in sparkles by the myriad sounds of nature. Pompous as he was, it was good of him to journey so far and take so much time with me. The bottom of Long Valley was very isolated; it was too prone to enervating warmfalls to be settled, so he'd come some distance from the comforts of civilization.

I wanted to find more lightstone, of course, but that was only part of the ancient question that had gripped my imagination. How deep could I go? The bottom of Long Valley's eponymous rift was by all accounts as far from the center and the land of the dead as one could get in the ice. It was kept clear by a periodic warmfall, so I had a good head start.

What was below the ice? Theology had long held that our universe was a bubble in an infinite volume of ice, and academic cosmology had no better suggestion, so the question itself was a minor heresy, but priests did not have the standing in Long Valley they had in Westeria. Some radical geometers had offered the idea that the ice was finite but unbounded; if I could dig down forever I would end up coming up on the other side of the universe, just as if one kept going west with the current from Long Valley, one would eventually reach Long Valley from the east side. That closure was of two dimensions and required three; the greater closure would be in three dimensions and require four.

The idea made my head ache. I didn't believe it, anyway. Something came up through the ice to make the plants grow. That something did not come down from the center, because you could cover the plants and they would still grow. And they would still grow according to the regular cycle. To me, this meant that something different had to lie below, something that changed with the cycle.

I took my prize lightstone axe from my thorax pouch and carefully tied its tether to my abdomen belt against its tendency to fly upward. I followed the path back to my pit, contemplating the universe. Icesplitter's model of weight held that water pushed things less dense than it out from the center, giving us weight and keeping us firmly on the ice.

It seemed to me that unless there were something pushing the ice toward the center, the universe would explode. Therefore, there should be a layer of water, or something, beyond this one. Perhaps more. The "layer" that lay beyond our layer must generate, or at least transmit, lightstones. And if I could find it, my people might have what they needed to defend themselves.

I checked my surface stores and rappelled down a knotted rope to begin again my painstaking routine: Thirty swings of the axe, then wait for my body to recharge itself as the ice chips settled back down. Then do it again. It took me a demicycle to lower the pit floor by a quarter arm.

With each new level reached, I gently laid my ear fronds on the cold ice-viewer, chirped a command to my vibrators, and watched for the dull fuzzy spots that would signify lightstones.

A quarter-cycle went by. Then I noticed something strange; not a dark, hard reflection spot that would signify a lightstone, but rather that half of my field of view seemed dimmer than the other half.

I raised my body on all four legs and directed my attention to the viewer itself. Designed from Valleyscraper's sonic wave theory of vision, it had eight-squared cones, each widest at the bottom and narrowing to a small plunger and plate arrangement at the top, on which one laid one's fronds. It multiplied by two times eight squared the slight motion of the waves emerging from ice in contact with the wide ends of the cones to those fronds in contact with the narrow ends.

The fluid in each cone was under a slight pressure, and if it leaked, the amplification would be somewhat less intense; and I would perceive part of the wave front as being dimmer. But I could not think of anything that would cause half the cones on one side to leak.

The viewer was anchored to the ice by a heavy tube frame; if the pressure on one side were not the same as on the other, there might be a difference. With effort, I braced all my legs and lifted the viewer off the ice; it did not seem unbalanced.

Still, I examined it at a wide range of frequencies – and nothing looked wrong.

I might, I realized, be sounding the edge of a huge object buried deep beneath the ice, its faintness due to depth, or softness. I went to the viewer and chirped for illumination. The dark half was still there. I moved the viewer slightly and chirped again. The edge stayed where it was – so it lay in the ice and not in the viewer.

Was it, I wondered, the edge of a physical change in the ice at that level? A field of soft ice? I thought I would have to expand my pit to test that hypothesis, and that would take cycles of work. But as I went to move the viewer to make room for digging, I tilted it and had an inspiration.

Suppose I dug my pit with a slightly concave bottom? I could move the viewer around scanning through the ice at various angles, looking thus in a different direction in each place and greatly expanding my field of view. I hastened to work.

It took another quarter cycle, but there was definitely something down there. It was huge; it was distant. It, I dreamed, might be a giant lightstone, more than enough for thousands of weapons. But I would never get to it before the Westerian armies got to us; I would need help to dig down quickly. I went off to find Threeclickson, snacking on local iceweed as I went; no time to stop for a meal now!

I found Threeclickson in his office with General Councilor Sharpfronds and four others.

"Loudpincers! Just the young body we need. You have saved me the trouble of sending for you. You know the general. I would like you to meet as well Prof. Lieutenant Farfronds, Mr. Crushpincers, Mr. Eightfold Longtail, and Goodmother Quickfronds."

"Goodcycle, all. Need? I have just come to tell you I've found something of potentially immense value, what is possibly a huge lightstone buried deep in the ice."

Spiracles flapped in humor. "What would you say, Loudpincers, if I told you we have gained access to where we shall not have to dig for lightstone?"

I waved my pincers upward in a questioning posture.

"Precisely. If you come into the courtyard, we shall show you. Are you curious?"

I decided to set my news aside for a moment; I had delivered it and need not argue or expound on its importance, and the possibility of a journey to the center excited me. I nodded agreement and followed the Colonel and the General.

The university offices form a hexagon, the center of which is an open area twenty bodies across. Much of the military development that we would rather others not hear was done there, and as such an invitation to enter was a mark of great trust – something I even more greatly appreciated as I approached its entrance, secured by three military personal and two sets of woven stiffplant doors.

We negotiated this gauntlet one by one and found in the open space beyond, with sonic beams illuminating it from all sides, a vast sphere, fully three bodies across. A windlass even larger than it was stood next to it. A small fortune in netterbug web fiber must have been wound around it.

"Young Loudpincers," Sharpfronds said. "There is a steady rain of lightstone skyward; it all must collect in the center. But how far is that? Now Prof. Major Crossfronds has received an echo from his instrument."

"An echo?" Were there layers above as well as layers below?

"Almost three times eight-to-the-fifth body-lengths above us is a reflection."

"Not a temperature ghost," Threeclickson added. "Something real that does not move. The center itself, or at least something that might stop lightstone on its way to the center."

I looked at the sphere and the windlass. Then I spotted its propulsion system: a small net filled with a fortune's fortune of lightstone waving gently in the current above the sphere, straining to drag the sphere upward.

My leg hair vibrated in spite of myself. "You mean to go where the dead go to reclaim the lightstone?"

"Exactly," Threeclickson said. "And you must come too."

It was said gently, as if in invitation, but it was an invitation, I realized, that I dared not refuse now that I knew what technology would accomplish this trip. Besides, if I had been told everything with a free choice, I would have begged to go.

"When?" was all I asked.

They were all still for a moment, and in the dark silence, the thumps of distant war machines made the horizon glow. Threeclickson waved an arm in Sharpfronds' direction.

"There must be no delay," Sharpfronds said. "We go as soon as provisions are loaded, in about thirty clicks. What you need will be on board, so there is no need to gather anything; however, I should not dismiss the danger."

He cupped his fronds toward each of us in turn. No one wavered that I could sense.

"Good. If you have affairs to settle, you, I, and all of us should do what we can in the time we have to resolve them. There are sonotube cubicles around the perimeter which you may use."

"You are going yourself, General?" I asked, not knowing then how impertinent that was.

Sharpfronds turned, then waved an arm, dismissing any idea of offense. "My style is to lead from the front, Loudpincers."

With that, he departed.

I stood and looked in wonder at the sphere for a few clicks, then proceeded to the perimeter.

From the standpoint of few affairs to complicate things, they had chosen me well. I had only my eggmother to tell, and my project for an inheritance. Eggmother was away, so I called the university recorder, who took my message for her and recorded my will. For the project, there was nobody but Softtipspawn. Because she was an early teacher of mine, our relationship was still a bit spiny, and for her to consider spawning with a student was to mix things better not mixed. But I would be a student no longer in a few cycles, and her eggs carried an intelligent heritage. We were of similar age, three moltings each, and this was thought best for reproductive success. If she would not get my seed, at least she would get my data; that in itself was seed for something.

The next step was the hardest. One wants, more than anything, for one's existence to have meaning. My discovery would, perhaps, cause my name to be immortal. But if it fell into the hands of the Westerian Empire, every being in the universe would be in jeopardy. With great reluctance, I told the recorder to place my will among the things that would be destroyed should the university fall to the empire. Not until that moment had the impending invasion really hit home.

A horn pulsed deep long waves. Our departure signal, probably, though I had not been told that. I left the cubical and headed for the sphere. There, Mr. Crushpincers directed me toward a hinged section of the sphere. He was, despite his name, quite small.

"It is a hatch. Pull it outward," he said.

I did as he said and it opened easily, almost pulling itself from my fingers as it swung hard toward the ice. "It seems too heavy to be strong," I said.

"It has many layers of fiber joined with a glue made from iceworm skin. It is both stronger than ice itself and heavier; this is a secret which you must keep now."

I moved the door back and forth, thinking about how strong and heavy it was. "If we have this, what do we need of lightstone weapons?"

Crushpincers clicked with good humor. "Not as much, certainly. But we need lightstone for much more than for weapons; we need the lightstone to fly over the enemy. A lightstone-levitated gondola with four archers could neutralize an eight of eights of infantry, if even a quarter of their load of poisoned daggershells found the target."

The instinct of a daggershell was to seek the ice at as high a velocity as its water jets would take it, its hard, notched shell penetrating deep enough to hold it until its next molting. They could stab completely through a thorax and still stick in the ice below. Many cycles ago, I had come close to being under one, and the wonder and fear at hearing its bright landing so close to me was one of my strongest youthful memories. To us such a thing as a weapon spoke of our desperation. To actually swim above the ice levitated by lightstone fired my imagination.

"What a project! Are you coming along?"

"No, someone must mind the windlass, I fear. Now you're the last, so on your way."

I nodded and entered the sphere. My companions were on benches against the side around the equator of the sphere, each with a portal that had been invisible from outside. Cabinets, no doubt filled with the equipment we would need, lay under the benches. I took the remaining free bench and looked around.

I felt I had entered some new and strange universe. The inner wall was smooth to even the highest frequencies, like an egg. Apart from the benches, the cabinets, and a cylinder covered by what sounded to be a taut drumhead at the very bottom, it all seemed very stark and featureless.

"We ascend," Sharpfronds said. Only the slightest motion betrayed the truth of what he said.

"Loudpincers," Goodmother Quickfronds said. "I have prepared something for us all to take that will ameliorate the effects of the rising pressure. I assure you, despite what it tastes like, that it will not harm you—I have taken it several times myself in pressure chamber tests."

"Pressure chamber?" I had never heard of such a thing.

Quickfronds raised her fronds in pleasure. "It lies beneath the north side of the University. We carved a cylindrical room, then froze a plug that, after some grinding, matches the opening almost exactly. The 'almost' we take care of with a caulking paste of crushed iceweed. A great screw can push the plug down, compressing the water beneath it."

I made postures of admiration. "This must have been in work for some time."

Sharpfronds clicked his spiracles. "It has. Fortunately. Dr. Quickfronds is our greatest expert on this, and we trust her to keep us alive. Now let me show you another wonder. Crushpincers?"

"Yes, General?" The voice had a tinny quality, missing some of its lower register glow, but it was clear and understandable. But where was Crushpincers?

"How far?" Sharpfronds asked, directing his voice to the drum.

"Two eight cubed and six bodies of line out," the voice answered, lighting up the drumhead.

Crushpincers must be outside the sphere, I thought. Observing the play out of the tether line. But, I remembered, the reel was on the ice, and we'd been rising for some time. We'd have gone through the reflecting layer beyond which unaided acoustic senses could not see. So how?

Sharpfronds leg hair vibrated in excitement. "Good show. Loud-pincers and everyone, there is enough tension in the line to carry the sounds we make, as amplified by the big drum head you see in the center. Another drum is attached to the line by small lightstone rollers, so that Crushpincers' voice can vibrate the line and carry up to us. The same works in reverse."

"Crushpincers is still on the ice?" I said, half asking, half stating.

"Yes," Sharpfronds said.

I could think of nothing to say. The implications of being far, far above the ice and still being able to talk to those below ran riot in my mind. Speaking tubes ran only a few eights of body lengths before the voice faded to inaudibility. Beyond that, messengers had been needed.

We rose and rose. There was no way to keep track of cycles, save through the voice of Crushpincers or one of his students from the drum below; but they told us that two had passed. Dr. Threeclickson said, based on his geometrical analysis, that we had ascended a hundredth of the distance to the mathematical center. Sharpfronds said we should reach something soon; occasional holes in the reflecting layer had revealed another reflecting layer at about this distance.

We were all feeling somewhat ill. The pressure, Goodmother Quickfronds said, was compressing the heavy fluid cavities in our bodies, interfering with our ability to produce energy. We would be able to tolerate it based on the pressure chamber experiments, for quite some additional distance. But it would be uncomfortable until we got used to it.

I felt tired, a little woozy, and lighter and lighter. I began holding onto my shelf instinctively, as if to keep from floating off it like I was made of lightstone. The very physics of my body was changing; it was as if I was being drawn to the land of the dead. Should we really be doing this, I wondered.

To keep my mind off my innards, I tried discussing cosmology with Quickfronds, explaining to her my idea that the universe was like an egg with multiple shells.

"Egg, universe – it's an interesting analogy," she said. "Shells exist to keep out parasites, but allow water and dissolved heavyfluid to enter and nourish the embryonic larva. The larva exist between the shell and the center, which has nourishment, but is not alive. An idea is a bit like an egg, too, I think. It should stay in the shell of one's mind until it is ready to emerge, no sooner, no longer. A real egg has only one shell, Loudpincers, and hatches only once. And before crèches and culling, most larva were eaten when hatched. If our universe is like an egg, are we really ready to crack its shell?"

War, ice, egg, universe – individuals were laid, hatched, lived and died. But everything else seemed to stay the same. "For how long have nations risen and fallen, for how long has knowledge been won and lost, how many generations of soldiers have died fighting over the same ice?"

Quickfronds nodded. "For longer than we know. Sometimes a warmfall will expose relics; Steadylegs of Crossvalleys has looked at the distribution and frequency of such finds and thinks warmfalls are less frequent now than when they were deposited, and the ice is on average a few body lengths thicker. But there is no discernible change in these rates for the five and three-eighths great greatcycles for which we have records."

I imagined all my research lost to the Westerian invasion and then, greats of greatcycles later, being duplicated by someone else, only to be lost again.

"What happens to a larva that stays too long in its shell?"

"The worms come, in time. An eggshell is not forever." Quickfronds waved an arm around her, "Our present shell only seems like it. Your analogy of the egg seems to repeat itself on several scales, and both in abstract and concrete. There may be some wisdom in it on how the universe does things."

"Thank you, Goodmother."

She nodded and turned away, signaling the end of conversation. I, too, was having trouble concentrating as what the pressure of the ascent was doing to my body distracted me. On and on we went, and we grew quieter and more unsure. How much cable did Crushpincers have on the reel? I couldn't remember.

If we did not find something soon, I thought, we might be in no shape to do anything with it.

"Comrades," Professor Lieutenant Farfronds called. "Something lies..."

The impact came as a surprise, throwing us off our shelves.

"...ahead of us."

We floated together into a jumble on one side of the sphere. Or the bottom, now, for, pulled however gently, we stayed there. It felt as if up had become down and down, up.

Then, before anyone could even groan in astonishment, the sphere began tilting back and forth, and we slowly rolled as a mass to the top. After much embarrassed and apologetic moving of limbs, we sorted ourselves out into a rough circle around the top.

General Sharpfronds gathered himself, jumped and swam up to the drumhead, and latched on. "Crushpincers!" he bellowed.

There was no response. The sound transmittal system depended on tension, I realized. And now there was none. We rocked slowly, feeling upside down and helpless.

Finally, there was some more rocking and a kind of sucking sound. The motion of the sphere changed, now feeling like it was tethered again as opposed to sitting on something.

"General? Anyone?" Crushpincers' tinny voice sounded.

"Thank goodness," Mr. Longtail sighed.

"We're here, Crushpincers. We're seemingly, uh, upside down, but everyone seems okay. Ah, Goodmother?"

"It was a gentle crash, we should all be undamaged."

"I'm undamaged," Sharpfronds echoed. Others followed his lead.

"Good." Crushpincers voice came after a discernible delay. "We noted when the line went slack, but there is some lag since you are so far up. I have had to reel you back a little to restore tension to the tether, but you should still be close to what stopped you. Can you open the top hatch?"

It was at our feet now; top had become bottom.

"We shall attempt that presently. Thank you, Crushpincers." Sharpfronds waved a limb at us. "It seems we have arrived."

"We should gather the lightstone quickly," Goodmother Quickfronds said. "I don't know how long our physiology will hold up under this pressure."

Actually, I felt somewhat better than I had earlier. Perhaps my body was adapting to the new conditions. I was conscious of, well, slowness, in my thought and movements. But quality seemed unaffected.

Sharpfronds nodded. "Loudpincers, Farfronds, unscrew the latches. Longtail, wind up the beacon."

We all jumped to our tasks, though I wanted a look at the beacon. Wind-up implied a spring of some sort; I had never heard of a spring driving a beacon before. The threat of the Empire had made the University busy indeed, and I found myself very curious about things that, apparently, no longer were to be hidden from me.

But first things first. I went to work on my latches. As I did so, the sphere began to develop a slight monotonic glow; the beacon, I presumed. Soon the hatch swung aside, and revealed "below" us a vast, smooth, featureless plain starkly lit by the tone of the beacon. I didn't see anything at all that looked like lightstone.

"So that is the land of the dead. Not quite what we were told before molting, is it?" General Sharpfronds said. "No eater of souls, no pleasure gardens, and no piles of lightstone, either."

"No, sir," said Farfronds. "It looks like another layer of ice, though darker, less reflective."

"The multishell cosmology," Professor Colonel Threeclickson said. "When the lightstone hits it, it must work its way through to another layer of water, perhaps one that is inhabited. As for the darkness, we have no idea what our layer looks like on the other side. It could be a debris field."

My leg hair wilted. That was my idea and Threeclickson had stolen it. I felt vindicated but disappointed that I had not gotten any recognition.

"And what happens to the dead?" Longtail asked. "I have a bad feeling about this. It is not what we expected. If we cannot see any lightstone, perhaps we should go home."

Silence greeted that remark. Not finding the lightstone made the expedition a failure and could have grave consequences for our nation.

"The area of this land must be over eighty percent of the area of our land." Professor Threeclickson said. "We can only see a small portion. Where do the warmfalls come from? We should take more of a look."

"You are welcome to stick your head in the crack," said Longtail.

"I volunteer," said Lieutenant Farfronds.

"Thank you," General Sharpfronds said. "But I would like one experienced soldier to remain aboard the sphere at all time. Since I shall have to make the decision of what to do, I shall get the information first hand. Your orders, Farfronds, are that if anything happens to me, have Crushpincers pull you all back. You hear that, Crushpincers?"

"I hear, General. May I suggest that, in that event, we pull back a little way and reevaluate. We would not want to lose you."

"Oh, bother that. Very well. Pull back a little and, Farfronds, you do as you think best. But should I meet my end up or down there, whatever it is, honor me by making sure that nobody else meets a similar end."

"Sir!" Farfronds replied.

"Enough discussion. 'Ware above, ah, below!'"

Sharpfronds let go of the communications drum and dropped slowly through the hatch and onto the plain. So far, so good. But then he kept going *into* it, though very slowly.

"Soft!" he said. "Like so much rotten tissue. Slime. I'm sinking into it! Totally unexpected! Throw me a line, quickly."

Farfronds leaped up to the cabinets below our benches and clinging with three arms managed to open a cabinet with one, extract a coil of rope, and toss it down to me. "Loudpincers! Tie an end to the latch and throw the coil down at Sharpfronds.

A glance down at Sharpfronds showed only his head and fronds still echoing above the surface. His voice holes were beneath it, but he had two of his arms just on the surface, waving slowly back and forth, trying to swim in it, it seemed. He could keep that up only so long, I realized. He was suffocating.

I glanced up in time to catch the coil of rope, but instead of just throwing it down to Sharpfronds, I followed the coil and lowered myself claw by claw toward the surface. The exertion made me incredibly tired.

General Sharpfronds had vanished entirely just as I reached the surface; there was nothing to show that he'd caught the coil. I began to lower myself into the surface, head first, to keep my spiracles above for as long as possible. Voices called to me to stop, but there was no time to argue.

The material was viscous, clinging, and dense. I tried chirping to see, but the viscous mass seemed to absorb every sound I made; it was as black as deafness.

I reached as far down as I could with my upper arm, feeling my energy wane as the substance began to block my spiracles. I felt something, and grabbed and held. It could be Sharpfronds limb. Or something else entirely. Something long dead.

Shuddering, I held on and began to back. Slowly at first, as the holding and the motion took every available bit of energy I had. But as more of my spiracles emerged into clean water above, I felt a little more strength.

Then the rope started to move up. My comrades must have seen me try to back out, I thought, and helped by pulling the line in.

My head broke into the water and I started rising faster. I shook myself back and forth to try to clean my fronds and vision returned. What I had in my hand was definitely someone's wrist, just inward of his pincers.

I looked around for a moment as my flapping spiracles desperately tried to restore my energy. In the monotonic glow of our beacon, every bump in the surface cast long, exaggerated shadows. One of the shadows moved, undulating toward me. I had to stare for seconds to be sure of what I was seeing; the rise in the surface was huge.

Suddenly, the slime fell away and a great round hole slowly broached above the slime, then waved right and left before descending again. The hole appeared to be a mouth with six huge triangular teeth around its rim, pointing inward. The Eater of Souls, I thought – mythology become real.

Clinging with both hind arms, I reached down into the slime with my other arm, grabbed my prize, and pulled. With the group above pulling as well, an entire arm emerged: pincer, wrist and up to the second joint.

The huge surface undulations moved nearer. Not enough time, I thought, not nearly enough time. But I continued to pull. Suddenly, the strain on my arms seemed to double and I had to cling, both to rope and the arm, with all my remaining strength. The eater? One slice of those teeth and I would be left holding only an arm, if that.

But before I let go, I saw that the arm I held was emerging rapidly now; we were being pulled faster from above. The winch, I thought. They must have told Crushpincers to reel us in. The General – for it was he – began to emerge. He came clear; thorax, head, abdomen, and his limbs trailing limply, but still in one piece, the muck streaming away from his body.

The slime swelled up next to us and a great arch, the upper part of the eater's mouth, broke the surface and rose inexorably up beside us. Slime fell away from two, then three huge triangular teeth.

This would be very close, but the general's body was free now and we were rising even more rapidly than the eater's mouth. Maybe it would miss. I freed one hand from the General's arm and got ready to try to bat or push us away. Hopeless, perhaps, but I would not give up.

Then something large and bright fell rapidly from above – incredibly quickly, the speed of its passage creating a brilliant wake behind it. I recognized it; it was our bag of lightstone, the one on top of the sphere that suspended us up/down from the ice. What a thing to see lightstone as *falling*, but that was the current perspective.

It struck the mouth just a body length from me and cracked it, caving it in between two huge triangular teeth. The mouth tore open, its parts waving uselessly.

Bright, dense material began to flow from the wound toward the center. Then we were above it, and rising (falling?) rapidly with the sphere.

I was pulled into the hatch, still holding the unconscious General Sharpfronds by his arm.

I released him to Goodmother Quickfronds and collapsed near the hatch with my limbs tucked under me, chrysalis style, shaking uncontrollably. My hands, my head, my body had plunged into the remains of others, accumulated over the ages. Even as I lay there, pieces of the dead clung to me. I had sought treasure in their land and they had guarded it well. I had seen the eater of souls itself. I abandoned myself my shudders, and lost conscious thought.

When I woke, I had been cleaned. Also, I floated; down had become ambiguous again. There was no need to chirp for vision; the hull glowed with many sounds – a sign of a robust slipstream. Were they reeling us back so rapidly? Crushpincers must have an eight of helpers turning the wheel!

Professor Lieutenant Farfronds came over to me and touched me with a limb. It was the gesture of an equal and a friend, and without his saying anything, I realized my status had changed. "The General survives, for now. But we are all in great danger; we have lost our lightstone and our fall toward home is too rapid. There is no tension on the tether. Indeed, it trails behind us now. We shall have to do something desperate, and soon, and we may not survive. I wanted to talk to you a moment first." He raised a pair of limbs. "I speak to you as one who, despite my professor title, has always been more of a military person. I have fought the bandits in the countercurrent reaches, and I have witnessed courage, so I know it when I see it. Some will judge this expedition a failure, for the loss of lightstone. But I think we have found a good and courageous soldier."

"Thank you, sir," was all I could think of saying.

He nodded, touched me again, then swam over to Goodmother Quickfronds and the General.

Some time passed, then Professor Colonel Threeclickson called us to attention, the first time he has said anything for some time. While he was the ranking officer after the incapacitated Sharpfronds, he'd let Lieutenant Farfronds, who must have been far more experienced in emergencies, take charge of details. But apparently there were responsibilities of leadership and rank that one does not duck.

"Companions..." He hesitated.

I clenched my pincers. It would, I thought, be so like Threeclickson to make some kind of acerbic, imperious, cautionary speech or lecture now, putting us all on notice. But there was no time for that. I had always feared him more than respected him, and now when a greater fear ruled, I had little confidence in him.

"Companions, if we stay with the sphere until it falls to the ice, we shall be crushed. Therefore, we shall have to abandon it. Lieutenant Farfronds, tell what must be done."

Short and to the point? While his logic remained, the manner did not seem to be that of the Threeclickson I'd known.

Farfronds crawled quickly up to the hatch, then dropped toward the drum, spreading his limbs and fingers as he did so. He did not fall rapidly.

"See," he said. "The more area you present to the water, the slower you fall. And, after a certain amount of time, no matter how long you fall, you do not fall any faster. Our bomb-throwers call this 'terminal velocity.' If you spread yourselves wide enough and so fall slowly enough, you should land on the ice uninjured. You must only have the courage to do it."

Neither I, nor anyone else, had the instincts of a floater or a swimmer. It was our nature to cling to the surface, anchored by our weight, to not be swept away by currents. I grabbed my bench all the more tightly as I listened to what Farfronds said. I saw the glow the walls of our sphere emitted from its too-fast passage and could easily imagine the crunch as it hit.

"How much time?"

I could barely hear that voice, but I recognized it immediately. General Sharpfronds was back with us.

Farfronds raised his upper arms. "Soon, sir. We have no idea of how far back we've come. We could strike at any moment."

"Very well. Open the hatch."

"General, you aren't ready yet..." Goodmother Quickfronds said.

"Am I ready to be crushed?" His voice seemed a bit stronger. "I will lead us out. You will come next."

"Me!" Quickfronds exclaimed.

There was a moment of quiet. Then Sharpfronds said, "I may have need of you when I hit the ice."

There was some nervous clicking of pincers at the General's small joke, but it seemed to break the tension. Farfronds motioned to me, and I joined him in undogging the hatch. But when we were done, we couldn't budge it.

"Pressure," Threeclickson said. "The sphere is at the pressure of high above. We must let it out to open the hatch."

Lieutenant Farfronds scrabbled down from the hatch, reached into the cabinet below his bench, and pulled out a military spear. Then he stabbed the tip directly into the communications drum. The sound of its ripping almost blinded me, and I felt an immediate and terrible discomfort all through my body, as if I were about to explode. Groans filled the sphere, but gradually the pain got less. Also, I suddenly realized I was back to my normal weight, and almost fell from my hand-hold near the hatch. What did pressure have to do with how much I weighed? Compression, I remembered. As my body expanded and gained more volume, it fell more rapidly.

"Loudpincers, the hatch!" Farfronds shouted. I pulled with as much strength as I had, and it opened, grudgingly at first, with a bright hiss of water jetting through the crack. Then it opened more easily. I reached down, to take the General's hand—he was too weak to climb up to the hatch.

Before he left, he gave what might be his final command, "Follow quickly, all of you." Then he was gone.

Goodmother Quickfronds quickly leapt up and followed him. After a moment of hesitation, Professor Colonel Threeclickson followed. Mr. Eightfold Longtail, however, stayed clinging to his bench. Lieutenant Farfronds went over to him.

"Go, now! You must."

Longtail shuddered in denial.

Farfronds tried to pry his pincers from their grip, but got nowhere.

"Get out of here, Loudpincers," he told me.

Again, I disobeyed orders, dropped from the hatch and tried to help pry Longtail loose. But it was hopeless. I touched Farfronds and drooped my fronds.

He nodded. "Go. I will follow."

This time I did go, leaping for the open hatch and pulling myself out and through almost in one move. The scream of the water passing by it made the falling sphere below me visible, if in a wavy, uncertain way. Below, to my right, I could make out the courtyard of the university—too close, I thought. I spread my arms and legs as Farfronds had told me, and my fall slowed immediately.

I stared at the sphere, receding below. Where was he? There! A dark shadow appeared in the glowing slipstream, and began sliding off to the right.

The sphere suddenly exploded in a million frequencies of sound and went dark. I chirped, and saw the ice below me, coming up too fast. Now my height and fall were very real; every muscle in my body tensed with terror. I struggled for control and stretched myself as much as possible and flailed at the water with my claws, trying to swim back. At the last moment, I put all eight limbs down to break my fall.

The landing was an anticlimax; I didn't hit any harder, I thought, than if I'd landed after jumping as high as I could. Terminal velocity, Farfronds had said. I had learned, I thought, a great lesson of mind over instinct. Feeling myself whole, I chirped in the general direction of where the sphere hit, saw it, and headed that way to see what I might do to help poor Longtail.

On my way, I saw a bright crunch, chirped, and recognized Colonel Professor Threeclickson. Of course, having left the sphere before I did, he would have had longer to fall. I went over to him, and ascertained that he had come through the fall as well as I had.

Then I told him the bad news. "Sir, Longtail wouldn't leave the sphere. I was headed over to see what I could do."

"You should stay back, Loudpincers. You would not want to see what must... Forgive me. You have already... I... Yes, let us go see what we can do."

Threeclickson had asked me to forgive *him*. I sensed again that whatever happened now, my life had changed greatly.

Goodmother Quickfronds landed just then and scuttled over to us. We told her what had happened. "Threeclickson, tend to the General when he comes down. Rest should be all he needs, and a little cleaning off. Loudpincers, you're young and strong. Come with me."

We were halfway to the wreckage before I'd realized how easily Quickfronds had given orders and how uncomplainingly Threeclickson had obeyed. Five cycles ago, he had been the terror of my life. An act for the benefit of the student, I surmised, by one whose real nature was to defer to others. Yet I almost felt sorry for him.

We reached the crumpled sphere and found our way in through a hole in the wreckage. Lt. Farfronds, of course, had gotten there before us, but there was nothing to be done. A jagged section of the hull had neatly severed Longtail's abdomen from his thorax. He had, uselessly, extricated himself and tried to hold his severed half against the wound, but that, Quickfronds said, only hastened his death, as certain fluids from the nether part should not mix with those in the thorax.

Quickfronds turned to us. "Should you ever find yourself in such a situation, do what you can to stem the bleeding from the thorax. You will still die, but may have as much as a cycle or two to say and do whatever last things you have to say or do."

Threeclickson and General Sharpfronds arrived next. We removed the unfortunate Longtail from the wreckage and all stood vigil for an eighth of a cycle as his body became light and ascended to the land of the dead, to become part of that slime in which I had been briefly immersed. I shivered, thinking about what I had touched. I thought of my conversation with Quickfronds as I watched Longtail ascend. If our universe was an egg with a single shell, what lay outside? What laid it?

We were a sober group back at the University, arms at sides, fronds still. General Sharpfronds, now much recovered, addressed us along with several military commanders and university staff.

"Gentlepeople, we took our best shot at it. We learned much of cosmological and perhaps theological interest, though the eater of souls we encountered seemed a very physical creature. Looking at echoes, I might have worn a rope and been pulled back with much less bother. But such an encumbrance could itself have been risky. Again, we took our best shot.

"Now we are in a very grave situation. Lushole has fallen; nothing remains between Long Valley and the empire. Highfronds has delivered an ultimatum: we should submit peacefully as inferiors to his superior government, or be crushed by his armed forces. We have five cycles to reply." The General snapped a pincer in contempt. "He has that little respect for our ability to improve our defenses significantly in that time. Hubris may be his undoing. Highfronds is a charismatic leader–do not underestimate him. But the juices of his abdomen run his mind, and we shall make that our advantage. We will do the unexpected, the unanticipated. We will fight creatively.

"The good news is that our war floaters are ready. With enough lightstone to float a dozen of them, we should be able to even the odds and make advance against us too expensive for them. If we can float all thirty, we may be able to repel them without significant loses of our own; a result that might guarantee our independence for some time. But that is a still-sealed chrysalis; we need more lightstone, for we can float only one as things stand.

"Lieutenant Lecturer Loudpincers has found a possible source of lightstone deep within the ice."

There were murmurs in reaction to this news, creating far more of a stir when it came from the General's voice holes than it when it had come from mine only a few cycles or so ago. But I barely noticed: Lieutenant Lecturer Loudpincers, he had called me. Graduation eight times eight cycles early and a field commission, too! If only I proved worthy of it.

The General continued. "It will take some time to dig it out, six to seven cycles. We will move civilian population and the war floaters deep within our territory, back in the cracks where they will be hard to find and may easily defend themselves. The University hexagon we shall turn into a citadel, capable of holding out for a hundred cycles against any attack machines we have heard the Westerians possessing. They may yet come up with some new weapon to save, or revenge, our people—but that is a very faint hope indeed. Our best chance lies with the war floaters.

"General Highthorax and General Stronglegs have prepared maneuvers and delaying actions which might give us three cycles or so beyond the ultimatum date. In that time, which will be purchased with the lives of the brave, we must find Loudpincer's giant lightstone, section it and launch the war floaters. Unless someone has a better idea."

Dark silence covered the gathering.

"The sacrifice will be great and the timing very, very tight. So we had best start digging."

Later, when I happened to be close to the General, I told him, again, that what I had was a theory, a speculation, at best a good idea. "Now soldiers will lose their lives on the idea that it is true."

"So you tell me now that you think you've oversold your idea," he said this with cold stillness.

I trembled; I had never been so frightened.

But General Sharpfronds rested a pincer on my arm, the reassuring touch of a father on a larva. "I am not so molt-damaged that I did not recognize the risk; nor did you mislead anyone by stating possibilities as certainties. The one certainty, which everyone in this country knows now, is that without some miracle, we are all slaves or dead. Well, miracles occur in combat as well as in craft, but they are done by soldiers who have *hope*. If we had not had your lightstone find to give them hope, we would have had to invent something of less substance.

"But I would prefer not rely on miracles of any kind, so let us get about the digging. We have some equipment here that will be useful; my people will take care of it. Refresh yourself and be out there in an eighth cycle."

I nodded, then, remembering my new status, clapped my pincers, military style. "Yes, General."

I headed for my student quarters, perhaps for the last time. I tried to contact Softtipspawn, but she had already been evacuated. Whatever happened, nothing would be the same. I gathered a few mementos to fit in a pouch, then lay on my bench and rested.

When I arrived at my dig the next day, General Sharpfronds' people had spread a great panoply of cloth and pipes around my hole. After a moment, I recognized it – a warmdrill. If one seals a certain flatweed against the ice so that water cannot flow through it, in time a heavy compressible fluid will collect at its roots, against the ice. This fluid, if allowed to flow into a container of dead plant material, will displace the water with its very heavy essence. Such heavy fluid makes plant material grow very hot, and water is pumped through that heat. The hot water, forced down by means of bellows, cuts through the ice rapidly. As a mere student, I had never had access to such inner University wonders. As the chief of a potentially nation-saving emergency project, I had as much special equipment as could be conveniently placed in the area.

We drilled cylinders, a body length deep at a time. First we carved a circle in the ice and made it deep, then, with a special sideways-facing nozzle, we cut in horizontally and so detached the cylinder from the ice. Ropes were frozen into each cylinder, and it was hauled up. Then the process was repeated.

In the distance, the glow of the battle of the University had begun to light the sky.

Down the shaft went, just spinward of the large mass I so fervently hoped was lightstone.

"Water," someone yelled. "We've struck water."

My first thought was multishell cosmology. My second was about how wrong that first thought had proved far above.

"Melt water, not seawater," the person in the bore shaft yelled, as if he could read my thoughts.

"Great central heavens!"

There was silence. "What is it? Can you see it?"

No answer.

I turned to one of our draftees, Premother Longlegs, a first-molt apprenticed to a sweettree farmer, now a refugee. "Longlegs, go tell General Sharpfronds that we've reached the objective, but something strange has happened."

Someone had to go down. There were only four of us above. Who to send?

At that moment, for some reason, I thought of General Sharp-fronds and his pronouncement: "My style is to lead from the front." The organizing had been done; what remained to be done was below.

"Tell him that I'm going down to investigate. Platoon Sergeant Shinyclaws will be in charge, up here, until I get back."

Like most officers who rose via the academic rout, I'd taken special pains to learn the names and procedures of the pure warriors; but was still uncomfortable. A seasoned troop might be holding his spiracles in amusement at how I did things, but Longlegs was as new to this as I was. She snapped a claw as if she were at drill, turned and was off.

"Sir!" Shinyclaws said. She was a veteran, and there was a sharp-ness to her voice that made me worry that she resented my rapid rise; she perhaps didn't take in the three moltings of academic training that had preceded my one act of physical courage. I should, I thought, deal with it now.

"Sergeant Shinyclaws? I'm new to this, I know, but we're very pressed for time. If you're unhappy, I'm sorry. I didn't choose the circumstances."

"Oh, sir. Not that at all. Well, not with you at any rate. I'm maybe a little unhappy because I'm not at the front. I'm still of egg-laying age, I'm afraid, and the General Professors are looking ahead to replenishing the population. But if we don't... I mean there won't be any point."

I thought about that. Both positions had a logic to them. I thought it through. "Shinyclaws, the work behind the lines still has to be done. By having that done by females of egg-laying age, the Generals cover two needs with one action. Personal happiness is secondary in such times. Sorry."

"Yes sir. I understand. But I would rather die fighting them now than be overwhelmed here and forced to bear their eggs later."

I could only nod. I had not realized the full implications of her assignment.

"Anyway, Lieutenant, ah..."

"Loudpincers."

"Loudpincers, sir. You'll be wanting to take a runner down with you, sir. Betterthinker would be my choice."

"Right, thank you. Carry on, Sergeant. The optimistically christened Betterthinker was actually one of the slower troops on the uptake, but he was fast and strong. "Betterthinker!" I shouted. "Come on. You're with me."

We'd built a tripod over the hole and a tube of rope netting hung down from its apex, enclosing the hot water tubes. The netting also functioned as a ladder of sorts, and on these we descended.

As we went, I reminded myself of who was below. It was the third shift; Sergeant Raspyclaws, Mr. Icefronds, the water jet technician, and able soldier Larvasaver. None were evident as I reached the level of my suspected giant lightstone. The shaft went further down; the plan had been to approach the lightstone from the bottom.

Only a half body-length or so of ice separated me from it and I could easily see it by holding my fronds and mandibles against the ice and chirping. It certainly looked like a lightstone; its rugged surface was full of shiny pits and sharp edges. But it was huge—several body lengths across, at least.

I felt warm water at my abdomen. My first thought was that it was the cutting water, but that had been turned off some time ago. The warmth was enervating; I wiggled my abdomen to increase water flow, then switched my body around, hanging upside down so my spiracles would be in higher, cooler water.

The warm current was issuing from the horizontal shaft. I moved down further so my fronds could see through it. The warmth made me forgetful and fatigued, and I had to fight to concentrate on moving each limb, but I persisted in descent.

Finally, I was level with the shaft, chirped, and saw the thing hanging below the giant lightstone. It was long, rounded at each end and unnaturally smooth, as if turned from a lathe.

On the ice in the shaft beside it lay the bodies of my crew. If I went to them now, I would probably suffer the same fate. I turned and began to climb up the cutter's suspension ropes, but could only move a little at a time. I had to get to colder water.

"Betterthinker. The ropes. Pull me up."

I was incredibly tired. If I let go right now, I would literally fall asleep. A very pleasant....

The ropes jerked upward, again and again. I should let go. No, I should hang on. It was getting cooler. I was thinking again.

I resumed climbing, and spotted my savior amidst a jumble of rope and tubes. "Good, Betterthinker. I'm awake now."

"Handholds, sir. On the wall. I need to let go."

I saw the notches in the ice and grabbed onto them with two claws as I let go of the ropes with the others. As soon as I had detached myself from the ropes, they slid back down. Betterthinker had, I realized, pulled up not just me but the whole cutting apparatus as well, weighted as it was with superheavy fluid tanks. Well, Sergeant Shinyclaws had said he was strong.

I looked at the tubes and ropes, straightened out again. If they were to pipe down cold water instead of warm, I might stay awake long enough to rescue my colleagues. But I would need something to keep the cold water around me. I scrambled back up the shaft as fast as my legs and arms would take me.

Tailoring is a skill the career military know well, I found out. We took one of the woven flatweed covers and made a rough tube of it for my body, cutting slits to allow my limbs to stick out and tying it around my neck and around a heavy fluid tube just beyond my abdomen. We knew how much tubing the cutter had used, and coiled twice as much for me. The tube served two purposes; to give me cold water to keep me awake, and, in an emergency, they would be able to pull me back with it. I also took the end of a coil of rope, in case something or someone else would need to be pulled back.

With Sergeant Shinyclaws and Ordinary Soldier Bristlelegs pumping cool water around me, I headed down again. It seemed to go more quickly this time, despite my encumbrance. Though I could feel the heat on my head, I had not the slightest loss of energy. The cloth tube that surrounded me, however, puffed up and deflated with each push of the bellows above in a way that would have caused amusement, had the mission not been so serious.

I traversed the horizontal tube quickly and reached the bodies of my comrades. Asleep or dead, I could not tell, but I dragged each one back to the shaft and harnessed each to the spare line. Then I called for Betterthinker to haul them up.

Then, alone, I encountered the wondrous object that had apparently followed the lightstone up through the ice. It was as wide as the shaft, and its warmth had melted a path all the way up to the lightstone. The thought of the lightstone reminded me of how much we needed it, and how quickly. The entire crew, I realized, would need cold suits like mine. No matter how curious I was, there was no time to investigate. We could work around the thing, whatever it was.

Lightstone! It must be after the lightstone just like my compatriots and I had been after lightstone in our ill-fated expedition less than three cycles ago. Less than a three cycles ? It seemed like a greatcycle ago. The thing seemed like more proof of layered cosmology—but, the layers were different. Alien. My mind was dizzy with change and happenings.

No time, no time to investigate. I turned to leave the shaft and get help.

"We've struck water – meltwater, not seawater. Great central heavens!"

I turned back. It was Sergeant Raspyclaws' voice, much more clearly than I had heard it at the top of the shaft, but it came from the object. There must be beings inside the thing, I thought, from the next layer; it seemed obvious; the large object was their version of the sphere I had ridden to the land of the dead. They were trying to talk to me, but all they knew of my language was what Sergeant Raspyclaws had shouted—so they were repeating that. Could they see me, somehow? I saw nothing from them but that burst of language.

Time, I had no time. But maybe they could help. Help us in our war? How. Perhaps they could carve lightstone – they were apparently after it themselves.

Perhaps they wanted it for themselves.

Where did my greatest hope lie? I decided to invest a few moments and pointed to myself. "Loudpincers."

"Loudpincers," it repeated in a golden burst.

I showed them my body parts: pincers, claws, fronds, arms, legs, and mandibles. I shouted LOUD and whispered soft. I backed up for go and went forward for come. I showed them ice, water, and lightstone. I tried "cold water" spilling some from my suit, and "warm water" waving my arms around. It repeated everything correctly and I said yes. I wished it would make an error so I could teach no.

I curled up in a chrysalis posture. "Sleep, I said." I unfolded myself. "Awake."

"Hot water sleep," it said

"Yes." I was getting somewhere.

"Cold water sleep."

"No, no. Hot water makes sleep."

"Cold water makes awake."

"Yes. Cold water makes awake? Question. Yes. Answer." Would it understand inflection? "Cold water makes awake. Statement. Hot water goes down? Question."

"Come Loudpincers up?"

"Yes." It was quick, picking up everything, forgetting nothing.

But I was getting tired and running out of time. How could I ask them to help?

I chipped some ice and showed them "take" and "move." They understood.

"Loudpincers take lightstone up."

"Lightstone go up?"

I moved my arms frantically, upward as fast as I could.

"Yes, up. Loudpincers take lightstone up fast!"

The effort wore me out. I felt warm. Then I noticed that the pulses of cold water in my tube had stopped. That could only mean the empire had arrived. I had only moments of consciousness left, time for one last plea. I took my ice chipper and swung it at my head, stopping just short.

"Kill. Kill above. Cold water stop."

Silence greeted that. What an idiot I was. What could our problems possibly mean to them?

Unable to stand any longer, I collapsed to the floor of the shaft.

"Help," I said. How does a person alone act out help? "Help." I tried to move an arm...

I woke with cold water flowing into my tube again. My first thought was relief – perhaps we had won above. My next thought was that the Westerians had figured out that I was down here and were on their way to enslave me. I found strength enough to chirp. My tube, I saw, was now running into a squarish hole in the alien thing and providing a steady stream of cold water. Hovering around me, swimming, were tiny circular things with little claws. One of them stopped in front of my fronds.

"SEEN-DEE" it said, pointing to itself with one of its tiny claws. "Cyndi help?"

"Yes," I said. "Cyndi help." Then I remembered the situation above. What hope for them there would be now, I had no idea. But I had to ask.

"Cyndi help kill above?"

"No, no, Cyndi no kill."

They could not understand, not yet. They could not understand my nation being raped and enslaved, its heroes and my friends rising to the land of the dead. They would understand in time, but too late, too late.

"Cyndi help above sleep?" it asked.

Great center, that would work! "Yes. Help above sleep. Stop kill. Stop war."

It was not done simply. The Iceprobe, for that was what they called it, had to back off and come back at an angle to intercept our shaft. There was no room in it for me; I clung to the lightstone while all this happened, and nearly fell asleep again. But before I did, Cyndi brought me a small squarish pack, which she fixed onto the back of my tube. It took water in and pumped it out, cold, into the tube feeding my cold suit. For this reason, I was the only one awake to witness much of the defeat of the Westerian army, for Cyndi's artificial warmfall put our soldiers asleep as well.

It was not done instantly. The Iceprobe could swim on jets like a daggershell, but it was alone and the Westerians had overrun almost everything. But they had bypassed the University after Crushpincers stopped their effort to breech its walls, intending to starve it out later. And they had been slowed by the deeply cracked area in the Far East where General Sharpfronds had planned Long Valley's last stand. The terrain and our deployment had broken the massed Westerian armies into smaller groups, and Sharpfronds' creative engineering had worsened the obstacles.

There was time to talk; Cyndi learned our language quickly, forgetting nothing and able to understand more and more of my descriptions. I learned that Cyndi was not the tiny machine, nor in it, but existed far from it and talked to us and the machine as Crushpincers had talked on the drum, but without a tight line. She is female – indeed she told me that should she reproduce she would retain the egg in her body and a larva would emerge from her abdomen. Horrifying, but natural to them – and having been in the land of the dead, I am no longer squeamish. She did everything quickly; she came from a place, she said, which had cycles called "DAZE" that were only a fifth of a real cycle.

"How long such wars repeat?" she asked.

I gave her Quickfronds' assessment of great-greatcycles and thickening ice.

She was quiet for some time, then said. "That long be eight to the fourth times our notched history maybe. Stop war cycle now be good. Maybe."

We went to the university first, putting asleep the army that besieged it. Crushpincers had ascended, but the university walls were still held by students and old professors. I was acclaimed a temporary general by the chancellor, and under my command, the university folk made cold suits and sortied out. The line that had tethered the sphere on its journey to the land of the dead was put to another use, shackling a Westerian army. We left eight to guard eight-cubed.

There was no rest. Each Westerian battalion we encountered presented its own problems. We ran out of lines and had to come up with new ways of shackling. Cyndi at first objected to the threat of violent force in restraint. But as she heard the tales of rape and dismemberment and saw the evidence, she exhibited fewer qualms. We ran soon out of Long Valley guards for captured Westerians and had to change our strategy to find more of our own people. In this, my senses proved superior; I spotted and recognized the glow of a battle. We went there and put both armies to sleep.

That was the end of my generalship; the army we found was commanded by Goodmother Quickfronds, whom I was very glad to see. But the fact that she was in charge of an army spoke volumes on how many had floated above while I had been teaching Cyndi our language.

I expressed my sorrow and apologies that I had not succeeded more quickly.

"You have saved us," she told me. "You must not berate yourself for not dying uselessly."

"Colonel Goodmother, I could have argued more strongly to dig for the lightstone first."

"The center seemed like a better idea at the time," she said. "What was done was done."

Cyndi interrupted this. "Colonel Goodmother Quickfronds... your title... healer? Know bodies?"

Quickfronds turned her attention to the tiny machine. "I did research at the University. In better times, I healed. Now I bring death."

"No longer. Teach me. We end this less time."

After a long talk, Cyndi asked for as much inedible vegetation as could be found or spared. We put it in the hole in the Iceprobe's side. An eighth of a cycle later, a cloud of very tiny machines issued forth. Two cycles later, all the Westerian soldiers that remained marched home in shackles.

Such is my history. Of those of us who ascended to the land of the dead, only Goodmother Quickfronds and I survived the war. General Sharpfronds died at the front even as his contingency plans were being executed, even as I remembered his leadership style. He has the large and deserved memorial outside the university.

But perhaps as great a story was how blustery, inadequate Professor Colonel Threeclickson and a student battalion held off an entire Westerian brigade at the entrance to the northern crack into Long Valley with warmdrills and bombs hastily made from daggershells and tricks of chemistry for half a cycle. Most of our population was able to flee in that time he bought with his life.

What remains is another story. It is the story of contact with the outer shell, where down is up and up is down; of many eggs, some of ice, some of lightstone, some of heavyfluid. It is the story of the beings who exist around other centers at vast distances that circle great hot centers of heavyfluid producing an energy we can only vaguely sense as heat. It is the story of meeting Cyndi in person, standing on the top of a cave of ice, head down and telling me how she thought I was upside down. She is tiny for so powerful a being, only an eighth of a standard body length, even in the lightstone covering she must use in our water. It is the story of her 'STAR,' 'SOL' and her center 'URTH,' which she assured me had places here and there where I could exist quite comfortably. It is the story of all that has changed us so much and of which so many have written about with much more grace and elaboration than I.

Was my meeting with Cyndi an incredibly lucky coincidence? Certainly it was to me, but it was less so from other views. She was coming anyway. Given our species, she would likely have come during a war; it happened to be the Westerian invasion. She found the thinnest ice to seek inward, I found the thinnest ice to seek outward; the location of our meeting was no coincidence. Yes, the survival of the Long Valley nation was determined by mere fractions of a cycle, but, patriotism aside, that is probably not crucial to the greater story. Cyndi's people are explorers. Contact was going to happen in some random way; it went this way.

Now, nothing can ever be the same. Between war and contact, it will be a long time before our scientists catch up to the standards of Cyndi's people. Our academics are as new larva in learning and our military traditions but an unfortunate history. But this is not without promise.

Allow me but two items of postwar personal interest. The first is that, a greatcycle after I returned to the University, I had a visitor I had never expected to see alive again. A female veteran with a half-regenerate arm appeared in my door with a military click.

"Colonel professor, do you remember me?"

"Shinyclaws?" I was astounded.

"The same. I was captured, but they didn't think a female would sacrifice an arm to escape. I linked up with General Highthorax in defense of the southern cracks. We were winning when your alien girlfriend came along and spoiled the game."

"Oh?" I'd heard the story. "Casualty ratio?"

"Maybe ten of them to every one of us. Defense versus offense, and we had a prepared position and daggershell archers."

"And how many of you were left before sleep came?"

Spiracles flapped in amusement. She knew she'd been caught. "Two eights of us. Against eight to the fourth of them."

"I'm proud to have known you."

She came up to me. "How much do you mean that?"

Suddenly I realized that I was the one who had been caught. "Well, a lot."

"Enough to give me your sperm?"

It wasn't, by any means, the first offer I'd had. But it was the first one I accepted.

The second and last thing I have to say was that, before Doctor Cynthia Lord Mallagues left to explain her actions to others of her kind – which I gathered would take some explaining – she made an appearance in the Westerian capital that will not be forgotten for a long time. As a result, the Westerian Empire is no more, for they no longer have emperors there.

The Westerians executed Highfronds themselves. They have a unique method in that land; the abdomen and the limbs are severed and the thorax is tied off. What remains is lightened by pressed flatweed and ascends, still conscious, up and into the land of the dead.

I am, perhaps, the only one alive who can truly appreciate what that means.

# STORY NOTES:

This was inspired by Jupiter's second large moon, Europa, but isn't specifically set there. At the time of its writing, the Europa ice layer was estimated to be too thick (circa 100 km), and Jupiter too far from the sun, for any significant transmission of light through the ice, or hopes of penetrating it with something like the "iceprobe" above. But just recently (December, 2013), we have received word of the discovery of possible geysers on Europa's southern pole. So the ice may not be so thick, after all, at least in some places. Time and exploration will tell.

Nonetheless, this world was conceived to be a satellite of what we now call a "warm Jupiter," at an unspecified (in Earth's frame of reference) distance and time from here and now. The ice bottom buoyancy-pinned ecosystem described here has some Earthly analogs in polar regions, but here, it is the dominant one with the local sense of up and down reversed from our gravity-dominated environment. This was more difficult to write than one might think, as conventional ideas of up and down were difficult to suppress. One really has to imagine oneself in the environment.

Are these aliens "too human" in character if not in form? At some point, one has to admit that one is writing a story for human beings to read and to which they will be able to relate. But I think there is an argument for a certain universality in the underlying motivational programming of intelligent beings; we see much of ourselves in the behavior of life around us, even that whose last common ancestor lived hundreds of millions of years ago. One might expect to see reciprocity, hierarchies, collective aggression, and even sacrifice for the sake of the greater gene pool. Details may vary, but such traits have survival value here and may have survival value elsewhere as well.

—GDN, Jan. 2014

# HELL ORBIT

Time. An ancient gold watch sits on the rough-hewn wooden table in my log cabin on an island on a lake a hundred miles' walk from nowhereville on a planet around a nondescript M1 star in a galaxy now a hundred million light years from home.

Home was Haven, the terraformed moon of a planet locally called Hell, then just over eight light years from ancestral Earth – I'd had cousins that lived in the ancestral Sol system. How young I was then, how young the human race was!

I wind the watch up every century and let it run for a week or so. Perhaps someday it will no longer run. Perhaps someday I will be free.

I was there at the landing ground when she came off the starship shuttle.

She was the first one to appear in the door and before the gangway reached the ground, jumped lightly down onto the green grass of our landing field, her long red hair flowing behind her like a comet's tail. She wore a tight, thin, black t-shirt, and such things made a big impression on me then. I often wonder how different the next two hundred million years might have gone if she hadn't looked like that. Below the t-shirt she wore some tan walking shorts, the kind with all the pockets. They made her bottom half look a little bigger than it was.

She looked around at those of us gathered to greet the first shuttle down, and, like a cat, fixed her eyes on me and pounced. A mistake on her part! But I was tall for my years and a little tired, which maybe she took for age and reserve. I was also the only male around not clearly some years older than she was, nor apparently attached to someone else. Anyway, there she was, bouncing right in front of me.

"Hi, I'm Karen Kelly."

Deep breath. "Alain Lecarrée." I held out a hand, trying to seem older, gentlemanly.

She took it and laughed. She was almost as tall as I was and her voice was lower than I might have expected. "Are you going to show me around?"

"Uh..." Other people were filing off the shuttle and being greeted by people they'd contacted before coming down. I'd just come out of curiosity. "Aren't you supposed to be meeting someone?"

"My folks were meeting the Richardsons, about Church stuff. That included me. Until now."

Her eyes sparkled.

This, I began to realize, could be a come-on. My first. I'd never had a girl come on to me, and I'd never done anything but make casual conversation with female classmates who were more interested in other, older, more assertive and self-confident young men. To tell the truth, I had no clue as to how to distinguish generic politeness from real interest. But Karen Kelly certainly seemed interested.

"Well, okay." Trying not to sound too eager, I may have sounded too mature. "You've gone through the orientation package?"

"Kind of. I'm on the habitable part of a tide-locked double planet and that," she pointed to Hell hanging over the horizon in half phase, its red and orange bands mostly hidden by tree tops and somewhat washed out by the misty air, "is the uninhabitable part."

"For now," I said, just to be contrary. Hell's atmosphere was a two-hundred-kilometer-thick brew of hydrogen laced with poisonous hydrocarbon fumes of almost every known variety. Its surface pressure was almost a hundred bars and the temperature was around a thousand kelvins, more over the lava lakes.

"Forever, I'd think."

Truth to tell, I doubted it ever would be, but something inside me made me want to establish my sophistication. "It's basically just a big iron ball. Dad says we could blow that stuff off and replace it with something breathable in three or four hundred standard years."

"You can change the atmosphere, but two and a half gravities! I'd sag!"

I must have looked really flustered, because she laughed.

"Okay. Back to the orientation. This part is half the size of Earth with four-tenths of a gravity and just over Earth normal pressure. It's habitable north and south of about 50 degrees latitude with high, hot desert around the equator. You've got small oceans roughly centered at each pole; we're on a big island in one of them."

She'd done her homework.

"Right. Just add water and seed. Dad said it was the easiest terraforming job yet reported."

"So, do I pass the test?" She grinned and touched my arm. She must have moved closer to me as we talked and I remember how her nearness made it hard to think clearly.

"Uh, sure."

"So, we're supposed to, like, be in the largest city on the planet." She looked around. "All I see is trees."

I pointed to the south. "Look over there. That's the capital clock tower; I guess it does look a little like a big tree."

She frowned, then smiled as she picked it out of the pines. "Okay. Is it within walking distance? Do you have, like, roads?"

As if to answer, a big maglev platform hummed out of the woods headed for the shuttle and the small crowd of people gathered around it. Robot helpers were busy off-loading luggage and cargo and the sound of people's voices had blurred into a general din.

"Yes. They're paved with grass; the magnetic stuff is under-ground."

"Hmm. They think concrete roads, bridges, and aqueducts are beautiful where I come from; at least the historic site preservation committees won't let anything be changed or grown over. You have anything more scenic?"

I grinned – she was talking my language now.

"Wait until you go spaceboarding."

"Spaceboard?"

"A rocket board you strap your feet onto. In a spacesuit, of course."

"Sounds exciting."

I made up my mind to ask her on my club's next trip around Hell.

"It is. Here, well, we've all sorts of trails. We can take a shortcut by Abdullah's Lake. There's some climbing, but it's only a couple of kilometers as opposed to three and a half by the maglev road."

"You said something about a lake?"

"Yeah, about half way."

"I could use a swim. They don't have any dumb rules like you have to wear swimsuits here, do they?" She grinned at me with her mouth slightly open and winked like she knew exactly what was in my mind and that was just fine with her. The trouble was, I didn't know the answer to her question. I decided to bluster it out.

"People go skinny dipping all the time, I hear," I said with as much nonchalance as I could muster, "but they're real quiet about it."

"Hmm, if I walked down your main street naked, they'd probably arrest me, right?"

I just shrugged my shoulders and cleared my throat to disguise an inflamed imagination.

"The bluenoses would get upset."

"Yeah, some girls on the starship got upset about me showing myself around like that, like it degrades them somehow." She shrugged and smiled at me. "For me, it's just fun."

My pulse started racing and I thought I should change the subject. "I thought you slept through the journey."

"Not all of it. Bodies need some up time to take care of radiation damage. I was up for about half a year out of sixteen. Time enough to color outside the lines a bit, so to speak. You ever break rules?"

"Uh, not that I know of, at least not on purpose." For the first time, that little small voice in the back of my head started to whisper that with Karen, I was getting into a little more than I could handle. I couldn't think of anything more to say.

"Not even just for the fun of it?"

I shook my head. Mom and Dad didn't have many rules, but the ones they had seemed pretty sensible to me. The only thing they'd said about girls was that I should study my biology, and that when I was ready for a relationship, I'd know. That had happened three years ago, when my voice changed. I was ready, and the more I looked at Karen, the readier I was.

She got a faraway look in her eyes and a frown stole over her face like a cloud. "I was known for rule-breaking, back on Earth. And they didn't know the half of it." Then she laughed, bright again. "It's more fun when you don't have to. What's your name again?"

"Alain Lecarrée."

"Okay, I just left a message with my folks so they don't look for me. Lead the way?"

I smiled, bobbed my head in a way that must have looked awfully silly, and headed off into the woods. The robots had cleared the trail after the last storm and we set off at a good pace. She had no problem matching me: her long legs just ate up the distance.

"It seems very tame," Karen said. "The woods back on Earth are, well, more crowded, more different sizes of trees, more, well, gnarly."

"Uh, there aren't any trees here older than thirty years. Some younger; they did think about it. Over there," I pointed, "are some saplings. Lodgepole pine, I think."

"Is it always so hazy?"

"Yeah."

I kept looking back to get a look at Karen's body. When the trail curved the right way, she was backlit by the sun and I thought I could see her breasts through the thin shirt, but it was probably only their shadow.

"Is Lollipop going to set soon?" she asked, pointing at our reddish sun.

She used the local name instead of Lalande 21185, but apparently the orientation hadn't covered everything. I smiled, feeling a bit superior.

"It won't set for a while. Our orbit around Hell is tilted a bit with respect to its orbit around Lollipop, and it's retrograde, and the eccentricity goes up and down, and things are precessing, and we're at a high latitude, so predicting sunrise and sunset gets kind of chaotic. It circles the sky every sixteen hours, so if you can see Hell, which you can on this side of the pole, you know what time it is from its phase, 'cause Hell always stays put. Except for a little libration, which…"

"Okay, okay, I have the picture. And I know it's hot more because the atmosphere's so thick rather than the sunlight. But Lollipop feels like a big infrared lamp up there and I'm really sweating."

I could tell that. Her t-shirt was starting to cling.

"Hope that lake isn't too far," she added.

"Naw. Just a klick or so," I said, trying to keep the excitement out of my voice.

As we got close to the lake, my heart really started pounding. Was this really going to happen?

It did, with almost an anticlimactic matter-of-factness. When we got the shore, she simply kicked off her sandals, dropped her shorts, pulled off her top, and waded in. It happened so quickly, I hardly got a look. When she was up to her waist she turned around and looked at me as if to say: what are you waiting for?

I fumbled with my waistband. Then I noticed we weren't alone. There were some people over on the other shore.

"Karen, uh, there are people over there."

"Yeah. Come on."

Already, less than an hour after meeting her, her wish was my command. So, with nervous glances across the lake, I stripped and quickly walked into the water, warm where the sun had warmed it near the shore, but meltwater cold as it got deeper. I ignored the chill until I got safely up to my waist; I was sure someone across the lake was staring at me. But they were too far away to recognize me, I reasoned, because I was too far away to recognize them.

Karen lay back in the water and glided on her back, her hair streaming over her shoulders.

"Chilly," she said.

"Yeah," I said, unable to take my eyes off her as she circled around and pulled me to her.

She put her open mouth over mine, sealed it with her lips, and stuck her tongue against mine, precluding any speech. Wasn't I supposed to start this? I thought. Everyone across the lake would know exactly what was happening.

But Karen didn't care and if I felt confused, my body did not. Nature took its course.

So I'd done it. Just like that. I'd never realized a girl might *want* to do it just like that – all the discussion in my spaceboarding gang had been about how to persuade, woo, or trick a girl into doing it and now one had just kind of grabbed me and done it with me. I was totally confused.

Karen sat up, grinned at me, and waved at the lake. "Ever swim across this thing?" she asked, as if nothing of any particular significance had happened.

That was all there was to it, I surmised. You got off together, then got on with life. As I wondered if she'd ever want to do it again with me, I tried to bend my mind back to the proposition of swimming across the lake.

There were the people over there on the opposite shore, but I could figure out that if I mentioned that she'd just say 'so what.' I had to be as cool as she was.

"Uh, yeah, sure."

"Race you," she said, then rose up, ran a couple steps into deeper water and dove in.

I followed, as if tied to her by a cord. From the middle of the lake, you could see almost down to the horizon; the northern part of Hell stuck up like a huge, banded, semicircular mountain.

We swam back and got out of the water. No towels, of course. I shook myself off as best as I could and dried myself with my shirt. Karen simply slipped her shoes on, picked up her clothes and started walking, making me feel like an overly self-conscious idiot.

"Don't worry, I'll air-dry long before we get to town," she said, laughing. "Not that I give a damn, but," she shrugged, "no need to get in too much trouble on my first day. So, tell me about yourself."

I shrugged, flapping my shirt in the air to dry it as we walked. "Not much to say. I'll start my junior year in high school in a couple of weeks and..."

She grabbed me and stopped us in our tracks. "*Junior* year?"

I grinned. "Yeah, a year early. And I'll be going right into tensors and numerical simulation with...."

"A year *early*??" Her eyes were wide as saucers.

"Yeah, uh, it's not that unusual here, small classes, most parents pretty smart. And we tend to mature a little earlier here; lower gravity, lack of ultraviolet, long days–no one really knows why. A couple others are going early too, Ted and Myrna."

"Alain, just how old are you?"

"Uh, fourteen standard years?"

She just stood there open-mouthed for about two minutes, then shook her head and chuckled a bit the way you do when something awful happens that's hilarious anyway. "Now I've really done it. Alain, I just raped you."

"Uh, you kind of took charge, but I didn't really mind. I kind of liked it. So I don't think you raped me."

"Well, I'm glad you didn't mind. But it doesn't matter. You see, I'm eighteen standard years old, biologically, which, by IPA common law that applies here unless you've set up your own, means I'm an adult and you're still a kid. Even if I just let you force yourself on me, I'd still be at fault. So I just broke a law again. More than I intended to, anyway."

I thought hard about that. Did I have to tell someone? If someone asked, would I try to lie about it to keep her out of trouble? What would happen to me if I got caught?

What would happen to her? Something in me said I'd feel better about myself if I did everything I could to keep her out of trouble, regardless of how much trouble I got in.

"What will they do to you?"

"Nothing if you keep quiet. If they find out, they'll... they'll probably decide something's wrong in my head and fix it." She was quiet for a while.

"Alain, I don't want to get my head fixed. I don't believe in it. I like myself the way I am. So please don't say anything."

"I, I'm not a good liar."

She stared at me, looking really scared then, the only time I'd ever seen her look that way. She didn't look eighteen at all then. She looked like a ten-year-old caught stealing cookies.

"I want to show you something," she said after we walked a few more yards. She rummaged in the clothing she held in her hand, reached into her shorts pocket and came up with the gold watch.

"It was my great-grandmother's. She gave it to my Mom before we left, and I, uh, borrowed it. To show people. Like you. It's a man's watch, you know."

"Yeah, I think I've seen pictures of people with them. They kept them on chains in a pocket. About three hundred years ago?"

Karen nodded. "Grandma told me how great-grandma got it. She never told Mom."

"How she got it?"

Karen laughed. "It was payment for services rendered, off the books. Great-grandma was about as law-abiding as I am. But her men protected her."

We walked on into town with me wondering what other laws she'd broken. She didn't tell me, then.

A week and a day later, the first weekend after the starship people were all settled in, I took Karen on a space-boarding session. You need a whole day – three hours to get to the jump-off point on the Hell side of the L1 tether system, an hour at least for check-out, five hours for one orbit around Hell, an hour for check-in, and three hours back.

The spaceboarders were mostly my schoolmates, but Karen seemed to fit in okay. In some ways she was too grown up, in others, not at all. The Earth girl was curious about spaceboarding, I told them, and I was her designated guide, seeing as we'd met the first day she was on planet. I kept the nature of our relationship secret – its revelation would have been almost as disastrous for me, socially, as for her. Oh, some of the other guys were dating, but spaceboards and girlfriends and boyfriends were in different compartments of our lives.

We took a shuttle up to the L1 station – the tether head is near Haven's desert tropics – with my usual group; Jed, Lofti, and Song-Li, and at first everyone was a little too well-behaved. We were halfway through the two-hour ride and nobody had said anything. Finally Lofti spoke up.

"Earth people are really strong, aren't they?"

Karen shrugged. "Not genetically. But just getting around in that gravity was a workout. You can be as strong as anyone from Earth if you work at it. You look like you do."

Lofti, who did work at it and was now almost as tall as I was, looked embarrassed and proud.

"Earth had the highest gravity of any visited solid surface planet in the galaxy, until they found Hell," he said. "I'm going to go there some day."

"That's for sure," Jed said and everyone groaned. Puns about Hell were an unavoidable hazard of this planetary system. We'd started out as a New Reformation colony and most people still went to churches that taught the old mythology.

"Are the pyramids real?" Song-Li queried.

Karen nodded. "Sure. You can walk right up and touch them, or at least the one they've restored. They put a layer of fake diamond-coated marble on it to protect the stone and show people what it looked like when it was new."

Jed asked, "Don't they let you touch the real stone?"

"No way. They're going to make them last billions of years and that won't happen if they let everyone touch them." A billion years? No one knew how long we would live, then. A genetic change that would end aging at about twenty-five or so was just around the corner, they said. All the really old people were trying to hang on as long as they could. At twelve years old, I'd counted to a thousand, once – in about five minutes. A million was counting to a thousand, a thousand times. A billion would be a thousand times that.

We kept talking about things until we arrived at the L1 station and floated over to the waiting tram down to the jump-off point ten thousand kilometers toward Hell.

Our weight gradually increased as we went down. The L1 angular rate is too slow for a circular orbit closer to Hell, so everything tries to fall down. When we stepped out of the cab we had a fifth of our Haven-normal weight.

When we got to the equipment room, Mr. Grimes gave us the same lecture he always does. He's a big guy with a deep basso voice, a shaved head and a moustache, and so powerfully built that you don't even think of not listening to him.

Karen beamed a megawatt smile at him and I chuckled to myself. She didn't know about him.

"Now, do not go to manual unless there is a genuine emergency. You've got 150 kilograms of liquid $CO_2$ reaction mass and an aneutronic lithium-hydrogen nanochannel reactor that will put out up to 8 megawatts thermal. Exhaust velocity is 12 kilometers per second, so thrust is up to a kilonewton, depending on how you throttle the reaction mass flow. Max acceleration, depending on your mass, is about a quarter Earth gee – over half what you're used to at Haven, so be careful. Karen Kelly, you're the adult in this gaggle so you'll be legally responsible, but you're a novice on the board so keep your ears open. Lecarrée, I don't really give a damn about who's the oldest; you've the most experience and I'm holding you personally responsible. Repeat, do not go manual unless there is a genuine emergency. We don't want to have to come and get you. Any questions?"

Dead silence. Even Karen looked serious.

"Okay, you've got about 7.5 kilometers per second to play with as long as you do it within limits. You've got about 40 minutes at max thrust. If you get too far off rendezvous orbit, the computer will cut you off with rendezvous plus ten kilograms of reaction mass reserve. I don't have to tell you to be back on time – orbital mechanics will take care of that. Suit up!"

With that he left us. We suited up in number tens – the conformal hard suits. You can live in one for ten days in a pinch.

"Let's go," Jed said. "There's a big storm on the far side I'd like to see up close before it hits the shadow line."

"Do *not* hurry a checkout!" Mr. Grimes' voice rumbled from the overhead speakers.

"Uh, no sir, uh, I just don't want to, like, waste time," Jed said, looking around.

"That storm won't hit the terminator for another four hours. You'll get a real good view. No hurry."

Once we pumped down, Lofti put his helmet on mine and gestured to Karen, in her orange "novice" spacesuit. The rest of us wore white with red detail. "You've got a real thing for her, don't you?"

"Huh?"

"You should have seen your face when she came onto Grimes. She's too old, or, like, you're too young, right?"

"Uh, she's pretty, but I'm not anything to her." I shrugged. "She's got lots of other guys."

"Right, so they say. Tell me, Alain, that you haven't been to Hell with her."

"It's none of your business."

"Get smart with me and I'll make things really bad for your pretty pedophile girlfriend."

I couldn't believe what was happening. I tried to backpedal as much as I could, and sound sophisticated. "I'm really sorry, Lofti, I didn't mean to sound that way, it's just that, you know, you have to keep that kind of thing private or everyone's talking about it. She's a friend."

"If you say so." He laughed slyly. "You think maybe she'd do it with me?"

So that was his angle. It didn't help that as he talked to me, Karen was looking right at us, just as if she realized she was the topic of conversation. Karen would do it with him, of course, to keep our secret. But, damn it, I hadn't confirmed anything. I was momentarily saved by the door swinging open.

"Don't know. Gotta get our boards," I said, and pulled away from him. I couldn't help but look at Karen, and the look on my face must have told her things weren't right.

We pulled the boards off the wall. Though they massed 250 kg fueled, they weighed only 212 newtons here, about half our body weight on Haven. But they still had all that inertia, so you had to move carefully. Karen didn't seem to have any problem with it and pretty soon we had our boots clamped on and were ready to go.

"Everyone ready?" Grimes asked. He got positives from everyone. The hangar magnetic field came on and we lifted off the floor. Karen wobbled a little until she got used to trusting the board's gyros. When she got steady, the floor swung open and the mag field lowered us to about twenty meters below the hangar. Then it cut off and we dropped away.

"Whoopee!" Jed cried, and did a hundred-meter loop.

"Wow!" Karen exclaimed. "What do I do?"

"Your accelerometer's calibrated in centimeters per second per second. Squeeze the hand throttle until you get ten, and try to go straight by shifting your weight."

She started gliding off, and I vectored after her. "That's right. Now rock back on your heels a little to curve your trajectory thataway."

She wobbled at first, then seemed to get the hang of it. I followed her as we arced back toward what was more or less the centroid of an expanding universe of space boarders. Hell was in half phase below us, its stripes and swirls of Technicolor clouds vivid now from the vacuum of space. I shifted to the back of my board and maxed the throttle for a pinwheel that expanded until my centrifugal force equaled my thrust, then I cut my jets with a vector toward Hell and waited, staring at the waxing vat of poisonous gases below me.

When I looked back at the gaggle, they were a long way away, but I could see that Karen had linked up with Lofti, heads together, doing an S-turn in tandem. He didn't waste any time. My biggest worry was that he'd tell Karen that I'd bragged. Nothing to do about it here and now. I just had to hope that Karen, who didn't panic easily, would check things out with me before going off the deep end.

With all sorts of maneuvers to try and the universe to stare at, the 150 minutes to perihellion, our closest approach to Hell, seemed like fifteen. In no time at all we were zooming down on it, board tips on its horizon, with just enough thrust to steady us.

"I see the storm!" Jed called out. It was impressive: a huge wall of white and gray, raised high above the rest of the atmosphere, its thunderheads sculpted in high relief by low sun shadows.

"It's huge!" Karen exclaimed. "From space, Earth storms look like they're painted on. This looks really 3-D! I thought the high gravity would squash it down."

"It does by a factor of two and a half," I said, "but the atmosphere's only about a tenth as dense to start with. So you get four times the vertical relief. Stuff that's twenty kilometers high on Earth goes up to eighty kilometers here."

"We're headed right for it – right for that wall of clouds!"

"We'll pass some 400 kilometers above it. Raise your board tip if this angle makes you nervous."

"Nervous? Can I get closer?" I could hear her breathing rate go up. "Just imagine plowing right into it, like a meteor. What a way to go, don't you think?"

"Are you okay?" Song-Li, who usually says very little, asked.

To answer, Karen tilted back and did a very good tight loop, for a novice. "I've never been so fine in my life. This is fabulous!"

At perihellion we were close enough to see things fall away behind us, zipping over the clouds only some 320 kilometers over the highest wisps. At nearly 23 km/s, we could easily imagine ourselves surfing on the atmosphere rather than above it. The hurricane-like structure of the storm became apparent as it moved from the horizon.

Suddenly, the majestic storm spiral was below us and we looked down into its dark red eye. Its farthest clouds cast incredible long shadows toward the shadow night.

"Look, Alain, the sun's setting," Karen gushed.

With amazing rapidity, Lollipop, reddish to start with, became blood red and squashed, streaked with clouds, and vanished. Our running lights came on as our eyes adapted to the night side of Hell. Down below, the glow of lightning bolts lit towering cloud formations, and every now and then we could see the red glow of some lava field on the actual surface.

I slid my board over to Karen and grabbed her hand.

She put her helmet next to mine. "Hi there," she said, squeezing my hand.

"Hi. Look, I didn't admit anything to Lofti – he's just guessing."

Karen laughed. "Don't worry, I'll take care of it."

"I wouldn't betray you, ever," I said, my heart speaking faster than my head could control it. "I love you."

"Oh, Alain. Crap. You shouldn't. I'm too..."

"You're beautiful. You make me feel wonderful, grown up, good."

She sighed and squeezed my hand hard enough that I felt it all the way through the space gloves. We watched a huge lightning bolt light up half the dark side of Hell.

Then, as quickly as Lollipop had set, it rose again and we were zooming back out to the counterweight.

None of us, as usual, had come anywhere near to using up our 7.5 km/s of delta-vee, so we threw ourselves into an orgy of high-acceleration maneuvers, spirals, and loops. I taught Karen the whiplash, where you and a partner spin yourselves up until you are dizzy and let go, whipping out away from each other. Then Lofti grabbed her and did it with her, too.

All too soon, the computers took full control of our boards and positioned us for rendezvous. We rose in formation below the hangar, and its magnets grabbed us and brought us in.

The next two years were the most idyllic of my life. I didn't own Karen, of course. Apart from the fact that she was inherently unknowable, she had men her own age to explore. I had no complaint about this; between school, athletics, spaceboarding, and my Earth-coin collection, the part of her appetite that came my way was as much as I was able to absorb. But with me, she was always a little nervous, and a little earnest. I learned to reassure her, to make her feel comfortable. At one point, she said I was getting really good and called me her favorite. I think she meant it.

My parents, however, weren't all that happy with me spending so much time with a twenty-year-old vamp. Karen was majoring in the performing arts and I told Mom she was a good spaceboarder and was teaching me stuff about Shakespeare, theater, and so on. Mom wanted me to date girls my own age but I pretended not to be interested.

Haven was pretty conservative, really. A lot of the first settlers had been New Reformationists and, while the local version of NR had come a long way – they even had a woman bishop – there was still a kind of the everybody-knows-sex-is-bad ambiance. And as Karen became more involved in her arts, she was more inclined to challenge that conservatism.

She sang the title role in a student production of the Strauss Salome and in the first performance of the dance of the seven veils, she took off all her clothes right in front of everyone. There was a great hullabaloo, the student director was fired, and the remaining performances were done more modestly.

I couldn't get her off my mind. Finally, after one really great date, I told her that I wanted to marry her as soon as I could and have children with her.

"Alain, you're only sixteen."

"I was only fourteen our first time."

She groaned. "I know, I know...."

"I fell in love with you, Karen. So deal with it."

She shook her head. "You *are* growing up. Look. I'm not respectable. I've left the church. I don't think there's any God and I tell people that. I think Thomas Solacus was a fraud. And there are things you don't know about me. Things I did back on Earth. Things that might catch up with me."

"It can't be that bad!"

"You'd never want to be seen with me again."

"I wouldn't do that, ever, Karen," I said and put my arms around her again, holding her tight against my chest.

There were little tears in her eyes. "I might not get to see you again."

"Won't happen!" I said.

We held each other tightly, giving each other soft little kisses. Then she let go, turned and walked off with a little wave and smile.

The week after, Karen was expelled from Haven's only college. There wasn't any announcement, but Lofti caught me between classes.

"So our dirty slut got her tit in the wringer, didn't she?"

I shook my head.

"What's wrong? You think she didn't get her tit in the wringer? Or do you think she's not a dirty slut. She is, you know. She's got to be screwing a dozen guys."

I shrugged. "Okay, maybe she's kind of slutty, but she's not dirty."

"Hey, you called her a slut," he said, grinning.

"No, you...."

"Oh grow up, 'Lainy boy. She's a slut, slut, slut, slut. And you know what?"

I shook my head. I wanted to kill him. "I don't know anything; you said she screws a lot of people and that's what a slut does, so I can't argue, because I don't know anything different. But she's my friend and I know she's not dirty. She's a nice person."

"You think she's a nice person. News came in last week from Earth that she did something really bad back there and they don't want her running around loose before they deal with that. You didn't hear that from me, because the person who knows would get in trouble."

"Sex?" I asked. "Nobody cares about that anymore." That wasn't strictly true; New Reformation roots ran deep here. But you certainly didn't get arrested for it. Lofti had sex with Karen too, I was sure. Blackmailing her about the age gap to get it; so he didn't care about her at all. But I didn't dare say anything more. I just shook my head.

"Maybe she killed someone."

"Go to Hell." I walked away from him then, so he couldn't see me cry. I thought of going to Karen's place, but knew that was a bad idea during the day. Then I thought about going to the school library, but that would mean going back and maybe running into Lofti again. Finally, out of options, I turned for home.

We lived in a tall, tropical style A-frame with smart transparent aerogel barriers front and back so it looked open. If you lived there, the aerogel got out of the way when you walked in the entranceway, but you couldn't see it unless you looked very carefully when the sun was on it. That was not now. But the house knew I was home and notified Mom before I could get to my room.

Mom was tall, still a bit taller than I was, with dark brown hair cut short, and her dark brown eyes hardly ever blinked. She'd always dressed modestly, even on the hottest days; and my parents had shown so little affection for each other when I was around that I wondered how I ever came to be. Seeing the tears on my face, she zeroed right in.

"Karen Kelly?"

I shook my head. "Lofti."

"But it was about Karen Kelly."

I shrugged.

"Has she had sex with Lofti?"

"I don't know."

"Has she has sex with you?"

In two years, I had never been asked that directly by anyone other than Lofti, who I'd put off. I couldn't lie to Mom. I couldn't betray Karen. I stood mute and looked up at the high, open-beam ceiling and started counting beams.

"Alain, I asked you...."

"Excuse me, Collette..." Dad had walked in.

"Henri, we need to have a family discussion about Karen Kelly."

"Eh?"

"Henri, I think that our son is not a virgin. That woman has no restraints, none at all. And she's hurt him. Oh, I doubt that she meant to but she has, and she's hurt him terribly."

"She has not!" I said. "I love her!"

Dad took a breath and sighed. "It would be a wonderful universe if we could all spend eternity with our first love, but..."

"Love? Henri, he has no idea of what that means and neither, I think, does Karen Kelly. She's barely more than a child herself. She has romantic ideas of being some kind of liberated artistic courtesan, far above the ordinary social rules of behavior. And there's something she did back on Earth – everyone's talking, but no one knows what."

"Yes, she's from Earth!" I said. "And she's been to all those places we see in history and language studies. She's a natural on a space-board – she can make one dance. So what if I were in love with her? We're all going to live a thousand years or more, so what difference will it make if she's a bit older when I'm a thousand and sixteen years old and she's a thousand and twenty? What difference will it make what she did on Earth when we're ten million years old? Why can't you – why can't everyone – just let her be herself?"

Dad put a hand on my shoulder. "Alain, I don't know what this is about, but she doesn't fit in. Not here. There may be places where she would fit in just fine, but she's trying to make this into one of those places and that's not fair. People here have a right to be who they are, too. Now, I'm less concerned about your feelings than your mother because I look on this as a growing experience, and you're due for one. That's part of the process."

"Henri, he's just…"

"Sixteen standard years. Two years older than many cultures back on Earth used as the date of their manhood rituals."

"Other times, other places," Mom said.

"What are they going to do to her?" I asked.

Mom pursed her lips.

"Nothing horrendous," Dad said. "If they're not comfortable with her being free the way she is, they'll put her to sleep, make a few adjustments to her genome to reduce glandular rewards, add some inhibitory memes to her… uh, whatever stores our habits. She'll be just fine afterward and probably a bit embarrassed about how she's behaved. And she'll fit in."

"Can't she just go somewhere else?"

"No starships due in for almost a year, and we don't really have a jail here." Dad shook his head. "Loyalty to one's friends and keeping one's word are pretty damn important, too, Collette. Let's let him think about it for a while. Meanwhile, we have a comet inbound."

"Huh?" I said. Lollipop had lots of comets, a couple generally visible every night.

Dad smiled. "Really inbound. It's going to graze Hell, maybe break up, go around a couple of times, then get perturbed by Haven to crash right into Hell. Some of the pieces might end up headed for impact on Haven, except we'll push them out of the way first."

"How?"

"Well, as I hear it, they'll identify which pieces might hit, and then everyone gets on spaceboards, picks up the pieces around perihellion, then just pushes them out of the way. The spaceboards could be programmed to do this by themselves, of course. Or we could make a maser gun to produce a lopsided boil-off. Or something else. But folks thought this might be more fun."

"Wow! How does one get to be a part of this?" I asked.

For the next three weeks I was super busy getting my school work done early so I could spend a couple of days in space pushing comet chunks. I'd heard nothing from Karen; she normally contacted me for our rendezvous, using the code name of Sarah, her great-grandmother. But there were no messages, and considering all the trouble, I thought that was probably just as well. But I missed her, especially late at night when I would hug my pillow and remember how beautiful she was and how good her body felt.

She had not forgotten about me, either.

The comet crash happened just as predicted. The comet was a big one, almost three kilometers long in its biggest dimension. It broke into seven large pieces, all roughly a kilometer across, plus tens of thousands of building-sized comet chunks. Eight hundred twenty-three of these were identified as being big and dangerous enough to push.

Some sixteen hundred spaceboarders were assembled, one or more to a chunk – the largest chunks got ten spaceboarders. This was too big a crowd for the counterweight hangar, and besides, its equatorial orbit was wrong. Instead, they built a huge ferry ship in orbit around Haven. We were all ferried up to that, and it maneuvered to match orbital planes with the comet debris.

We got a great view of comet pieces coming in from about a hundred kilometers' distance, the bigger hunks comets in their own right, sputtering and spitting out gas and dust. Almost all of this would survive the second pass around Hell, but then Haven would perturb most of it into atmosphere entry on the second ascending node of the third orbit.

The spaceboarders buzzed out of the open hold of the ferry like a swarm of bees. It looked like chaos, but the computers had everything straight. The heads-up display in my suit guided me right to a fifty-meter-wide coal-black cinder full of pits and ridges. It was spinning around at almost a revolution per minute, so I headed for the pole.

Karen was there, waiting for me.

"Hi, Alain." I got that on my private frequency as I approached.

"Karen? Is that you?"

"Not my ghost. I'm in a pit on the south pole. You're going for the north."

I bent my board, zoomed south in an arc, found her, and did a perfect flip to end up motionless beside her. She handed me a bungee to tie down with; the gravity of this little dirty snowball was inconsequential. Anchored, I put my arms around her – not very sensual in a space suit, but the symbolism mattered. I hadn't realized how much I'd missed her.

"How did you...?" I asked.

"They're using every spaceboarder on the planet for this. I guess they figured I couldn't do much damage in a space suit."

"I guess not."

I could see her face clearly, lit by the reflection of the heads-up display in her helmet. Her eyes were wide and glistened, just like the first time we'd made love.

"Guess again. I brought a vacuum tent."

"Wow..." I said, both knowing and not knowing what would come next.

"First, let's get this rock on a different orbit."

Standing on our hands, with our boots in the toeholds, we let our boards fire under computer control. When they stopped, we tethered them, Kelly grabbed the vacuum tent and led me down into one of the many holes in the comet fragment.

We unfolded it, wriggled in, sealed and inflated it.

The first thing she said when we got our helmets off was "Alain, back on Earth, I killed someone. Just before we left."

"*Killed* someone?"

"A New Reformationist prophet. He said he was going to marry me and filled my head with all sorts of spiritual nonsense. And we 'practiced.' Then he found someone younger and prettier."

"Didn't you tell your folks? You were too young!"

The irony of what I'd said didn't hit me until after I'd said it.

She sighed. "It was a small community; we were 'different,' so we had to stick together and handle our own problems. Our prophet was our authority, and you just didn't... I think one of the reasons my parents wanted to emigrate was to put a lot of distance between him and me. We lived on an island the church built in the Caribbean. We were committed... to a bunch of sick nonsense. The more I thought about it, the madder I got, about using women, about teaching a bunch of lies, about preaching one thing and doing another. I went to him to say goodbye and give him a piece of my mind. He was alone. He took me to an empty beach on the parsonage and told me to take my clothes off. So I did, the veil last."

I remembered that in the old days, New Reformation women had to wear veils. I remembered her performance in Salome.

"I wound it playfully around his neck, then kept winding tighter and tighter. The look on his face as he realized what was happening was amazing. When he stopped breathing, I pulled him into the ocean and watched the waves take him. If I'd been older and smarter, I would have weighted him down, I guess."

"The surveillance camera would have seen you come back without your veil."

"That too, yeah. It was premeditated, but not very. But I have no regrets about doing it. I'm not into regrets – things have their own logic sometimes, their own necessity that transcends the social order. So no regrets; he deserved to die, and I was the right executioner. But getting caught is really, really lousy." She put her arms around me. "One for the road?"

My lips met hers and any thoughts of resistance fled. Something inside me told me it would be our last time.

When we were done, we dressed in silence, stopping to touch each other now and then. As I pulled my boots on, my chronometer beeped.

"We've passed aphellion. Gotta be out of here in a few minutes," I said. "This rock is burning in." On its way to Hell, as it was.

"Probably." She laughed. "We were a little too busy for a trim maneuver, if they sent one."

"Then they'll find us out!" I said.

She nodded again. "Haven't heard much from us for the last few hours, have they?" She laughed. "Well, I suppose it's time to face the music, as they say."

"But they'll wipe you, won't they?"

She smiled and shrugged, the waves of the movement propagating through her free-fall floating hair. "Not if I can help it. Alain... I have to say I'm really, really sorry for what I've done to you."

"Done what? I wanted you, I wanted you more than anything in the whole universe."

She nodded and sighed. "I know. So I couldn't go away without giving myself to you one more time, whatever the cost. And now I'm going to hurt you even more, because I... I fell in love with you too, in spite of all common sense. So I either tell you that, or I don't. And even if it hurts you, I thought you'd rather know I loved you."

I put my arms around her again. There were tears in her eyes.

"Yes, yes. We can get married," I said. "In a few years when I'm old enough. Get married, have kids, all of that."

She gently pushed me away and shook her head, serious, frowning. "No, it can't be that way. Even if it could, I wouldn't be the same person, but someone else, reduced, damaged." Then she grinned like the sun breaking through the clouds. "Not that criminal wild woman that stole your heart."

I laughed. "Karen, you're not...."

"I'm exactly all of that, by definition. In this society, I'm antisocial. In any society, I think. I'm a total rebel. Try to tell me not to do something and I'll make a point of doing it. I don't belong, period. And I *don't* want to change. I am who I am."

I heard a beep in my head. We had to get out of there; we really had to go.

"Karen..."

"Hold me tight, once more. Just hold me tight. Then we'll get our suits on."

We did. One last firm embrace. Then we hurried into our suits, ran an autocheck, and blew the tent with an emergency rip cord.

Hell was awfully close when we got to the surface, filling half the sky. I released my spaceboard and locked my boots on. Karen stopped halfway.

"Good God, I left my watch down there," she said. "I've got to get it."

I made to release my boots.

"Oh, no you don't. Get going. If something goes wrong and you get hurt, they'll be after me for murder or something. I'll be okay. I mean it. Get going."

"Alain Lecarrée, Karen Kelly, *Get out of there, now!*" Grimes' voice roared in our helmets. Then, before I could unlatch my boots, my spaceboard took off of its own volition, under central control, I assumed. Karen waved and vanished as the comet chunk's small horizon came between us.

Out and out I went, feeling helpless. Where was Karen? Where was her spaceboard?

I was three hundred kilometers above the rock we were on as it began to glow and break apart during perihellion. "Karen, Karen!" I screamed.

But, as I watched, some of the chunks survived the passage, a half dozen glowing dots tumbling back up. We hadn't changed the orbit quite enough. Maybe... maybe...

They'd burn in next orbit, for sure.

"Manual override," I told the board. Why hadn't I thought of that earlier? I don't know. Adults tell you things and you do it. Then the time comes when you make your own decisions. Mine, damnit, had come just a few minutes late.

"Alain, Grimes here, what are you doing? Over!"

"She might still be down there, sir. I'm closest."

There was a brief silence. His voice wasn't angry this time, not at all. "Not likely, I'm afraid. But you have to look. I understand that. Watch your propellant, and we'll have help on the way."

The pass through the upper atmosphere of Hell had shortened the orbits of what was left – only a three-hour period now. With only a couple hours to find her and almost out of fuel, I skimmed over each fragment, trying to find the bungee restraints we'd tied the boards down with, trying to find the tent fragments, calling Karen's name over and over again.

Then I spotted it, a glint of gold floating over the black surface. The watch. I jetted over and grabbed it, and looked down. Did I see a fleck of white? Her helmet?

I jetted down again, watching for the fleck as the fragment's rotation might take it under me again.

Suddenly I was seized by two mechanical arms and dragged away. I struggled. "Stop, I saw her. She's down there. She's...."

It was Dad's voice this time. "No, son. We've got radar on it now and whatever it was, it was about the size of a space helmet. I suspect she took it off before... easier that way. There's nothing in this debris field now big enough to be an intact person, nothing. The rest of the debris is solid, or it wouldn't have survived passage."

The robot grappler was not to be struggled with in any event. I relaxed and said, "Manual off."

"Okay. We've got to pull out now, perihellion coming up."

The robot stuffed me, with my board still attached, into the waiting lock of a spacecraft.

Six more black spots dotted Hell as I watched. I don't remember sobbing, but I must have, because Dad called me. "I'm sorry, son. She's gone now. You've got to keep going."

And so I did. I became an explorer, a wanderer, going on out farther and farther. I go somewhere, and then I stay long enough for my mail to catch up with me, and a little bit longer just in case. For there's a part of me that fantasizes that she somehow fooled us all, that she'd sequestered a cold sleep pod in that hole along with the vacuum tent and had somehow managed to hide it from the radar and somehow survived the perihellion passage and somehow made it to another star, or just to a starship, and bribed her way in. She'd have made a new identity and then, decades, centuries after the stories died away, she'd have started after me.

So I've never been able to change myself and edit out those memories and store them elsewhere like I have so much else. Karen had made a statement, and I had listened; I am who I am. I will be that for all eternity.

Maybe she will catch me some day. Maybe, tomorrow on the path to my cottage, out among those pines that are not pines, in this crisp, oxygen-rich air with its slight tang of ozone and ammonia, she will come and find me, and we will embrace again and never leave each other. For old as I am, the cosmos is still young and the watch still ticks, and anything can happen.

# STORY NOTES:

This story was written to an image, one of two occasions that I have done this. The original image was an unstoried cover for *Analog* by Wolf Read in 2001. I discovered that too late to submit a story in time for the selected issue, but some years later, I found out about *Visual Journeys*, a labor of love by Eric Reynolds' Hadley Rille Books. I suggested Wolf's art and my story, and the suggestion was accepted.

Wolf placed his "spaceboarders" around a Jupiter-looking planet during what looks to be an encounter with a broken-up comet, perhaps inspired by Comet Shoemaker-Levy's encounter with Jupiter, 16-22 July 1994. Jupiter itself wouldn't have worked for the story because fatally strong radiation belts surround it. I'd gotten rid of those, temporarily in another story "Out of the Quiet Years," but not in an era in which the recreational activity depicted by Wolf seemed plausible. So, I decided to go to another star. Hot and warm Jupiters were in the news and I hoped it seemed plausible.

I chose Lalande 21185, a "red dwarf" about 8.3 light years from the Sun. While it's technically in Ursa Major, it's well south of the Big Dipper close to the big cats (Leo Minor, Leo, Lynx) and is not visible to the naked eye. It's close enough for a relatively near term human colony at a time where human genetic engineering is still in its infancy. It may have a planetary system; it seems to wobble a bit in the sky and there have been several efforts to put planets to those wobbles, but this is all unconfirmed as yet. Unless we are looking down from the top of its planetary system's ecliptic (which is possible, though unlikely) – Jupiter mass planets would have been confirmed by radial velocity measurements.

So I decided to make Hell a mini-Neptune planet of a few Earth masses, big enough to have an atmosphere that looked like Wolf's banded, spotted illustration, but small enough to escape detection from planet hunters. No such planets were known at the time, but today, courtesy of the Kepler mission, they seem to be the most common type of planet in the cosmos. Hell is a bit unusual of its kind, though; it has almost no water. Perhaps it was formed closer to Lollipop and got thrown further out in the chaos that may accompany the formation of a planetary system.

Lalande 21185, aka "Lollipop," provides the imaginary Hell and its Haven with a little less energy than the Earth gets from the Sun, but because it is a redder star, most of that energy is in infrared wavelengths that are more effective in heating a planet and the thicker atmosphere lets less of the longer infrared wavelengths out. So Haven is comfortable only above sixty degrees latitude or so. With only 40% of Earth's surface gravity, Haven's atmosphere needs to have about two and a half times the depth of Earth's to produce an Earth-like surface pressure. It's able to retain that atmosphere because, like Saturn does for Titan, Hell provides an axisymmetric magnetic field that keeps the stellar wind from blowing the atmosphere away without creating high temperature Van Allen belts that would do the job themselves. The planet and its moon are mutually tide-locked, like Pluto and Charon, and revolve around their common center of mass in a period close enough to sixteen hours that only occasional adjustments need to be made.

Haven was (in this fiction) settled by members of the patriarchal "Church of the New Reformation" which had controlled Martian Politics for a while, but lost influence after the alien Kleth visited the solar system [See: *After the Vikings: Tales of Future Mars* by G. David Nordley, published by Variations on a Theme, 2013]. Many of them emigrated to new worlds and this was considered a win-win arrangement. The usual result was, after a few years of practical struggle, a more or less normal polity with a few residual patriarchal traditions, attitudes, and practices – perhaps too close to our own time for comfort.

Another thing in the news at the time I wrote this was a story of a statutory rape due to age difference, with the older party being a young woman teacher. So I went with a teenage boy's most fervent wish come true becomes his worst nightmare. Be careful of what you wish for. The future will present a few new wrinkles in these situations, but the basic dilemma should still be recognizable. The particular circumstance is not autobiographical, but I should admit an awareness that perhaps can only come with age of how time does not necessarily heal all wounds, and should we find our conscious lives extended to the end of the universe, there can only be one first love.

# THE FOREST BETWEEN THE WORLDS

A persistent buzz against his wrist drew Akil Mateo into reality from deep sleep. "Kita?" he mumbled, and reached beside him. Empty air. Where was she? Where was he?

As sleep faded, he found himself in a hammock of fine netting beside a hut in a clearing in a forest. Where? Memories flooded back into consciousness. He was 51 light years and change from Earth on the planet Haze and Kita was long gone.

He felt another buzz on his wrist and hit the wait-a-minute bump on his com patch; so much for sleep. He wanted to think it was a bad dream, but seven weeks ago, as he had experienced time, he'd come home to find her things gone and a message telling him that their sixty-three-year marriage was over. He'd jumped at a chance to head out here and put all the reminders far, far behind him. But his dreams and the emptiness beside him were the greatest reminders of all and they followed him everywhere.

His com patch buzzed again. Com patch: there was no net to touch here; everything was infrared or ultrasonic. He shook his head, yawned and stretched. After almost forty hours in the field, his body felt like lead in spite of the one-tenth gravity. It had better be important.

At least this was a cool day, not much over 30 Celsius, he imagined, and with just a faint but very welcome breeze. The vast cloudy globe of Shadow, overhead, was already a waning crescent and the upper reaches of the interforest were already lost in darkness; in less than an hour, their sun, Oshatsh, would vanish behind it for twenty minutes. Three hours later, true night would fall. Here, between the twin worlds, the exhausting pace of six-hour days nearly doubled.

Buzz. "Hello?"

He looked at the image on the tiny screen stuck to his wrist. The shaved head of a woman stuck out of the tall, gently undulating low-gravity waves in the nearby lake they used as a swimming hole. The subtext told him the call was from Marianne Jones, a biological researcher he'd met a couple of standard days ago when he'd come down to the base.

"Akil Mateo?" she asked.

In her Australian accent, the last syllable of his name came out "kill" instead of "keel" He sighed. "Ah-keel here," he said, exaggerating the pronunciation slightly. "Just woke up. What is it?"

"Sorry, but you're the only one around. Could you check Sharada Fina's hut and see if she's there?" Her voice sounded worried. "I've been getting no answer from her com patch for the last hour."

"Sharada Fina? The anthropologist?"

"She may be up in the forest. If so, she's overdue."

"Didn't she check out?"

"Maybe through her system, but it's got a privacy block. Base ops says her com patch is still in her dome with vital sign monitoring off. That's okay if she's in her dome, but I'll bet she left it here."

He automatically ran the fingers of his left hand over his com patch, feeling the discrete bumps of its few manual controls. A com patch was generally deemed too unobtrusive for the Forest People to understand as technology, as long as you didn't let them touch or use it in their presence. His matched his skin color so well that he could barely discern its circular outline. "Leaving the com patch behind is going a bit far, isn't it?"

"Tell me about it! Sharada talked Uma Weiss into keeping technology out of the forest. Uma made an exception for com patches, but Sharada doesn't like even that. Look, com patches record everything, so I think tech transfer is a smoke screen – she just hates people looking over her shoulder up there."

"How does she record her data?"

"She dictates it when she gets back to a stand-alone system, then puts out an edited report."

He looked at the darkening band of green between the worlds. While the interforest wasn't particularly dense, there was a lot of it and, he recalled, some vines were actually conductive. "Maybe she's shielded by the vines."

Jones shook her head. "I've never had any problem. I think she just wants to have her ducks in order without back-seat drivers while she fights the battle over how intelligent they are."

Akil sighed. "I see. I'll check it out." It made sense. In addition to technological hygiene, leaving the patch behind would help preserve Fina's data monopoly.

He got up, stretched, and swung his legs off the hammock. The curly "grass" smelled vaguely like ginger as it squished beneath his bare toes. He glanced at his shorts and shrugged. The heat led the ground staff to be very casual around the complex, for comfort. Well, he'd held out for two standard days to the likely, though politely unstated, amusement of everyone here. To hell with it. He smiled at himself; talk about going native.

He dug his toes into the turf and pushed off; remembering to lean well forward to minimize his air resistance and maximize his traction. People told him it got to be automatic in a few standard days; but it was still very artificial for him, fresh from the one Earth-gravity of the rotating star base. It felt okay as long as he concentrated and didn't have to react.

Two modest gliding strides took him across the compound's central area to Dr. Fina's dome. Like all the others, it looked like one of the three-meter ramshackle nests of sticks constructed by the pseudosimians. But there was a modern door set back in the shadow of the semicircular opening, and the huts came equipped with all modern conveniences. Not too surprisingly, the door didn't open as he approached.

"Open," he said anyway. It didn't.

Akil shrugged. She could, of course, be sleeping. Akil pursed his lips and ran a hand through his curly, jet-black hair. One didn't violate a colleague's privacy lightly.

"Jones? Are you copying this?"

"Yeah. She could be in there screwing that amber-furred Forest Person with the black ear tips."

"Screwing? Do you really think anything, uh, vaginal is involved?" The Forest People had only one area of anatomical resemblance to people, but that was a prominently displayed embarrassment. He considered himself open minded, but the idea of her letting one of the round, furry, vaguely spider-shaped beings stick its organ into her body in the name of science was a little beyond him.

Jones groaned. "Akil, everyone knows she's been screwing the things; she's said as much herself. She likes to shock people. Like standing in front of me covered with nothing but dirt and scratches and saying 'oh, yes, I did' when I'm open-mouthed and saying 'you couldn't have.'

"But she's serious. She thinks they do it to exchange data encoded in molecules as well as to bond with their group, like the Bonobo. Well, she's bonded all right. Addicted is what I'd call it. But I don't think the Forest People are doing anything more than following instincts."

"I understand there's some debate about that," Akil said, with some understatement. The dispute concerning intelligence, or not, of the Forest People was more like a minor war among the staff. He tried not to take sides, but if there were genuine intelligence on these worlds, it had reacted very slowly to their presence. Or maybe it was just watching.

"Debate, hell! We're just spinning our wheels. She's got all the data because she's the only human being on this planet the Forest People accept, because she's the only one that would ever be willing to do... *that!* I don't know why I care."

Akil found himself momentarily speechless at the display of feeling and wondering whether Jones and Fina had some kind of relationship. Meanwhile, he stood in front of Fina's door feeling like an idiot as he confronted her dome's cyberservant.

"I'll try again." He spoke toward the door. "Will you at least tell me if Dr. Fina is in?" Akil asked it. "I don't need to bother her, just tell me if she's in. We are concerned. If she is in and you don't tell me, she may be inconvenienced unnecessarily in our efforts to find out."

"I have been instructed not to answer any questions."

The hell with it, Akil decided, and struck the door with the flat of his hand. It made a low, hollow woody sound. "Sharada Fina!" he yelled. "We just want to know if you're home."

"I'm doing something private," her voice answered. "Please respect my privacy."

"Sorry," Akil said and turned away, embarrassed, then stopped.

Something seemed wrong with her voice, he thought – her intonation or timing. A lack of tension, perhaps, or natural irritation?

"Dr. Jones..."

"I heard, and I don't believe it either. It's a sim. That woman's headed for a disciplinary hearing. Base ops, I'm formally requesting authorization to take control of Dr. Fina's dome system. Explain things to Commander Richards. Hang on, Mateo, I'll be right up there."

The ground base computer acknowledged its instruction. Akil's intuition told him that after the ten minutes of lightspeed delay plus however long it took to get Commander Richards' attention and decision, they would find an empty hut with its robot AI dutifully following its master's instructions to simulate her presence for as long as possible.

Jones came bounding from her swim in long low-gravity strides, large droplets of water still trailing from her lightly tanned skin. She was a big, athletic woman, a bit darker than could be accounted for by the trickle of ultraviolet light that managed its way through the vast, distended Hazian atmosphere. Polynesian roots, he suspected. She was, perhaps, five centimeters taller than Akil's 175.

Like everyone in this hothouse climate, she shaved her head, but her fuzziness indicated the last time must have been a couple of weeks ago. She grabbed a tree to slow herself and her large breasts kept moving in low gravity slow motion for some time after the rest of her body. The effect was surreal and, involuntarily, Akil grinned.

She rolled her eyes upward. "Low gee, Mateo – get used to it. She's not in there, is she?"

He shrugged. "I'd guess not."

Akil's felt his com patch buzz against his skin. "Go ahead," he said.

"Marianne, Akil, Sam Richards here. We've done a minimal override of Sharada's AI instructions to let you in. We've had a little discussion up here, but the upshot is that she's not there and you should probably go after her, promptly, and reel her in if you can. The two of you should be enough – a crowd would probably upset her and the Forest People. Everyone else is out in the field anyway. So you two have got it.

"I'm sure it's not necessary to remind you, but for the record, please avoid doing any violence to the Forest People, not even to save Sharada's life; she knew the risks and took them voluntarily. If there is any hostility, we might lose any chance of a peaceful evacuation; not the sort of calling card we wish to leave. If you can't reel Sharada in a standard day or so, come back and we'll regroup. If you have any questions, handle them locally. Don't wait for another fifteen minutes of lightspeed delay. Okay, you've got the ball now. Get going. Stay in touch with the ground base and good luck. Richards out."

"*We've* got the ball?" Akil said, wondering how he'd gotten himself in that position.

"I guess so. I'll go in," Jones said, ignoring his qualms. She turned to the door. "Open."

This time the door slid open without a fuss.

Fina's hut was full of forest things and standard equipment. Everything was there in perfect order, including her field suit and survival kit. The com patch was lying on the pillow of her web hammock.

"This isn't like her, all neat and everything in order. It's as if she expected people in here before she came back. Chaos!" Jones exclaimed as she touched the field gear. "I wonder if she took *anything* this time?" She seemed worried to Akil.

"Is that dangerous?" he asked. He knew the biochemistry was different enough that people wouldn't be nourishing to Hazian predators. There were some basic compounds in common; water, methane, alcohol, and some sugars, and a few other simple organic compounds, but most of the complex stuff had gone in different directions.

She shrugged and pursed her lips. "Not as far as we can tell, at least for short periods. The biology generally leaves us alone, though you have to watch out for some plants that can't tell us from the natives. There's water if you know where to look and some edible fruit. We can do without the nutritional supplements for a few days."

Akil nodded.

Jones frowned. "But, Mateo, we haven't been here long enough to think that everything *isn't* dangerous. Sharada's given up thinking."

"You think she's in over her head?"

"You better believe it. A lot of people do. She claims she's gained acceptance by mimicking all this touching, stroking, and screwing, and she thinks she's picking up something at least on some level. She likens the process to averted vision. She says she now gets feelings about things after she does it, as if the Forest People are picking up on her chemical language and manipulating her feelings. But when you ask her what she understands, she can't translate."

Akil looked her in the eyes. "It sounds like there were all sorts of warning signals that something like this was going to happen."

She shrugged. "Mateo, a warning has to be exceptional. Alarms that are on all the time are just noise. Uma Weiss is getting ready to recall her, but I think that's more because of the time Uma's daughter, Olympia has been spending with her."

"Olympia's what, twelve? You're not suggesting...?"

Jones shook her head. "That would be going too far, even for Sharada. Besides, Olympia would never go anywhere without her com. But Uma's getting worried."

Feeling *he* was getting in over his head, Akil wanted to change the subject and gestured to some long pointed wood poles leaned against one of the walls in Sharada's dome. "Those look a lot like spears to me."

Jones shook her head. "No reports of them ever using them that way. I see them sticking out of vines here and there, with Forest People using them as perches, to avoid contact with the vine. If you come in contact with a vine, it starts to envelop you with sap and digest you; that's how the forest stays clean."

"So the Forest People sit on the sticks and don't get enveloped; that sounds intelligent to me."

Jones shrugged. "Look, 'intelligence' is a catch-all for a lot of different talents, and these things might even be able to do biosynthesis faster and better than we can, but for a race that's supposed to be on the verge of intelligence, the Forest People don't seem to interact with us as much as parrots or chimpanzees back home. Of course, I'm more of a biologist than an anthropologist."

Akil shook his head. "I wish we knew enough to make plausible similicrons."

"In a month or two, we will. The people doing that want more data on behavior and chemistry. We have to have similicrons that will fool beings that perceive right down to the chemical level – it's like trying to build robots that smell real enough to fool intelligent dogs – dogs that might resent the intrusion and be smart enough to retroengineer the robots. Until we get there, our data gathering has to be open and in person. And that person is Sharada."

"Look, I understand that much, about not wanting to leave everything to the robots. Maybe she thinks she can do something before they arrive. She's probably just ten kilometers up at their usual meeting place. It should take us three hours to get there, max. A stroll through the park." Jones smiled. "With a couple of surprises. You'll enjoy it."

"Like this?" He spread his arms to indicate his nakedness.

Jones shrugged. "She does."

Akil felt very uncomfortable about that.

Jones laughed. "You should see your face. I was just kidding. Grab your coveralls and the standard low tech survival stuff. I'll grab her kit, too; she's been away too long and may need the supplies."

Akil was still nervous. "I'm going to ask Stavros to follow up, just in case." The ground base geologist had struck Akil as reliable.

Jones, who had started to gather Sharada's things, turned and shrugged. "Whatever. It shouldn't be necessary. By the way, I'm Marianne." She stuck out a hand.

He took it. "Ah-keel," he said with a forced smile. He was not going to put up with "ackle" for hours on end. He looked into her eyes. He hardly knew her, but she'd been on the surface over a month. Was she someone he could trust?

Her eyes were steady as if she was checking him out as well. "Ten minutes?" she asked.

He nodded. "Sure. I'll meet you at the north end." Oshatsh vanished behind the limb of Shadow as he said this, and the sounds of the surrounding forest changed as the light dimmed.

Akil returned to his hut and found a fresh set of coveralls; they were light and roomy and as tough as a fabric made from local fibers could be. They had an open weave to allow plenty of circulation, but he started sweating almost as soon as he put them on. He pulled on some lightweight boots made from a stiff open weave with gripping soles made from some hardened local resin.

His field kit was still packed from his previous foray, but he double checked it. It held nutrient supplement pills, a roll of tissue, a pack of medical patches of various sizes, a polished obsidian knife in a fabric sheath, a mesh water flask lined with a rubbery native leaf, and some other useful things made of materials unlikely to surprise any natives. If, he reminded himself, they really had the wits to be surprised. He slipped the kit onto his back.

Thinking of the nutrient pills, he took a couple and gulped them down with a glass of water. They could forage for bulk; several Hazian fruits and leaves were edible, though of incomplete nutritional value. Thus equipped, he hurried out the door to their rendezvous and waited.

Full day came again as Oshatsh rose from the misty edge of Shadow above, this time on his side of the interforest. His feelings of irritation at having to use some of his time to rectify someone else's screw-up subsided. This expedition had all the makings of a minor adventure and a distraction to keep his mind off his failed marriage. He'd fled his loss, but it followed him in his mind. What had he done so wrong for Kita to discard him like so much excess baggage after sixty-some years?

Stop this, he told himself. Look around you and get your mind on the forest. The brilliant sunlit mountain of green crept up from Haze as if it was growing toward Shadow while he watched, too big to comprehend at a glance. But he knew that under it sat one of the largest volcanoes ever found; the inner pole shield was over twice the linear dimensions of Olympus Mons and the enveloping forest was likewise monstrous. It grew up from the volcano out through the L1 point and spilled down onto the surface of Shadow, a huge hollow tube of long hollow trees and alien vines that bridged the 250 kilometers or so between the twin planets. Even at the edge, the largest "trees" jutted more than a kilometer above the volcanic ash soil.

The biology and structure of these trees, Akil knew, had little in common with trees on Earth, but "tree" was what they looked like and "tree" was what they were called. At ground level, they stood an average of almost a hundred meters apart, like the pillars of some gargantuan temple. The biggest of them resisted even lava flows and scans showed that some of them extended down through a billion years' worth of built-up rock.

Black, pyramidal mushroom-equivalents jutted two and three meters up from the forest floor reeking both fetid and sweet. Like everything on Haze and Shadow, except where an eruption, storm or recent impact had caused a kill, it seemed to be a climax forest, or even more than that, a collage of living fossils some of which might be older than multicellular life on Earth.

The trees frequently hosted vines of comparable scale, which apparently did them no harm. Beams of light lanced through the mists of the upper canopy. An eerily ape-like pseudosimian cavorted in the vines far above them. Shape prejudice made them seem like relatives, but the consensus was that they were less intelligent than, say, terrestrial opossums.

"Damnedest thing you ever saw, isn't it?" Marianne said, coming up behind him. "Ready?"

"Ready," he replied.

"Grab a walking stick." She gestured to a stand of "beetle plants," whose overlapping iridescent leaves had reminded someone of beetle wing covers.

"Walking sticks? Marianne, it's only a tenth of a gravity up here and these packs mass less than four kilos!"

"Which means a lot less weight to steady you and less friction to stop you – though your momentum is as much as ever. We need the balance aid. Also they're useful for clearing plants away and avoiding close encounters with Hazing life of the slobbering kind. They can't eat us, but they don't all know that. We can't use anything technological but our com optronics in here. But what we can have is a stick. Take one."

Too warm and uncomfortable to argue, Akil just nodded and pulled the stiff leaves off what seemed a suitable staff, though with more effort than expected. It reminded him of bamboo.

Marianne led, bounding off toward the tree line. He followed.

The forest had a profusion of detail, but all the details looked much alike to Akil.

"How do you know where we're going?" he asked.

"Look for the yellow-brick-fruit tags." Marianne pointed above with her staff. "There's one."

Akil looked for a while and finally spotted a basketball-sized yellow globe hanging from a low branch, patterned with what looked for all the world like alternating rows of yellow bricks. A few more seconds of searching revealed another one about thirty meters ahead.

"Those are native to the outer pole archipelago, so any that you find here, we put there. If you pick them before they get ripe, they seem to last forever. At least they've lasted for the couple of months since we've been here."

"Okay, we follow the yellow-brick-fruit road, then."

Marianne laughed at the reference. "That's the general idea. The Forest People always come down the same base trunk to visit us. We'll assume she went up the same way. The path slants up the aureole wall, then heads straight up the mountain 'till we get to the first base trunk ring, about ten kilometers from the central caldera. Then we circle north until we hit the right main trunk and ascend about ten kilometers."

An hour into their trek, Akil noticed that the canopy blocked the view above, forming a green and yellow sky. Oshatsh, approaching the

horizon now, shone under this and the shadows of tree trunks became more and more numerous until the effect was one of shafts of sunlight reaching in, rather than individual shadows. But there would be no problem with light until the eclipse. Oshatsh set was a long-extended affair as light refracted through the least curved horizon of the deep atmosphere – and the vast half globe of a waxing Shadow would light the sky for another hour, though less and less as the umbra of Haze bit into it. He looked for spots, but Oshatsh was a settled old K5 star with a generally placid surface.

For the next hour, the path led up the slope of the volcano around which the forest grew. The terrain was awesome; huge blocks of jagged a'a lava as large as spaceships jutted up through the carpet of debris, massive trunks and vines headed endlessly skyward into the mist, and webs that seemed made of thin vines filled in much of the space. Though he had "flown" through it in virtual reality, clearly any real flight by anything much larger than a duck was impossible. Sticking close to the ground, they got under most of it and lifted up any obstructing web with their walking sticks.

"Where are the spiders for these webs?" he asked.

"The webs *are* the 'spiders'," Marianne said. "Sort of. Look, we've given these things descriptive common names according to whatever they remind us of from home. But never forget that webs aren't webs, pseudosimians aren't apes, and flying elephants don't act anything like terrestrial elephants. Look, over there. A web's got a butterball."

He looked in time to see a web collapse around what looked like a yellowish soccer ball. The soccer ball had a beak like a parrot's at one end and four ridiculously small, claw-tipped wings arranged around its belly. It squawked once, then vanished from view, as layer after layer of white netting wrapped itself around the struggling creature.

"Vicious," Akil said.

"That's why you don't often see butterballs this deep in the forest."

"Are the nets dangerous?"

"One of them started to wrap me up once, but spit me out before completing the job. I got an interesting pattern of acid burns out of it, but they healed in a couple of days."

"Sounds like fun."

She shook her head. "Cured me of going bare-assed out here. I wrote the page on the nets; how much study did you get in before they sent you down here?"

"Level three on fauna..."

"That was flora, Akil. Well, pseudo-flora. We're not in Kansas anymore."

"Oh." Unfortunately, Akil had never been that interested in plants.

"Just try not to touch anything but rocks, trees, and blackleaf vines, and you'll be okay. Don't rest on the large elephant-ear leaf vines. They grow around things – quickly, by plant standards."

Using paths filled in by forest debris, they made good time through the a'a field. The shade gave little relief from the heat; this deep in the distended Hazian atmosphere, heat was borne by air more than light. Akil brushed by something that looked like a loose ball of spaghetti with long thorns that made a sound like ripping paper as they scratched across his coveralls. He felt a sharp sting as one of them penetrated the weave.

"Porcupine Plant," Marianne said as she saw him pull it out. "The quills can be a nuisance."

He nodded, ruefully.

As they ascended, the lava field changed from the blocky a'a lava into a more smooth, ropy pahoehoe, but on a scale ten times what Akil had seen on Earth. The largest lava tubes under them would be immense and he savored the thought of exploring them.

What appeared to be a clearing opened beyond the trees to their right, looking at first like a slightly raised meadow. Akil suspected otherwise, and confirmed his suspicions through his com patch. "Marianne, can we hold up a bit?"

"Uh, sure. Whew." She looked like she could use a break. "We're almost there, anyway."

"Ever been over there?" He nodded toward the clearing.

"No. A crater?"

"The main east vent. We think it's going to be active again in a few days. Want to take a look?"

Marianne took a breath. "Eclipse is coming up. I want to be on the tree by then."

It was getting darker, and a bit cooler. Akil knew that far above the canopy, the shadow of Haze had started to cover the almost full disk of its sister world. Mid-eclipse would bring real night.

"Just a quick look?" he asked.

"Okay. Quickly."

They hopped up the slight rise in a couple of minutes and were rewarded by a kilometer-wide hole in the ground filled with smooth, flat, lifeless rock. Dim in the diffuse fading light, the forest rose around it on all sides like some kind of giant's cathedral. High overhead, individual trunks and vines lost themselves in the misty gloom.

"Chaos, what a place!" Marianne said in a hushed and awed voice.

Akil smiled. Then he saw what he was looking for. "Steam," he said, and pointed to his left. "Over there on the rim." Thin white tendrils rose there, easily visible against the almost-black of the forest.

"Akil...?"

"What?"

"Down below. In that big wide crack. I see a glow."

Akil stared, couldn't see anything at first, and turned to Marianne to tell her so, but as soon as he averted his vision, the red glow jumped out at him a little further along the crack than he had been looking. "Good eyes! If things go as predicted, that hole could be full of molten lava in a few hours. Okay, we'd best get going."

But Marianne stayed rooted, wide-eyed. "Is this what the main caldera looks like, on a larger scale, of course?"

Akil shook his head. "Radiography shows it's full of debris. No light in there, anyway."

"Okay. Ready to go."

Ten more minutes of bounding uphill brought them to an immense vertical trunk that Akil thought must be thirty meters across. It had two yellow-brick fruits hanging from a lower branch. A glance at the map displayed on his com patch showed them about ten kilometers out from the main caldera. So near, yet so far – but he was on another mission today. He prepared himself for a climb that would be long, hot, and tiring even in low gravity that had sensibly decreased as they ascended closer to the null-gee point between the worlds. But as they approached the tree, he heard a very low-pitched moaning.

"Hear that?" Marianne asked. "This is one of the first trunks that actually goes all the way to the L1 point. It's also our elevator."

"Elevator?"

She grinned. "That's the surprise. It's hollow. See that opening? What you hear is a draft blowing into it. In the trunk, the flow rises about seven meters per second."

It was a darker black on lighter, but Akil could make out a notch in the tree twice as big as a person.

Marianne stuck her staff on her backpack and approached the notch from the side. She grabbed a vine on the way and then moved in front of the notch, coveralls flapping in the first stiff breeze Akil had seen on Haze. She clearly needed to hold onto the vine to keep herself from being sucked in.

"Cool at last! Oh this feels good! See you upstairs!" She let go and was gone.

Venturi affect, Akil thought. If the shaft velocity was seven meters per second, and the opening half the area of the shaft, the inlet air stream would be about fourteen meters per second. He thought for a moment. Terminal velocity, where wind resistance equaled weight, for a spread-out person falling on Earth was around 48 meters/second. In 1/16 gravity, that was reduced by the square root to about 12 meters per second. Then the atmosphere was almost three times as dense; so a light breeze of 4 meters per second should be enough to support his weight here. So a seven-meter-per-second air stream should leave him with a net ascent rate of about three meters per second. Air density would trail off some with altitude, but here between the worlds, gravity would trail off even faster.

He followed Marianne's example and approached from the side, grabbed a vine, then moved into the air stream. He had to hold on hard, but the wind felt wonderful – cooling and drying him.

It was time to go. Still, to just let go and let himself be blown away worried him. What if he hit something? If he was going to hit the inside of the tree opposite the wall, he wanted to hit feet-first, so he grabbed the edges of the opening and lifted his feet.

The wind swung him up like a vertical hanging gate, and he let go when he was horizontal. He brushed some resilient foliage on the top of the notch a couple of times, and then he was floating up in the breeze. Turbulence near the sides of the tube pushed him back toward the center whenever he drifted away from it. He could barely sense his motion, but the spot of light below him grew steadily smaller. Then it vanished altogether. Eclipse.

"Marianne?" he said into his com patch, worrying about a collision in the dark. A comforting dim glow came from its screen, light enough for his dark-adapted eyes to see the insides of the hollow tree trunk as he drifted past them, if he didn't stare directly at the screen.

"I'm about a hundred meters above you." She replied.

Plenty of distance. "Just out of curiosity, how do we get off?" he asked.

Marianne laughed. "There's a net blocking the shaft at our stop – no worries; it's a dead one. Now I have some questions for you. Why is it so hot here? With the eclipses, the forest gets half as much light as the rest of this double planet!"

"Convection. This thick air and Oshatsh's redder spectrum means most of the incoming energy gets absorbed on the way down and distributed by air currents. Around the tree, the atmosphere is even deeper because the gravitational potential levels are further apart. That blocks more of the infrared radiation; so you get more greenhouse effect. Still, because of the eclipses and lower pressure, it averages about five kelvins cooler here than Haze's outer pole."

"Could have fooled me. Exercising too much, I guess. Okay, now tell me why Haze and Shadow even have an atmosphere. And why haven't Haze and Shadow merged?"

Very good questions, Akil thought; questions that formed much of the motivation for the expedition in the first place. There were plenty of models, all with a lot of free parameters and some good guesses, none of which was proven.

"We're still working on it; we've only been here for a few months, after all. I can tell you this much; because the atmosphere is so thick, water and any other hydrogen compounds tend to freeze out many kilometers below the mesosphere. So it's almost all dry nitrogen, oxygen, and helium above the stratosphere, and largely atomic helium with only a few nitrogen and oxygen molecules when you get to the top of the atmosphere where molecules might escape.

"That's the exobase and its temperature is about 23 Celsius below freezing. To escape Haze and Shadow, atoms only need to move about 1900 meters per second, like on Earth's moon. But the thermal velocity of neutral nitrogen or oxygen atoms at that temperature averages less than four hundred meters per second, so they pretty much stay put.

"Ion pickup is another matter, but Oshatsh has a lot less ultraviolet in that part of the spectrum than Sol and doesn't create a lot of ions. Nor does it have much solar wind, and what it does have is largely neutral. Still, there's a significant loss. But there are significant reservoirs of volatiles, too. Big oceans and large ammonia clathrate deposits at the bottom of those oceans, mainly along the orthomeridian."

"The what?"

"The great circle equidistant from the inner and outer poles; it's at right angles to the prime meridian and goes through the north, south, east and west poles. The term was invented in back in the twenty-second century by the geographers of tide-locked worlds."

Marianne sighed audibly. "Got it. So we think Haze and Shadow *are* losing their atmosphere, they just haven't had time to lose most of it."

"Yeah, more or less. Chandra thinks the time constant is something like five billion years. Sun-Oh used a different method and got three billion, but Oshatsh is easily eight billion years old, so there's something they don't understand going on here. That's why we do these things, I guess. Haze and Shadow combined still have about two and half times as much atmosphere, by mass, as Earth does, and must have started with a lot more."

"I see. Now," Marianne asked, "why haven't they crashed together?"

"We don't know. Tidal perturbations and friction should have done the job long ago. But there are a couple of contrary influences; you notice how it's always cloudier on the trailing hemisphere?"

"Yeah, come to think of it."

"Well, the greater reflectance on that side provides a small net push in a spin up direction. Also, the ongoing mass loss decreases the gravitational attraction. The geometry of the land gives a tidal slosh frequency that's out of phase with rotation, so that drag effect is tiny as well. Finally, the forest itself may pump-up the rotation like a Landis tether, by contracting slightly during in eclipses and relaxing otherwise."

"The Gaia effect?"

Akil shook his head. "Thermal if anything. Anyway, the length of the day may actually be increasing, but we haven't been able to find ancient coastal tide lines because all the land surface is volcanic and generally younger than the hundred million years or so of data we'd need. There's essentially no fossil record."

"Tell me about it," Marianne said, a hint of exasperation in her voice. "We biologists have nothing to explain evolution here, either, or where the interforest came from. Those volcanoes look weird, don't they? Like big nipples. Why?"

Akil laughed. "That one I can explain. It's the sharply curved potential surfaces between the worlds. If you measure the mountain surface against the local mean potential surface, they have roughly the same slope as Olympus Mons, Mauna Loa, or any other shield volcano in the known universe. What low gravity gives in vertical scale, it takes back in a reduced coefficient of friction. Remember, it has to get down to zero in the center where their gravities cancel each other, about a hundred and sixty kilometers up. It's like the two planets were trying to suck each other's guts out.

"On the interforest, my guess is that the shield volcano on Shadow's inner pole once reached almost to the L1 point. Surface gravity would have been down to less than one percent of Earth's at the surface. Trees of ten or fifteen kilometers height would have been structurally feasible, and their tops could easily have hung over into Haze's gravity well and grown down to Haze."

"Well..." Marianne sounded unconvinced, "the problem with that is that the main interforest trunks are more closely related to the local vines than the tall trees of the perimeter. It might have started as air weed at the L1 point that hung lower and lower until it touched the ground. Before you tell me the L1 point isn't stable going in or out, we've thought of that. The updrafts from the inner poles are enough to keep things up there. A kind of Sargasso air sea formed between the inner poles. The wonder to me is that the forest survive the eruptions."

Akil formed a basket with his fingers. "It forms a kind of natural Hoytether – an interlocking tube of branches that can be cut in many places without weakening. The occasional lava flows burn away only a few trunks at a time, and there are centuries or millennia between eruptions at the same place; the forest regenerates faster than it gets cut. If Sharada really can communicate with the Forest People, they might be able to tell us something about the frequency and effects of past eruptions."

"Don't count on it." Marianne said. "They may be as smart as chimps in some areas, but overall, they've gotten nowhere in at least the last twenty to thirty million years. That's about all the further we can trace them so far."

"You really don't think much of what Sharada's doing, do you?"

"I don't know, of course. But it sometimes seems to me like she's found an excellent excuse to indulge in what most folks would call a perversion." She sighed. "Please don't tell her I said that. I could be wrong, and I'd like to put things back together with her if and when this ever gets over."

"Back together?"

"We're lovers, Akil. Or were before the Forest People took over."

Marianne preferred women? Akil's thoughts about her skidded to a halt, and he felt almost relieved. This was dicey enough without such complications.

"Uh, sorry about the break-up. But it seems from out here that you might be better off."

"Maybe, but I sure don't feel that way. Akil, when it comes to sex, she has this uninhibited go-for-it attitude that *sends* me! Our own communication was so great we really didn't have to talk about it, we just stare in each other's eyes that way and then, uh!, I'm gone! What she did to me was just so damn wonderful. I want it back. Got the picture?"

Why Akil wondered, did people like to dump their private lives on him? He'd never thought of himself as a 'father confessor' type, but people kept doing it. He hardly knew Marianne.

"I see," he said, struggling to think of anything else to say. He had cared deeply for Kita and certainly had found her lovemaking pleasant enough, but the intensity of feeling Marianne was describing was foreign to him and didn't sound very safe. More importantly, the relationship could complicate their efforts to persuade Sharada to return. What had Richards been thinking when he sent Marianne after her? Or was that why he, Akil, was along?

"Uh, maybe things will work out," he finally offered.

"Not bloody likely, is it?" Marianne said. "Well, we've arrived."

Akil saw a tiny spot of light far above him; eclipse must be over. In a minute the spot of light grew large enough that he could see Marianne lying in a net above him. He felt unsettled as his eyes contradicted his inner ears and told him he was falling onto the net and her. He missed her by inches but the net stretched and pinched them together. It was a chance contact, but he was feeling a little sorry for her about her apparent loss of Sharada's affection and gave her what he intended to be just a brief and friendly hug.

She clung, and his heart started beating a little faster. They looked at each other seriously for a second, and he had to fight off a moment of instinctual desire. But she disengaged wordlessly and scrambled off the net and out through the hole.

What had happened there? he wondered. She was apparently oriented toward other women, and he really didn't like her that much anyway. So why?

"Akil! Come out, look at this!"

He scrambled out of the net to the hole in the tree and looked into an utterly alien environment. The vegetation was thinner up here, with shafts of light lancing through the huge spaces to illuminate a riot of color. Indescribable smells assaulted him.

The hole led onto a huge branch, almost as thick as the main trunk. That led to the next main trunk, perhaps three hundred meters away. He climbed out against an incoming air stream; the true exhaust of this hollow trunk must still be many kilometers above them. He looked around. Huge overlapping iridescent leaves – or were they flower petals? – grew in twin rows out of straight spikes that seemed to grow from the main trunks themselves. Outrageous red flowers that vaguely resembled Chinese lanterns ten meters across hung from impossibly thin vines that reached up to branches and vines overhead. They were lined with Japanese-fan leaves black as midnight, translucently thin, and at least two meters in radius from the vine. His mouth opened wide; virtual training had done nothing to prepare him for this holistic experience. Occasional weird sounds made the unearthly silence all the more noticeable by contrast. In the distance, a tone-deaf idiot tried to tune a violin. Something hit a gong so huge and low pitched that he felt the vibrations more then heard them. The call of a tortured cat punctured the relative peace in six-note clusters of tonal agony.

Huge, strange shapes flitted in the deeper murk, and the sight of familiar 'spider nets' hanging between close vines and branches almost reassured him.

"Down here, Akil."

He scrambled to the edge of the "branch," clinging to its rough soft "bark" and looked down. He spotted Marianne's dark blue coveralls a hundred and fifty meters or so below him, against what looked like a platform woven of some light sticks. A sky-eel nest, he thought, remembering his orientation. Things would fall on it and the sky-eels would eat them, dead or alive. This one was clearly uninhabited for now. Marianne was holding a light yellow something.

"How...?"

"Just jump! Jump *down*, right at me – otherwise it will take you forever to fall this far."

Intuition screamed *no* at him, but he realized she was right. Still, he couldn't make himself jump down very hard, and he seemed to float down like an oversized leaf in the giant wood. He protected his face with his arms just before hitting the platform and bounced up gently, forgetting to hang on.

Marianne grabbed him, pulled him down and shoved the cloth out to him. He recognized it immediately. "Human coveralls. Maybe Sharada wore them after all, at least this far."

"They're too small." Marianne shook her head and looked grim. "I think she has Olympia with her."

"Uma Weiss's daughter?" The implications of that took a moment to sink in. Suddenly, despite the heat, Akil shivered. "Did you tell base?"

"Yeah. Olympia's not there. Didn't leave word with her mother, either. She told one of the other children that they were going to talk to the 'caretaker,' whoever that is."

"I'd guess the 'caretaker' is one of the forest people."

"And I think you'd be right. Uma is upset."

No doubt, Akil thought. "Are they sending help?" he asked. "There's no sign of anyone here, and talk about a needle in a haystack..." He gestured around him. "I think it's time to forget about contaminating the Forest People with technology and fly some people and surveillance robots up."

Marianne looked frightened. "That's what I thought, but they don't agree. Not even Uma. They're worried about destroying the possibility of the Forest People developing as a non-technological culture; that's a real hot item in exosociology. So they're assembling another low tech climbing party, but they want us to start searching around here." She sighed. "I want a robot. I feel bloody damned expendable, right now."

Akil reached for his com patch, then thought better of it. This woman was far senior in ground experience and if her advice wasn't being heeded, his would just be so much noise. He thought briefly about just sitting tight and waiting for reinforcements. Then he thought about the twelve-year-old. "Where should we search?"

"This is the lowest of the Forest People's gathering sites we know about, so we should start on this plane, and work our way up." She looked at her com patch. "This group doesn't stray too far from their main trunk. So we don't have to search the whole forest."

"Got it."

"We're near the outer edge now. Suppose we work our way into the forest core, go up a hundred meters or so, back on out to the edge, up a hundred or so, and repeat? Unless you have better ideas."

Akil just shook his head.

Marianne pointed up and to her right. A twisted "rope" of vines with black leaves about the size and shape of elephant ears hung in a catenary toward the next main trunk inward. "Can you jump up to that? I'm pretty sure I can. Then we can go hand over hand."

They jumped and grabbed. The leaves obviously wouldn't allow a safety loop around it to slide freely, so they tied themselves together; in one-sixteenth gravity, either one of them could support the weight of both with one hand gripping the vine. Thus secured, they headed inward, got themselves into a rhythm, and swung along like a pair of gibbons. They kept going through a night that, lit by Shadow's reflected light, was not much worse than deep twilight except for the pitch dark total eclipse of Shadow. They reached the edge of the core in three hours. Nothing.

Akil called Stavros to report the negative results.

"We haven't left yet," Stavros replied. "We still have to discuss tactics, technology impact and leadership with everyone. On top of that, a new vent has opened up just west of the base; the lava is very gassy, liquid and moving fast. We're waiting for others to get in from the field and sort their stuff just in case. Going to be at least another hour. I'd be up to you already, except now I gotta coordinate with everyone else. Sorry, buddy. All I can do is wish you luck."

Akil thanked him and told Marianne.

She nodded and stared inward. There were no leaves here. "Less light in here than a full moon gives back on Earth," she said, glancing at her com patch. "Dry, too. Are your lips a little rougher? Feel any cooler?"

He took inventory. Indeed, his lips were dry and over the last kilometer or so he had felt much more comfortable. "Yes. That's as it should be; warm air rises from the planet through the core toward the L1 point. It's actually two kelvins warmer in here than out near the canopy, but the humidity is down so much it feels cooler."

"Hmm. I've got an idea for what these vines are."

"Roots?"

"Yeah, but going the opposite direction of what you think. Plenty of food here, plenty of oxygen. But no water. This," she pointed to a long black twisty fibrous thing, "I think is an aqueduct for that." She pointed to a bumpy, house-sized nodule growing on a piece of wood as thick as a ship.

"Upside down and inside out," Akil commented.

"Yeah. Like some other things I can think of. What's all the way in?"

"The inner two kilometers form a hollow tube, according to radar data, up to the Sargasso area."

"I'd like to stop and take a look at the inner wall; there may be…"

He held up a hand to stop her. "We're on a mission, Marianne."

She stared at him for a second, then sighed. "Okay, what do we do? Climb up half a kilometer and head out?"

Akil nodded. "That's a plan."

She started up, then stopped dead. "Akil..."

"I see it."

Off to their left, back in the direction of the core, one of the Forest People's spears protruded from a vast dead trunk. But some ancient strain had split this trunk lengthwise, creating a crack almost two meters wide that ran its length from the dark below to the dark above. The crack ran just above the spear and cut into the wood so as to expose almost two meters of embedded shaft.

"We can get to it – that way." She pointed at a "root" about ten meters overhead that crossed the open area between them and the split trunk.

"Time, Marianne."

"I know. Just a few minutes, *please*." She launched herself at the root, caught it, and swung over to the find. "The shaft is just like the ones in Sharada's hut."

But it was not the shaft that caught Akil's attention. It was the collection of alien bones embedded in the woodish fiber around it. "That *was* used as a spear, it seems."

Marianne nodded, quietly, and examined the remains. "The vines have evolved a way to get nutrients up here. But some parts of the bone are apparently indigestible." She grabbed a hunk of the trunk and it crumbled in her hand. She looked up and shook her head. "I don't understand."

"What?"

"It's been partly mineralized – desiccation, ages of dust, volcanic fumes, and an occasional drenching have caused most of the organic material to be replaced with silicates. That can happen in thousands of years on Earth, but here... look, there's the central void."

Akil looked up over the trunk, into a gloomy emptiness that must have been a couple of kilometers across. He must have stared for ten seconds before the importance of what she said registered on him. "This is *really* old to be this far in."

"How old?"

Akil looked at his com patch, his eyes selecting his way through a data tree. "The central trunk vines reach this thickness in about ten thousand years. Eventually eruptions take both ends and the vine dies. New growth pushes the dead old growth slowly toward the center where it either falls into one of the calderas or gets taken by the wind up to the center. The process takes forever; the latest models would require something on the order of a billion years."

"A billion. Akil, this is a pseudosimian skeleton, and it's exactly like, as far as I can tell, the pseudosimian below. Look, instead of a single backbone, the cycloskeleta have a loop of some sixty bones. In interforest, avian, and oceanic life, the circular plan held; and in the Forest People it was retained with a vengeance." She drew her fingers along what seemed to be a bony railroad track. "But in the pseudosimians and other Hazian ground life, this loop had stretched into something not entirely un-spinelike except for its double hump. But..."

"But?"

"If the pseudosimians are this old, it should have merged by now, fused into a true spine, but..."

Akil was no expert in evolution, but he got the point. "Stasis."

"A *billion* years of stasis. Akil, that's strange for that kind of life form. Very strange."

"Unpunctuated equilibrium? Living fossils?"

 "You're going to think I'm crazy, but I'm beginning to wonder if it's deliberate. As if the Forest People don't want any competition developing."

Akil shivered despite his coveralls. "Are you suggesting it was culled? But it looks the same..."

He fell silent as he realized that bones told only part of the story.

"Look at where it was, Akil." She touched the crumbling bone of the ancient pseudosimian. "It was like us. It was exploring. A behavioral mutant, if you like."

Akil shivered again. "We aren't supposed to be here either, are we?"

Marianne looked into the gloom. "No."

Akil touched her. "Look, we'd best get back to trying to find Sharada and Olympia."

"I suppose so. But that seems so futile and this is important." She sighed. "Well, it's recorded and uploaded now. Someone else can do the follow up." She looked up to a vine perhaps two hundred meters above them. "Up?"

The journey back to the canopy took about fifty minutes. The search became routine. A journey to the core and back took an hour and a half. There they would check in and wait out an eclipse. Then they would ascend and make another such journey. They did this three times, returning to the "elevator" trunk each time.

The last time, they found another hole in the tree, with its characteristic in-draft.

"We've gone up a floor, it seems."

"Uh-huh. One floor. Let's check in. Akil, I'm exhausted."

"Me too." He raised his wrist and spoke to his com patch. "Stavros?"

He answered immediately. "Everything's assembled and we should be about to start climbing. Finally. We'll have to detour about twenty kilometers around the lava, so it's going to take a while." The man's irritation showed and Akil could only imagine the discussions and politics involved. "Why don't you guys stand down through a couple of eclipses and get some sleep. You've done what you can. We should be up to you by then. By the way, don't try to return to Haze base, it's not there anymore."

"Sorry I missed it," Akil answered. "You're right. I hate to leave the needle in the haystack, but when we're this damn tired, we're probably not your best observers."

"Roger that. Marianne, take care of him. Good try, both of you. I'll see you soon. Stavros out."

Akil turned to Marianne. "Net hammocks from a vine?"

"Yeah. But use dead vines for suspension. You don't want our good line enveloped by the vine. You take this side of the tree, I'll take the other. I need to hang my ass over a branch for a bit."

Akil got out of his coveralls and found a hole something had dug in a branch to squat over. That done, he cut a couple of vines from which to hang his hammock, tied them into loops, hung the hammock from the loops and crawled in just as the eclipse hit.

It was a Shadow eclipse, and maximum, only a slight band of refracted twilight fell on the smaller world. Akil caught a glimpse of this ghostly arc through a hole in the high haze, and of a bright star or planet near it; that was the first celestial object other than Shadow he had seen from the surface of Haze. Of course, he thought as he slipped into sleep, he was no longer on the surface of Haze.

Akil woke from a dreamless sleep to the almost perfect silence of the interforest in Shadow eclipse and shuddered a little as he looked through the web of his hammock down further than he could see in the gloom. He was safe; even if he fell, he could body-glide to a vine before he was falling fast enough to hurt himself, but his Earth instincts didn't let him feel safe over that void. He called Marianne. She didn't answer. He checked her location, and the nav utility told him she was several kilometers below his position. What? Surely, if she'd seen something, she would have called him before leaving.

"Marianne?" he called.

No answer. Had she fallen somehow and not managed to catch herself? He swung himself out and headed for the other side of the tree. There was her hammock, empty. He turned back to get his things, jerked and froze.

There, only a few centimeters from his nose, floated a huge, wet, constantly blinking eye. Its translucent nictating membrane closed and opened vertically as if driven by some alien pulse. In the surrounding darkness, it looked disembodied. He shuddered and tried to back away.

With surprising strength, corrugated fingers grabbed his wrists and legs. Akil pulled his hand free, but his com patch stayed in the Forest Person's hand. The Forest Person tucked it in some unseen pouch or pocket and grabbed Akil's wrist again before Akil could think. The hand seemed to stick to his wrist like glue. It tugged painfully on his skin as he tried to pull away.

"Marianne! Help!"

A dozen other arms gripped him immediately. He struggled, but, while he seemed much stronger than they were individually, they didn't let go and thus each of his arms was burdened by two or three times his own mass of Forest People. Their smell reminded him of wet dog and he could feel their warm furry bodies next to him with that wet stuff at their centers, erect and probing. He screamed.

It made no difference, so, with effort, he suppressed the panic and concentrated on observing the anatomy and behavior of the Forest People. There was no report of any Forest Person ever having harmed or even approached a person except for Sharada. But the hands that weren't holding him, or carrying them all to who knows where, were feeling him all over, poking, prodding, even, it seemed caressing. They seemed particularly interested, if that was the word, in his sex organs and his spine.

Their plump, furry bodies filled the middle of the loop like a bubble of flesh with the head and five arms spaced around it with almost mathematical precision.

He examined the short-necked Hazian head and its sense organs. It was supposed to be a specialized limb; the other limbs had homologous vestigial organs; he remembered pictures of a very primitive form Hazian sea creature that looked something like a six-legged starfish with mouths, tentacles and eye spots at the end of each arm.

The jaws on the Forest Person's head were also homologous to the fingers on the other hands, he recalled. The brain was back within the ring, deep beneath its leathery flesh, inaccessible to whatever damage he might wish to do. An esophagus ran beneath the muscles to the central body. A general purpose cloaca opened next to the penis-like organ that was the cause of all the problems.

Akil tried very hard to ignore the fact that this part of the Forest Person in front of him was now very elongated and firm and trying to insert itself into Akil's navel. He felt a sudden sharp pain there and cried out involuntarily. The organ withdrew, with large low-gravity drops of Akil's blood clinging to it. Akil glanced down; the wound seemed minor and, thanks to centuries of genetic engineering, would heal rapidly. But that didn't keep him from shuddering.

What the hell would they be doing to Marianne? "Let me go!" he yelled, uselessly.

The Forest People just kept climbing. Their camp vanished in the haze of mist and leaves below, then, in the next shadow eclipse, he lost the trace of vine trunks he was trying to memorize to find his way back. They never let go of him, twice substituting in fresh carriers on the fly. In the darkness, which seemed to not affect the Forest People at all, they entered another elevator trunk. When they finally left it, the eclipse was over and he was weightless in the forest between the worlds.

In spite of his situation, he gazed around in awe. The distance between tree trunks had increased to several hundred meters and vines dominated the vegetation with their characteristic elephant-ear leaves. The air felt noticeably thinner, more crisp and dry, though not really cooler. Light breezes carried ridiculously huge objects with them; a dead branch the size of an aircraft and in the distance, a free drifting web – a flying carnivorous plant, no less.

He saw his first "flying elephant." Until it took off at their presence it was almost perfectly camouflaged, with its "ears" looking like leaves and its trunk like a vine boll. While its body was of pachydermic proportion, the thin legs ended in hands that looked like they'd been stolen from the front legs of a huge frog. Its "ears" rippled and scooted it along like the wings of a manta ray.

They towed him to a tree branch where four of his captors anchored themselves and held him there. The one in front, who had attempted to do whatever to his navel, apparently had other business. Within minutes of the anchoring, one of the side holders was replaced, following the pattern that had been established since his capture.

He first thought that this was the time to try to get away – while grips were being changed. But no, they would be especially vigilant then and, in addition, would have a five-to-one numerical advantage instead of their normal four-to-one. Patience. At least they didn't seem to want to kill him immediately.

He could feel a gentle warm dry breeze flow past him; the core wind, he assumed. Strange new scents tickled his nose. The air pressure here was down to twice Earth normal, and the partial pressure of oxygen down to two-thirds. The lower concentration would make the effects of that worse, should he exert himself. Should he get the opportunity. He made himself relax and took deeper breaths; he knew his body would acclimatize soon enough.

He wondered about the time and found a spot of Oshatsh light to watch; fortuitously it seemed to run along a distant vine. Twilight engulfed the interforest; a Haze eclipse. He couldn't see either world from this position, but a Shadow eclipse would have been darker. The Haze eclipse twilight brightened into crescent Haze light after a period of time he knew to be about twenty minutes, but seemed longer. Then day broke and he found his spot of light again, far to his right. The rotation of the worlds was so rapid that he could almost see it creep along the vine.

As the spot reached a major branch on "its" vine, one of his captors was exchanged. Shortly thereafter, it began to darken, gradually reaching the pitch black of a Shadow eclipse. Shadow, being slightly smaller than its companion, fit almost entirely within the larger world's umbra.

That made it just over three hours between captor switches, he thought. Possibly, none of the original group that he had struggled against were now holding him. Indeed, the grips on his wrists and ankles were noticeably less tight. In that he felt a ray of hope.

He gathered more information about his surroundings. The "day" following the Haze eclipse was significantly dimmer than the previous one, so he must be well on the eastern side of the interforest. There was no immediate way that he could use that information, but it made him feel better to have a rough idea of where he was.

An occasional "spear" protruded from vines at various lengths; the longest from slight mounds in the vine's surface. The thought of what grizzly remains might lie beneath those mounds sent shivers through him. But he thought the spears might be fairly easy to dislodge, or break off. He could use one of them as a staff.

A Forest Person, or even a pseudosimian trying to escape would seek to get all hands and feet on the tree trunk and scramble away. He would make no effort to do that. Instead, he would try to coil his legs between him and the tree and jump.

His bowels were crying for relief. Would they let him squat? He would make a virtue of necessity, if so.

He tried to assume a fetal position, but gently. He did not want to display the full Earth-gravity strength of his muscles yet. They resisted. To establish a warning signal, he hyperventilated, then he farted. Apparently, his rear captors didn't like that and adjusted their position.

He tried to squat again. This time they allowed it, and he tried to pass some fecal matter, but, straining his abdominal muscles, could only produce a small pellet that floated nauseatingly near to him. One of the Forest People swatted it away. Maybe that would be enough for them to get the idea.

The back captors moved him up the tree a bit after this and placed his nether end over a hole in the branch out of which some vines he hadn't seen before grew. Akil bided his time. His best chance, he thought, would be about two thirds of the way through brightest part of the day; when he could see almost as well as they could, when at least the one that had been there the longest might be a little fatigued, and before the relief was in the area.

Another Haze eclipse and he had his spot back. When it was about halfway to the point where the captor shift change had occurred, he hyperventilated, then started to squat. This time there was little resistance. He concentrated on making a supreme physical effort. As he performed his functions, with little problem this time, he imagined his captors relaxed a bit. He felt the vines move under his seat, probing for every last bit of the organic matter he was donating and he wanted to swat them away in utter revulsion. But he suppressed the reaction with the knowledge that they were doing him a service.

Finished, he relaxed himself completely, going as limp as he could, and took a couple of deep breaths. Then he exploded, slamming his feet against the trunk with every ounce of strength in his body and tore free of two of his captors as he shot into the air.

Two came with, but using his arms to get his legs in position, he managed to kick them away as well, leaving great red welts where their hands had been. Never mind, he was free. The Forest People left on the tree were madly scrambling through the foliage to where they thought he would land, but the velocity of his jump was, he hoped, far too high for them to catch him that way.

He straightened his body in an approximation of an airfoil and glided toward a large vine trunk. That cost him some speed, but appeared to work. Anyway, he came close enough to catch some of the vine's foliage and swung himself around to its surface. Using the foliage to hold himself down as he folded his legs under himself again, he targeted a likely spear and jumped for it, just as the posse was about to catch up to him.

He flew to it easily. Getting the knack of this, he thought to himself.

"Akil! Akil!"

Marianne. He resisted the urge to look around and concentrated on his landing, and grabbed the vine trunk with his hands. He hauled himself along its smooth surface to the spear with his fingernails and, like a Forest Person, used it to hold himself to the vine, but floating above its surface.

"Marianne! I hear you but I can't see you."

"Above you, to the right! No, your left. Above to your left!"

He stared and stared. Then he caught a motion; Marianne struggling with her captors.

He couldn't pull the spear out, but was able to snap it off near where it entered the vine, then grab its stub in time to keep himself from floating helplessly away.

Forest People flowed toward him from every direction – no time to think. He chose a tree branch near Marianne and jumped hard. Holding the spear shaft in his hand gave him a feeling of confidence that he hadn't had in a day.

Be wary, he told himself. Be doubly careful when you find yourself thinking you're hell on wheels. He planned as he glided toward the tree. He would be only ten meters or so from Marianne and her captors. Also, assuming they didn't move, he could approach them from the side. Could he hit the group hard enough to launch them all into free fall, where they could be kicked off one by one? Perhaps. At least he might stun them and be able to jump again with Marianne and whatever came with her. The Forest People could defeat that easily by moving, but he hoped that what he was doing was sufficiently unusual that they wouldn't anticipate it.

In midair he wondered why they weren't any smarter than they were, but had no time to complete the thought as the tree rushed up at him.

He belly flopped onto the trunk and grabbed on with his hands, then scrambled to find a good takeoff point. Marianne's captors had noticed him and were starting to move, but they were too late. He aimed a little ahead of the way they were going and jumped with everything he had.

"Oof!" Marianne grunted as he hit one of her side captors square on. The Forest People hung on to the vine but he apparently stunned the one he hit enough that he was able to pull it off and fling it away into the air. That freed one of Marianne's arms, and between the two of them, they were able to dispatch her remaining captors, who flailed helplessly in the air.

No, not so helplessly; they could swim in it, and they were swimming back toward them.

Akil felt a wave of exhaustion. Exercising too hard in too little oxygen, he thought.

Forest People were flowing toward them in all directions.

"Jump," he said. "Across the clearing." They did so together, but without much velocity, and ended up coasting slowly through a hollow in the wood with knots of silent Forest People staring at them here and there.

Akil breathed deeply and asked his heart to beat a little more slowly, trying to stave off hypoxia.

"Thanks," Marianne said. "I owe you one."

Akil looked at her. She was dirty, had numerous bruises and scratches, patches of dried blood. She probably looked a lot like he did, he thought.

"Yeah, I'm a mess," she said. "They did it to me and they knew exactly what to do, damn Sharada. They knew exactly what to do and it hurt. Oh, did it hurt."

"I'm sorry."

"Yeah. Just think about Olympia. That kind of puts it in perspective."

Akil looked up. They were drifting toward a branch filled with Forest People. "Damn. Here we are, representatives of a vast civilization with robot slaves and starships, falling into the hands of our enemies utterly naked and with nothing but a broken stick to show for our heritage."

"We have each other," Marianne said.

"So we do... so we do! Marianne, we can jump off each other. Put our feet together, coil up, hanging on to the spear for tension, then let go and jump."

She shuddered. "No way to do this without splitting up?"

He thought hard and shook his head. "I think it's that or get caught again."

She closed her eyes for a moment. "Okay." She grabbed the spear and they got their feet together. "Where do we jump and then what do we do?"

"Pick a trunk and steer for it, like you were sky diving. Then jump from it toward that big old gray trunk toward the core."

"It's not a tree trunk, it's a leafless scavenger vine. Never mind. I'll meet you there."

There wasn't much time, Akil thought. Their momentum was bringing them closer and closer to the branch full of waiting Forest People.

"You keep the spear," Akil said. "I'll let go on the count of three, then jump."

"Ready."

He looked up. They were only about ten meters from the Forest People and there was no time for "one" and "two." "Three, jump!" he shouted.

It wasn't a work of art, but they both shot off in opposite directions. Akil had the shorter distance and had to pick out a landing spot quickly. But he was getting to be an old hand at it. He absorbed the shock with his legs bent and slightly off center so that he rotated onto the vine and could grab it. Then he set himself, made a mighty leap across the clearing toward the scavenger vine, and looked for Marianne. She crashed more than landed on her target and was agonizingly slow getting herself oriented. Forest People swarmed toward her.

"Come on, come on," Akil yelled.

At the last minute, she jumped toward their target, but it was a good, strong jump.

Akil bent his body to sail past his target and land on a smaller nearby trunk. The Forest People started to swarm toward him. He waited until he could see forest glinting off their big wet eyes before he jumped for the rendezvous point. The decoy worked and he arrived about the same time as Marianne, ahead of the forest people.

"Where to now?" he asked.

"We don't see Forest People in the core," she said. "Too dry. Let's try that."

"Three quick jumps and we should distance them pretty well," Akil said. "There's a trunk with a split in it, branches coming off in a kind of K shape, up to your left?"

"Got it. You go first."

They didn't stop until they were so deep in the central gloom that it was difficult to see. Everything around them seemed hot, dry and mummified.

"I think we can rest now." Marianne said. "I don't think there's anything alive down here. We must be fifty kilometers below the green line."

Akil, exhausted, simply nodded.

Marianne looked at him as if she wanted to say something more, but apparently thought better of it. Finally she said, "Can you sleep first? I'm too wound up. I'll keep watch. I'll take my turn the eclipse after next."

That would give him about four hours. He felt like he needed it. "Sleeping in microgravity without anything for a restraint is easier said than done, unfortunately." He tried to pull a vine off to tie himself down, but it crumbled to dust in his hand.

Inspired, Marianne brought the butt of her staff down hard on the smallish branch they had chosen for their stopping place and was rewarded when a big piece of it caved in. "Hollow," she said. The hollow proved less than a meter wide and the "wood" inside seemed almost polished. Akil was able to wedge across it to hold himself with his back to the wood. Exhaustion did the rest.

"Akil?"

He cleared his head. This time there had been no dreams about Kita or anyone else. "I'm awake."

"Second eclipse. Look below. It's glowing."

Instead of pitch dark there was a deep, diffuse kind or redness. Even this far up, the air had a tinge of sulfur in it.

"The eruption is still in progress – I can smell it. No escape that way."

"Could we make it to Shadow?" She looked into his eyes.

This was a test for her, he thought. Hell, it was a test for both of them. "I haven't given up on Sharada and Olympia," he told her quietly.

"Look, we seem to be safe here, but there's no food, no water, and little oxygen and what the bloody hell are we going to do stark naked on the Forest People's home court?"

He squeezed her hand and smiled ruefully. "They aren't as smart as we are, or have you changed your mind about that?"

She shook her head. "Maybe someone's directing them. Maybe Sharada."

"Oh, in that case, what do we have to worry about?"

She laughed grimly at his irony. "Remembered what happened last time we went to sleep? Akil, have you ever been betrayed, I mean really dumped and crapped on by someone you loved?"

"My ex, kind of. Somehow, after sixty years, I hadn't expected it to happen. But she didn't hurt me beyond that." Though that, he thought, had been enough. "Sharada couldn't have planned for you to be the one to come after her. It could have been anyone. That's not really her fault."

Marianne sighed. "She set the stage. Can you imagine what Olympia's going through? I asked you whether you'd been betrayed. Have you ever experienced *anything* like this before?"

Unfortunate memories came back to Akil, and he shuddered. "Once, as a kid," he said. "A girl I knew talked me into doing it with her, then she changed her mind at the last minute after, well, I was ready. I didn't know she had a microcam on us; she showed it to all her girlfriends. I had to tell my parents and change schools."

Marianne touched his arm. "That counts. Chaos, our ancestors wanted real sexual equality, they changed the genome to get it, and be careful what you wish for."

Akil yawned. Most men were less assertive than their ancestors and women were more so. Women were also taller, stronger, less emotionally dependent, better at math, and so on than the previous norm. Men were less angry and more verbal. Humanity had become a race more suited to communitarian sensibility than survival in the primeval forest; less frustration all the way around. Those decisions had been made over a century ago, and it seemed pointless to Akil to rehash them now. But Marianne needed to talk more than sleep. *Whatever*, he thought. "As I remember, it cut the homicide rate way down and made adolescence tolerable. Anyway, it's all statistical; any given person can still be anything people ever were."

"Yeah, in theory. But that makes us a different species, really. All that's left of sexual dimorphism is the different reproductive plumbing. But once upon a time there was a rich dimorphic culture with all kinds of literature that feels irrelevant now, written by people who delved into a human nature that doesn't exist anymore."

Akil smiled. "Most of that part of human nature was just culture, I thought."

Marianne shook her head. "Most modern people have no idea of what Ulysses *felt* when he returned and saw the suitors after Penelope. *Othello* is a complete mystery. I can relate to some of that, the way I feel about losing Sharada to, to *this*. But I'm a throwback, 'the last human woman' I called myself in college." She laughed. "And then I fall for another *woman* and then she does *this*. What a bloody damn mess!"

Akil could barely see her face in the dim light, but it seemed as if she were near tears. He reached and touched her hand, to reassure her. Time to change the subject, perhaps. "What college?"

"Queen's on New Brisbane, the space colony. My folks were from royalist refugee stock. Conservative in other areas, too. I don't know that they retroengineered me, or anything like that, but it would have been in character. Why did she leave you?"

"Huh?"

"Your ex, Kit or something, what happened?"

"Her name was Kita. I'm boring, Marianne. Six decades of steady sensibility was enough for her." He smiled ruefully. "So if you want excitement..."

She shook her head and her eyes glistened. "Had enough of that, haven't I?"

She held tight on to his hand, then slipped through the hole in the trunk, slid herself beside him and artlessly pressed the rest of her bare body against his, trustingly, as a child might.

He put his arms around her and rocked her gently. It felt beautiful, but he thought this could have nothing to do with desire on her part, especially after her experience with the Forest People. So he simply held her until the tears dried and she slipped into a deep sleep.

Then he slipped away from her, adjusted the position of the staff to keep her from floating away, and left the hole. Far above, it must have been midafternoon, but even Hazian daylight was more like diffuse moonlight this near the dead core of the interforest.

People, he thought, as much as they were intrigued by the new also liked to conserve things, liked to keep them the way they used to be. Earth was turning into a museum; every species, every building preserved just the way it was in the era that people first became aware of it. If they could stop the drift of the continents, they would. Perhaps, as Marianne said, they didn't like to see the efforts of their forebears turned into irrelevant dust. He understood Marianne's nostalgia for times gone by. But Marianne preferred women, which was certainly not an ancient human tradition, at least not in most cultures. Was this a contradiction?

Or was it that Sharada was simply the most passionate and assertive person within fifty light years and Marianne had simply had to have *that*, the best cave man available, plumbing being beside the point.

The engineers had done a good job, Akil thought, at least with him. His libido was distinctly laid back. But part of him wondered what it felt like, back then, to be so compelled, so motivated. Two steps forward, one back.

He wondered about the Forest People – perhaps Sharada and everyone else had it wrong. Perhaps they were not a nascent culture, but one that had been intelligent once upon a time and had simply given it up to stop torturing themselves. The Forest People certainly could be the products of advanced engineering; as far as fifty years of data collection by sensors and two months with observers in the field could tell, they never got sick, they never aged, they never fought, they never seemed bored or unhappy.

He shook his head and looked around him. The L1 point was an atmospheric Sargasso sea; debris from all over the central part of the forest would be brought here either by gravity from around it or by the warm winds from the planets. The low oxygen and absolute dryness might mean that some of this stuff was very, very old. Maybe, he told himself, old enough to preserve some record of evolution on these worlds.

He wandered away from Marianne's sleeping place a little, exploring branches, logs, trunks, and dried leaves that crumbled when he touched them. He found more spears, bones, skeletons, and whole mummified animals, both on the primitive (he assumed) ring plan of the Forest People and the double-spine of the pseudosimians. The winged critters tended toward the ring plan, but put on edge so the lower part of the ring worked as a breast bone. In the monkey-like things, the limb opposite the head had become long and tail-like, though it still retained a functional hand on its end.

He wondered again about Marianne's concern with the fossilized skeleton they'd found embedded in the tree. Everything he found was easily recognizable from his training, though it had to be very, very, old. Yes, evolution seemed to have stopped dead in its tracks here and it seemed deliberate. But who had done it and why?

Then he found a rock. Probably a meteorite, from its rough, pocked surface. A tool. He broke off a dry branch from a nearby trunk and scraped it, then scraped it some more, putting an experimental point on the stick. It crumbled; he needed greener wood.

A large mass embedded in the trunk turned out to be volcanic glass, and a blow from the stone produced some obsidian shards that were sharp enough to use as a knife or a scraper. Akil laughed at himself. He'd progressed from precultural to Neolithic in an hour. Given enough time maybe he could build a starship.

He had nothing to carry his new found treasures in; for that he would need living leaves and root vines that had enough moisture to be tough and flexible. They would need to make an expedition back to the fringe of life, tap some roots for water, some food, and gather some material–if they could avoid the forest people. With a stone in each hand, Akil made his way back to the hole in the trunk to wait for Marianne to wake.

Four eclipses later, they had lots of stringy root fibers for "thread," numerous very straight sticks, a dozen tough elephant ear leaves, several fruits that Marianne assured him were edible, and a wicker cage with a big ball of water – about a kilo, Akil figured – in it.

They'd also had a close encounter with Forest People and had spent an eclipse frozen in place in a tree hollow shared with some understanding balloon birds; they were larger versions of the ground-nesting "bubble birds," and it had been disconcerting to watch the workings of their innards through the thin translucent skin stretched over their circular skeleton.

"Our own bones are starting to show, too," Marianne had joked.

Akil had smiled, but they both knew this could go on only so long. Searchers were out by now, he was sure. But they would be looking far, far below the null point.

After another four eclipses they each had a crude obsidian knife, a couple of dozen meters or so of crude twine, canteens made of hollow branches capped with elephant-ear leaf patches and sealed with megavine resin. They also had elephant-ear leaf capes, belly bags to carry their primitive treasures, and stout, springy staffs cut from tree foliage.

"The secret, I think, is not to stop," he told Marianne. "Just keep jumping out; we can move faster than the forest people. Once we get outside the trees, our bodies should show up like infrared beacons to every sensor pointed at the general area. They should see us."

"If they're looking."

"Sensors have been looking at the outside of this place at centimeter resolution or better for over a standard year. It gets down to freezing and below at the forest edge. The sensors will see us. We'll just have to trust that they're programmed to notice us. Or some person looking at the data sees us."

Marianne nodded. "Okay. That's our best shot, I guess." She took a deep breath. "I suppose, if we get out of this, we'll look back and say, 'What an adventure!' I hope I remember how I feel right now if that time ever comes."

"It will," Akil said, trying to convince himself as much as Marianne.

They planned. It was approximately 120 kilometers out to the edge of the forest in the thinner air that surrounded the L1 point. Thin by Hazian standards, Akil reminded himself – it would be still thicker than Earth's at sea level. But with very little oxygen and cold. It would feel even colder than it was because dense air conducts heat more efficiently. The cold would be uncomfortable, but survivable. Assuming, he told himself, they didn't run out of fuel. It had been five days since they'd had a real meal with all the vitamins, minerals, and proteins they needed. You can't live on sugar alone.

It grew dark outside. "Shadow eclipse. We should get another night's sleep."

"First shift," Akil volunteered.

"Akil, we haven't seen a Forest Person or anything else living down here for three standard days. I think the rest will do us more good than standing watch, or to put it the other way, being run down is a worse danger than getting found here by the Forest People. We're way down on energy stores; if food is sleep, sleep is food. Our bodies need the down time. Mine does, anyway."

That made sense to Akil, and they settled into the log together. Marianne cuddled up against him like a child. She looked into his eyes, and slowly, tentatively, began to caress him. He began to respond, and felt embarrassed.

"You're gay," he said.

"Shut up," she said. "That was a million years ago. Now I'm scared."

When they woke, he lay awake looking at her for several minutes, thinking she was the most beautiful person he'd ever seen. Then he slid out of the hole and did his private things over a hollow that was "up" to the few microgees that remained here. Marianne was awake when he returned, and he automatically gave her a hand to help her out of the hole in the trunk. She held it a little tighter than usual.

"Ready?" he asked her after they'd tied their meager belongings around their waists.

"Yeah. No, wait."

She took her obsidian knife from her pack and scraped "M&A" in the dry surface of the dead, hollow trunk that had been their home for the last three standard days. "I don't have a camera, so that will have to do." She grinned, one of the few times Akil had seen her smile in the last few days.

Akil laughed. "You realize that tourists will be come to see that for millions of years, or longer?" He put a hand on her arm. It was inevitable, he realized, that he would feel protective toward her; the ancient genetic programming that governed pair bonding, however muted, was asserting itself, and the ache in his soul where Kita had lived was becoming a memory.

If they got out of this, he knew the time would come for an effort of will to return to his chosen life and commitments. And Marianne would inevitably feel hurt by that, but, if he judged her right, she had enough understanding and will power to take that in stride.

Then, he thought, remembering the skeleton around the spear, this could be all the life they might have together before an end filled with desperate efforts and pain. He imagined being transfixed by one of those spears and left alive against a vine like a still-living butterfly pinned to the backing of a collection box. He imagined being absorbed by it, woody fibers slowly covering his limbs, torso, head and finally his eyes and nose. He returned Marianne's embrace, needing the comfort as much as she did.

Their bodies urged them to dally, but they knew any further time lost lessened their already slim chances. After a moment, by some common unspoken consent, they released each other.

"Okay." Marianne said. "Let's do it. Out the way we came?"

Akil shook his head. "Aside from trying to avoid the place the Forest People gather, the forest is a little thinner along its north-south axis because gravity constrains it more. It will be a bit cooler that way too – better contrast for the optics."

"We stick together?"

Akil thought. Separate efforts would have the significant advantage of redundancy, but two going together would give them more eyes and hands and combine their complementary knowledge of the Hazian system. Where logic didn't give him a clear choice, his feelings did.

"Together. But, Marianne, if one of us gets caught, the other should press on. Our best shot is to let everyone else know where we are and get help."

She nodded, tight lipped. "Which way is north?"

"Good question. Thinking out loud, uh, where they took us when we were captured..." He pointed. "...that way, was on the east side I think. Haze's inner pole is that way, toward the glow. Those directions define a plane, so at right angles to that plane, this way..." He pointed through a relatively dense section of dead wood and vines. "...should be north. Once we get away from the core, we'll be able to judge by how even the light is."

"Good," Marianne said. "In twenty kilometers or so, we should start seeing patches of sky. It isn't as dense as it looks."

"Thank providence for that. Okay, I'll take the first point." With that, Akil found hand holds on "their" trunk, pulled his legs under him, and pushed off for the north.

Marianne followed. They usually jumped, but occasionally found a vine going the right direction and pulled themselves along it with a kind of pull-glide motion.

They set out as the next shadow eclipse ended.

Eclipse followed eclipse until they had reached the first live roots that tapped the ancient debris for minerals. Another hour brought them to where house-sized microgravity versions of the "mushrooms" lived.

"Time to be more alert?" Akil spoke the first words they'd shared in several hours.

"Yeah. We should probably hole up and get some rest now. It might not be safe to do so later. Let's find some water, too. We can make the big push tomorrow."

After tapping a "mushroom" root, they found a hollow in a small dead branch, just big enough for both of them, and slithered in. Akil couldn't remember when he'd been so tired; he fell asleep almost instantly.

When they woke, they realized that they'd lost track of eclipses, and thus time. Marianne found some sweet fruit, and they made a meal of it as they waited for the next eclipse.

The eclipse twilight started to brighten without reaching complete darkness. "Haze eclipse," Akil said. "So, assuming we've been out more than three hours, we've either slept for nine hours or fifteen."

Marianne yawned. "If anyone ever finds us, they'll tell us what day it is."

Akil sighed. "Knowing would make me feel a little less helpless."

She wrapped herself around him. "How do you feel now?"

"Helpless. Look, Marianne, shouldn't we save our energy?"

"What energy? Probably. Shut up. Make me forget all this for a few minutes." She sealed his mouth with hers before he could say anything else. He found, to his surprise, that his need for this temporary oblivion was as great as hers. When they were done she wordlessly slipped out of their hideaway and went to the other side of the tree.

After a moment of contemplation, he came out as well, grabbing their belly bags on the way. Wondering how far they'd come, he broke off a twig, let it go and counted to ten; it drifted about a meter in that time.

"Acceleration is up to a couple of centimeters per second; that's about sixty kilometers above the center on the last isogee map I saw."

"That high? I think we'll make it, then. I feel like, like it's worth trying. I didn't when I woke up. Thanks." She shrugged into her cape, and tied her pack around her waist. "I'm ready."

Upward. They climbed more than jumped now, as the growth became more dense. Akil's movements became automatic; grab, pull, coast, grab, and pull. Marianne took the lead; she knew the wildlife. She was also in better shape, and he had to force himself to a faster pace to keep up. Dry twigs and thorns scraped him so he was occasionally thankful for the loin pouches they'd made.

The canopy went by fast enough that even he noticed gradual changes in the surrounding ecology. Large branches, of the main trunks that ran between the worlds oriented to the local vertical as if they were trees themselves. There were splashes of color among the gray and black of the vegetation. Mugginess and humidity returned. Breath was no longer a problem for Akil. But fatigue from lack of normal nourishment and water were also taking their toll.

"Hush!" Marianne said suddenly.

Akil grabbed a branch, held still and looked around for forest people.

"Flying elephants. Right in front of us," she added.

His perception of the shapeless boles on a tree ahead morphed as if by magic. He nodded.

"Maybe we can ride them," Marianne suggested.

She approached slowly, then leaped at one, grabbing it on the back. It jumped in panic and flailed its ears, turning ponderous elephantine cartwheels in the air. With relatively little effort, she managed to wrap her legs around its neck, and grabbing the "stems" of its elephant ears as if they were the handlebars on a bike, steered it on an erratic path to the other side of the clearing and back.

"Woof – I hope this gets easier. Well, what are you waiting for? Grab one!"

Akil did, imitating what Marianne had done. He managed to steer it about as well as she did, and followed her on the way up. They covered about twice their usual distance before the next Haze eclipse, but the effort of steering left them exhausted. In the growing dimness, they almost ran into a huge water ball, maybe ten meters across, floating in a gentle updraft like a huge soap bubble.

"A bath!" Marianne squealed. In unspoken consent, they let go of the difficult flying elephants, which fled, as quickly as they did anything, back toward the core. Marianne handed her cape and pouch to Akil, took a breath, and eased herself into the mass of water. It quivered and wobbled alarmingly, but didn't quite break apart.

Akil searched the gloom for Forest People and saw none. Now that the flying elephants were gone, he realized that in addition to transportation, their clinging to the large creatures had probably hidden them from the Forest People.

But first things first. His body was an itching stinging mess of scratches and dust and he felt attracted to the water ball as if it had the gravity of a Jovian planet. He tied their pouches and capes to a convenient branch and slid his body into the shaking mass. It was like being swallowed by a live thing; the surface tension drew him inside the cool liquid. While not uncomfortable, it was easily several kelvins below the temperature of the ambient air.

He took a deep breath, and being very careful not to disrupt the drop, eased himself in the rest of the way. He tried to peer through the water ball, but everything was bizarrely distorted as the surface of water undulated. He rubbed his body with his hands everywhere he could reach, longing for a sponge or a wash cloth. Marianne swam over and ran her hands over his back. He returned the favor. They stuck their heads out for air together.

"I could stay in here all day," she said, "if I weren't so hungry. By the way, did you see the air fish? They've gone back to their ancestral habitat!"

He looked into the wobbling globe of water and after a few seconds found one of the microgravity flyers swimming like it had been born to it. A small rain of amber bubbles trailed it.

"Marianne, it's spawning. Laying eggs. That train of bubbles."

"Wow! Nice eye, Akil. I'm sure that's what it's doing. These water balls must be an important part of the ecology up here. This place warrants a lifetime of study."

He spotted another water ball, and a third. There must, he thought, be a storm above. The water stung his eyes a little and tasted vaguely sulfurous. The warm, saturated air from the eruption must have reached the L1 point. There must be a huge cloud over the forest, he realized. He and Marianne would not be seen unless they could get above it somehow.

They stayed in the water ball through totality. As light returned, they tried to swim out of the water ball, but emerging turned out to be less easy than anticipated. Simply rising out of its top wouldn't work, it drew them back in. Finally, Marianne pushed Akil out and he pulled her out in turn. They shook themselves dry as well as they could, found their things and resumed climbing.

"I think the eruption's triggered a big storm." He shivered. In the dense Hazian air, a slight breeze signaled a major blow. "Feel the wind?"

"Yes. A little chilly."

"You don't usually lose much temperature with altitude here, but a storm is a different matter. Cold air tends to spill down on the outside of the forest. That's why it's more or less comfortable at the base."

"What do we do; climb up into the cold and freeze until it clears up? Normally we'd survive, but we're run down – not much energy."

An air snake rippled its three meter body by them turning its jaws aside in a quick snap at something too small for Akil to see.

"It would be nice to be able to fly ourselves," he remarked.

Marianne let go of her vine and made vigorous motions, as if she were trying to tread water. She was able to hold herself aloft, even rise a little, but soon grabbed the vine in exhaustion.

"I'd need some kind of real wings," she said.

Akil thought of trying to sew elephant-ear leaves into a crude wing, with sticks to stiffen them, but a look at his already-fraying cape told him they wouldn't have the kind of strength to hold a seam. "Maybe we can make some, but not out of what's around here."

"Yeah, it'll get a little cooler and dryer in the canopy top with some stiffer flora."

They plunged on up into the murk. Two, three eclipses went by. The clearings in the forest got larger, bubbles of empty space for them to jump through. It was a great relief, each jump giving them a minute or so of total relaxation.

He shut his eyes for twenty seconds.

"Akil!" Marianne yelled.

He opened his eyes just meters in front of a branch with a Forest Person on it who was reaching for him with its hands. Instinctively, he swung his staff at it. It grabbed the staff and pulled.

But Akil wasn't heading exactly for the Forest Person, and its pull swung him down toward the branch. Akil let go of the staff and jumped with everything he had left as his feet landed on the branch. He felt the rough sticky surface of the forest person's hand scrape his foot as he left the branch, but it couldn't hold him.

"Akil, run! I'll be all right, just run!"

Free, he looked around, trying to find Marianne and figuring out where he was going to land.

She was nowhere to be seen. He called her name and heard nothing but a rustle of leaves. The clearing was inundated with Forest People, swarming over the foliage like so many ants, heading toward him.

His words had been: "Our best chance is to press on alone," or something to that effect. Maybe, just maybe, she had done that. He jumped in the only direction he couldn't see Forest People, in through the forest, brushing leaves and vines but somehow avoiding being snagged. He grabbed a tree and had a moment of confusion as to which way was up or down. But the moment passed and it was clear to him. He seized a vine and yanked himself upward.

The forest here was dark gray on black and he couldn't see much in front of or behind him. But he could hear them, rustle, rustle, rustle. Oh, he could hear them.

Then, suddenly, the eclipse passed and he was through the canopy and into a clearing above a magnificent cloudscape. Only a few branches of the tree he was on jutted out above him and similar tops stuck out of the mass here and there. There was wind here, and it even smelled cold.

He looked down; he couldn't see any Forest People for the moment. He climbed.

He reached a place where the trunk split into three branches and formed a kind of cup, almost three meters across, with a flat patch of soil. Marianne would go wild, he thought; a cloud island that likely had a dozen unique species, though he wouldn't recognize them.

But it did have one he did recognize; a grove of beetle-plant of the sort that they'd made their staffs from. He could use another one after surrendering his last to the Forest Person. He broke a branch off and was about to tear the bottom leaf off when he noted that moving it moved all the other leaves up the staff as well; they overlapped like scales.

Or feathers, he realized.

He waved it experimentally; if he held a leaf as well as the staff, he felt a lot of resistance one way, where the overlap of the leaf he held kept the next from trailing in the wind and so on down the line. In the other direction, the overlap went the wrong way and the leaves trailed freely.

A Forest Person appeared over the edge of the cup and scurried toward him.

He snapped off another beetle-plant staff near it roots and jumped for the sky. The cup filled with Forest People, waving their arms at him and making grasping motions with their hands. Some jumped and began swimming toward him.

It took him a few tries to figure out how to hold the beetle plant just right, to brace the severed stump in his armpit, grab the staff with his thumb, and use his fingers to stiffen the second leaf. He was falling again by the time he made his first coordinated flap, but when he did, it sent him upward. So he did it again. The motion was more a kind of swimming or rowing than flying, but it did propel him upward. He rapidly outdistanced the air-swimming Forest People. A lone tree projecting through the clouds to his right was strangely bent as if it were missing some of its crown. The remaining portion pointed, more or less, a third of a right circle away from him. He fixed it in his memory and settled into a stroke, rest, stroke pattern that he thought he could maintain for a while. The deck was far above him, kilometers perhaps, but there was nothing to do but keep trying.

The wind changed direction; up until now all he'd felt was the wind of his passage, but now a warm gust was coming from below him, gently but persistently. Was he dropping? No, the sky above seemed to be getting lighter. An updraft. Even though the clouds were his goal, he looked at them with apprehension. Hazian storms did not have the violence and power of high gravity planet storms, but there were still tremendous amounts of total energy involved.

He blew by a water ball on his left; a huge spherical droplet several times the volume of the one he and Marianne had bathed in. Even in this incredible scene, the thought of her burned in his mind. He belonged with her, he realized. How had that happened?

Suddenly, it was completely white around him. Wind changed direction and changed again, his mass acting as a kind of accelerometer; the longer it took him to reach terminal velocity in a particular air mass, the faster the wind. In the clouds, in the low gravity, it was hard to tell up from down, and he had to stop occasionally and toss one of his stones to see which way it fell relative to him.

Shadow eclipse robbed him of any light. He was cold, wet, and struggling to stay vertical for minutes. Then a white twilight faded in again.

Something smashed him in the back and almost caused him to lose his wings. He twisted around to look and saw a ball of ice that must have been over a meter across drifting down below him. He looked up just in time to see another one float grandiosely by him on its way down. He stroked his wings to build up some velocity in the air mass and give him some maneuverability, and did have to dodge a couple of them. His, cape, in tatters, fell off.

Then, so suddenly it made his eyes hurt, he was in Oshatsh light surrounded by billowing pillars of gleaming white clouds. Up and up he went, like being in an elevator that did not stop. His lungs burned;

oxygen at this altitude must be so low, he thought ruefully, that he couldn't remember how low it should be.

But as he scudded up out of the cloud forest the scene below made him forget his fatigue. Huge worlds filled his sky on either side of him, while the cloudscape seemed fantastically sculpted. He could trace the Hazian jet stream by wind-shredded clouds as it spiraled down south of the interforest, then back again on the other side, as geometry and Coriolis force made their topological compromises. There were holes, vast slashes in the cloud formation that revealed the interforest far, far below.

Somewhere, far out to the east and west were satellites that should be imaging him now, a black, hot spot against the cold cloud tops. He tried to hold his wings behind him, so he looked less like some errant item of Hazian fauna.

"I'm here, damn it, I'm here," he muttered to himself. "See me!"

Exhaustion caught up with him and he trembled with cold. He had to get back down into the warm fast. The updraft that had been his salvation was now his enemy. With aching arms, he rowed himself sideways until he sensed the chill of a downdraft, pointed his head at the clouds and flew down, resting several seconds between each stroke. Eclipses came and went.

He was far past exhaustion when he finally broke through the clouds amidst a sunlit shower of glistening wobbling raindrops as large as himself scattered every few hundred yards or so. He spotted the tall tree with the bent crown a few kilometers down and away. He rested, gliding toward it, descending, descending...

He got the scare of his life when he woke up over it and realized he'd fallen asleep while gliding and shivered at the thought of the disaster that could have caused. He shook his head hard to clear it and looked a third of a circle left from the slant. The tallest tree that way must be the one he'd climbed. With incredible good luck, Marianne, if free, should be nearby.

He missed her terribly. How, he wondered, could you get so used to a person in only a few days? But those few days seemed like an eternity. His universe of instant communications, on-demand equipment, and the support of unlimited reasoning power seemed to have evaporated like a dream. His reality now was the forest and survival.

He had to get down into the warm, find some fruit, find a hole, and see if he could rest long enough to recharge his batteries. He was almost to the crown when he thought of his rescuers. How would they find *him*? He couldn't rest yet; he had to leave some kind of sign or message. The letter A, he thought, for his name. He arranged some beetle plants in the form of an A about three meters by three meters, nearly filling the treetop island. Then, for good measure, he carved an A into one of the branches and under it carved an arrow pointed down.

Then he started climbing down. Despite the way his senses protested, he found he made the best progress by ignoring the minuscule gravity altogether and pulling himself along head down. Oh to be warm again!

He was well into the canopy by the time he recognized some of Marianne's fruits. He husked and wolfed down three of them on the spot, looking up and around for Forest People every moment his eyes weren't needed to manage his hands. As a child, he'd always thought it was amusing the way a squirrel's head would jerk up and glance around every now and then while eating. Now, he understood. He found a half dozen more fruits and stuffed them in his pouch.

Now for a place to sleep. He found no holes on this trunk, so he hurriedly carved an A and an arrow on the trunk, and jumped in the direction of the arrow. Still no Forest People.

A half dozen more such jumps gave him a ten-meter diameter trunk with a hole full of butterball birds, which he unsentimentally evicted. Once in, he found a warm nest covered with straw. He darted out and cut some beetle plant staffs that he used to bar the entrance of what was now his nest by right of conquest. Shadow Eclipse came, and he slept.

It was pitch dark when he woke again – Shadow eclipse plus clouds, he thought, leaving not a glimmer of light. With each passing hour the likelihood that people looking at the satellite data would have seen him above the clouds and followed him into the forest was getting less and less, and with it any chance that they would be looking for the women here near the L1 point as opposed to around the more usual Forest People haunts.

If he could only find Marianne again. He shut his eyes and tried to get some more rest

"Akee?"

His eyes shot open. Who was out there? Marianne?

"Akee?"

Something bumped him in the back. With a flick of his hand, he levitated himself and looked down. A tiny butterball bird, its eyes shut, but otherwise looking like a miniature of the adults, was calling.

A quick investigation revealed that it had just hatched, and, under the straw "floor" of his nest, lay some broken eggshell and two as-yet intact eggs.

He couldn't resist petting the top of its furry little head with the end of his little finger. "Sorry, kid. I can't take time to be a father just now. Maybe if I get out of here, yours will come back."

"Akee?"

"Yeah, whatever." Akil pulled the beetle-plant staffs from the hole, stuck his head out to see if the coast was clear, pulled the rest of himself out and got set to jump. As he crouched, he happened to look down at the trunk. There, very clearly, was carved the letter "M" and an arrow.

Small world, he thought. He jumped in the direction of the arrow and looked for another "M ->."

He lined that one up with the trunk with the butterball-bird nest and jumped for the next trunk. Another "M". By the next eclipse, he'd found another empty nest with an "M" over it, and a crude note: "Stay here."

He stayed through the Haze eclipse and through the next Shadow eclipse. It was the longest wait in his life, but just before the umbra of Haze reached the center of Shadow again, she came in the hole, saw him, and threw herself and a leaf bag of fruit into the nest and into his arms.

Unable to think of anything else, he stated the obvious. "You got away."

"I wasn't that far behind you; I saw you fly away. Then I went aloft each period between eclipses scanning the sky for you. I was going to give it a couple more sunny periods, then try it myself. Do you think they saw you?"

"How long?"

"Seven eclipses.

"Chaos, over a day. I'm afraid they didn't, then. I'll be in their data, but what person or machine would be looking for a man-sized infrared source there?"

"Should we try to fly back?"

"All the way to Haze?" Akil could see the planet from the opening of their nest. "The eruption's still going; see the orange in the clouds? Less than half that distance down to Shadow. There's a base there."

He was silent for a while. "And there's still Olympia."

Her lips tightened. "I need to have my head examined. Yeah, there's still Olympia. And Sharada, she could be captured as well, in spite of her relationship with the Forest People. Akil, I really, really don't want to go through that again. But then I think of them 'communicating' with Olympia. So I guess I've got to risk it."

"Maybe not. Could we find that place again," Akil asked, "in any reasonable time?"

"If we can find our trunk near the center... oh!"

"Right. Down in and out again, that's two hundred kilometers of dodging Forest People – we'd be able to reach the Shadow base and fly back on an air scooter with reinforcements in less time than that would take."

"Okay," she agreed, almost sounding relieved. "We'll make some wings and fly for the Shadow base. First, I need some rest." She lay on the straw in their nest.

He lay beside her, and she embraced him.

"Oh, is it good to have you again!" Her hands started to caress him, but to no avail this time.

He managed a soft chuckle. "Too tired, Marianne, and probably lacking several key nutrients. I really do need sleep."

"Mmm, sure. Good night, then."

He dreamed about Marianne that night. They were at some sort of party and she came toward him from across the room and interrupted his conversation about the ammonia volcanoes of Shipapu and asked him why he was naked; he hadn't realized that he was naked until then, and, embarrassed, excused himself from the conversation and tried to flee the room, but Marianne, as naked as he was, caught him and threw him down on the floor and started to make love.

"People will see," he protested. "They will tear us apart."

But no one did. A colleague ignored what was happening to ask him a question about viscosity in low gravity as she pressed her breasts against him and bit his shoulder. He answered that it was unaffected, and then he wanted her so badly he could scream. He tried to tell her that he wanted her somehow in *him*. But she guided him into her with one hand, caressed his body with another, held his arms helplessly down with two others, and pressed her soft furry chest against his.

As in most such dreams, he began to wake before reaching climax. But as he began thinking, the dream didn't go away and he realized that the fur wasn't right and Marianne had too many arms. Terrified, he tried to force himself awake, to force himself to breath in and out, to move *anything*.

He came out of it, opened his eyes and saw the single huge central eye of a Forest Person.

He convulsed and screamed, then screamed again as whatever was in the Forest Person's analog of a vagina bit into the most sensitive part of his anatomy. His arms were helpless and he arched his back in a spasm of agony.

He fainted.

When he regained consciousness, he was being bundled out of the hole in the tree – the same one; he caught a glimpse of the carved "M" and the "Stay here." Every motion brought pain to his nether regions, with the small consolation that this showed his nether regions were still present. "Marianne?" he called.

No answer. He got dizzy again.

When he woke, it was warmer. The foliage seemed to be flying by as if the Forest People were in a hurry. He was being held tightly, tighter than before, if he judged it correctly. They weren't letting him turn his head. Learning? Had the Forest People followed Marianne's carvings right to their nest?

Time to see if Marianne was with them. "Marianne?" He tried to shout, but it came out more like a hoarse croak, as if his throat had dried out completely. He'd probably fainted with his mouth open. He shut his mouth.

"Akil, behind... you."

"Are you all right?"

"What do you think? Are you all right? Get me out of here," she yelled, "someone please get me out of here!" Then she started sobbing.

What could he do? Held by a dozen arms and weak as a kitten, there was nothing he could do. What could he say? What could he do for himself? Wall it off, maybe. Stick it in a mental compartment and think about everything else as if his experience didn't affect anything. Concentrate on other things; deal with it by not dealing with it. Psychological first aid.

"Marianne, try to set it aside in some kind of mental compartment. Deal with it later. We need your brain, your knowledge; we can't fight our way out of this one. Can you do that? Try?"

There was a minute of silence. Then, "Yeah, I'll try. In a minute; I have to empty the compartment first." She let out another blood curdling scream. Then she said in a voice that sounded more detached, "That felt good. I may need a few more."

"I don't blame you," he said.

"Thanks. Well, I guess we solved our problem of finding the Forest People's clearing. I'm seeing more striped air fish. They like heat of the east and west poles of the interforest. They're a meter across and look something like a flounder or a sole, with black stripes head to tail. And I think we're following the East main; see the longitudinal depression? We think it's a merger of two trees. There are only two main trunks that look like that and one of them is far south."

"It seems a little warmer and it's brighter after Shadow eclipse," Akil added, straining to try to turn his head back in the grip of his captor to throw his voice behind him. "I think we're on the East side of the interforest."

"Can you piss, Akil. I can't"

"Why?"

"Molecules for our rescuers to track, wherever they are."

He tried. Nothing. He couldn't remember when he'd last had a drink of water. But maybe he could spit. He really had to work at it, but finally managed to send a small mucous ball flying out toward the trees.

"Try spitting," he said.

"Good idea."

Akil felt very tired, and let himself doze off again, taking care to shut his mouth. He awoke in Haze eclipse. He let Marianne know he was still alive and then tried to relax to watch the forest. He wondered about its quiet. Earth forests could be cacophonous, but here, calls were few, clear and individual. The air had a tinge of sulfur. Was the eruption still in progress, he wondered, or did the smell just hang around for a long time in the dense atmosphere?

"Oh no!" screamed Marianne. "Akil, to your left!"

He almost missed it, and wished he had. It was Sharada, flat against a huge Elephant-ear leaf vine. She was pale white. A shaft stuck out from a wound just below her sternum. Shiny, sticky fluids from the vine had already started to spread over her legs, torso, and the back of her head. There was a whiff of sweetness as they passed.

But she was alive; still able to turn her head as they passed her.

"Don't worry, Marianne. It's okay. It's how the forest does things. Accept it." She smiled, then turned away to complete what was apparently the business of dying a slow, grisly death.

Marianne screamed "Help!" at a note so high it punished Akil's ears. He joined in, but by some unspoken mutual consent, they gave up after three screams. Neither the forest, the Forest People, nor anything unseen appeared to notice.

Then they were back in the Forest People's clearing, held against tree trunks stripped of even the meager belongings they had managed to make in their few standard days of freedom, at the mercy of something they could not comprehend.

The Forest People didn't wait long. A Forest Person was in Akil's face, stroking him, pressing its cloacal cavity against his recently abused penis. "Get away from me," he said, without any hope of being understood. "Get away from me."

"Akil," Marianne said, "the spears."

Some nearby Forest People were holding them. Was that the deal, he wondered. Give them a few inches of hard flesh or get skewered like Sharada Fina? It was no use trying to explain that human anatomy didn't work that way. Should he close his eyes and try to forget what was happening and imagine something? Go back to his dream. Could he do that to save his life?

No, he would not. But he could shut his heart down, if the spear didn't do it, but he would not lie there pinned like some insect, watching Marianne get raped. As a young boy, he had once pierced a fly with a pin and watched it struggle for ten minutes. He had been ashamed of himself later. Was he up against some being as incomprehensible to him as he must have been to the fly?

He had never believed in any kind of Galactic oversight. Here and there people had found nodes of what they called "the galactic library," but other works of ancient sentients were spread very thin, and there was no reproducible evidence of the slightest interference in the development and occasional demise of any intelligent beings. But his own oncoming fate had all the markings of the humor of some sadistic, omnipotent judge right out of the god mythologies of many cultures.

"Akil..." Marianne's voice was soft.

"I think we're done for. Don't worry about losing control. No one will know how we die."

"I'll know. You'll know. But that wasn't what I want to talk about. Over to your right. I think I see some field kits. The yellow one is

Sharada's, the one you brought. It might still have her com patch in it."

He looked quickly. "Got you." Was there any way to get it?

The Forest Person in front of him suddenly gave up and turned its attention to Marianne. Akil waited for the spear.

"*Get The Bloody Hell Away From Me!!!*" Marianne screamed as the Forest Person came at her to do its thing. She wrenched her body this way and that, and even in the grip of four of them managed to resist it.

She would soon wear out, he knew, but he was full of admiration for her struggle.

A pale lithe figure drifted in, seemingly from nowhere, and touched the struggling Forest Person. It noticed her and acted confused. Olympia. She stroked the Forest Person and, as it turned, presented herself to it.

"Olympia," Marianne said in a hushed voice. "Oh, no. Don't. Not that. Turn it back to me. I won't resist anymore. You don't have to do that."

"I don't mind," Olympia said, letting the Forest Person embrace her. "It doesn't hurt that much. Sharada says they're just exchanging encoded proteins with us. It's not any worse than the medical robots. You just have to get used to it." The girl shivered a little. "I'm still working on the 'getting used to it' part, but I think I can tell them to leave you alone. I think 'please no' real hard, and that puts something in my blood that they understand." She floated clear of the Forest Person, which scrambled purposefully away to somewhere in the gloom. There was a bright drop of red clinging to her thigh. She brushed it away.

"Olympia," Akil said, hardly believing what he was seeing, "Olympia, do they know we're aliens?"

"Uh, not them. But the Caretaker does. Sharada says the Forest People are like the eyes and arms of the forest."

"The forest? The Caretaker? Is the forest conscious?" Marianne asked. "Can we talk to it?"

She shook her head. "We're too fast. It thinks too slowly – very deep, very parallel, but slow."

"So..." Akil said, "the Forest People aren't smart enough themselves to understand us, and the forest itself is too big and slow?"

"Something like that. Sharada was trying to fix that, and it's caught on, she says."

"Olympia," Marianne said. "I think something's gone very wrong. Can you help us get away?"

She looked around "I don't think so. As long as I don't try to get away, they let me float around and stuff. It took a couple days for them to trust me that much."

"Do you," Marianne said quietly, "know what happened to Sharada?"

"She said that a marvelous thing was going to happen, a transformation. That's the whole reason we ran away like that, so she could do this thing and I could witness the results. She went that way..." Olympia pointed with a free hand back along the double main east trunk. "...with the yellow-eared group."

Marianne turned her head to Akil and shook it. The message was clear to him; say nothing about what they'd seen. Not yet. But he did have something to say about something else.

"Olympia, do you recognize Sharada's backpack?"

"The yellow one. She didn't want them here, but the Forest People brought them."

"I put Sharada's com patch in it before we left."

"Oh!"

"Olympia?" Akil's voice was anything but steady. "Can you get it, put it on and call for help?"

"I don't think Sharada would like that."

Marianne said, "Olympia, we're very tired and we haven't had any real food or much water for the last three days. I've known Sharada for a very long time, and she wouldn't want us to die like this. I'm sure she won't object. There's nothing anyone can do to stop her now."

Olympia thought about it and looked around at the Forest People, who didn't seem to be paying any attention to her. She pushed herself toward the backpack.

Nothing moved to stop her.

She rummaged, then stuck both hands in. When she withdrew them, she was holding a nutrient pill container and a canteen. She pushed herself back to Akil, popped a pill in his mouth and gave him a squirt of water. "They say you shouldn't have too much all at once," she said.

The com patch was on her wrist. There was no way for Akil to tell if it was activated.

Olympia looked at it intently. "I think it's working. They've got a record-and-transmit only protocol for when Forest People are around."

"Hold it next to my mouth," he whispered.

She looked around, then did as he asked.

"Stavros, This is Mateo. Please forget the damn protocols and get an autodoc in here now. Let us know you hear us, please. This is an emergency; Sharada's been badly wounded and she's shutting down."

"Mateo, Stavros. I'm breaking protocol, but to hell with it. Cristos!"

"What?

"Do you know what you guys look like?"

"Worse for wear I'd imagine."

"You're both stringy thin, dirty as hell, and Akil, you look like you've managed to turn brown. I can imagine what you've been through. We've been copying all of this, and the chiefs don't know what to make of it. I'm afraid Sharada's welfare isn't high on the priority list. We're evacuating the planet."

"Huh?"

"Look, my advice is to get out of there and head outward if you can. I've got a fix and if I can get you without a major Forest People incident, I will. Forget about Sharada – if she shuts down she shuts down. Stavros out."

"I'd better give Marianne some pills and water, too," Olympia said.

Akil nodded and she went over to Marianne. He couldn't hear what they said to each other, but he could see the tears in Marianne's eyes.

Very gently, Olympia tried to pry the hand of one of Marianne's captors off her wrist, but the captor held firm.

"They learn," Akil said. "They knew about our previous escape."

"You got away?" Olympia asked, in apparent wonderment. "Why didn't you run home?"

"We came for Sharada and you," Akil answered. "We didn't give up soon enough."

"Gee, I'm sorry. I don't think I'm in any real danger. But Sharada's going to be really upset."

"I don't think, so." Marianne said.

"That is true, Marianne. I am not upset."

Three heads turned toward the new voice. Sharada pulled herself into the clearing on a vine from the opposite side of the clearing. She seemed very subdued.

"Dr. Fina?" Akil asked, in wonderment. She looked no worse for wear and there was no evident wound below her chest but something was different.

"The new me, Hazian version."

"Oh! You're... you're a hermaphrodite," Marianne said.

"The forest came up with something that can transcribe DNA to what Hazians use. My new body is made from Hazian cells and has a compatible interface. Because of the low gravity, the interface has to be protected, internal. The resemblance to anything human was a coincidence, but a useful one. This is too important for squeamishness. I will demonstrate."

Sharada touched and stroked the nearest Forest Person. It turned to face her and simultaneously held and stroked her. Their bodies hid the rest of what happened, but after some gentle pelvic thrusts, Sharada sighed and turned back to them.

"I have just passed some instructions that my brain has encoded in the Hazian equivalent of DNA, what we call Hazian transfer genes, or HTG."

She repeated the performance with another Forest Person, while the first one proceeded to communicate with yet another. In a few moments Akil and Marianne were released.

"Olympia, that is my com patch." She reached for it. Olympia let her take it, looking as confused and terrified as Akil had ever seen a person look.

"You were dying," Marianne said.

"My old body served as the template and the process of learning it is necessarily destructive. The Caretaker demonstrated my change with one of the Forest People. A damaged one lay down on the trunk there, they put a spear through it to hold it there, and soon a new one with the same markings and no scars floated out of their factory—a special vine half a kilometer further toward center. The new body communicated with the old one; there's some final calibration that needs to be done. After that, the old one was absorbed. That is how they... we dispose of bodies around here. The same with all... effluvia. The vines need the minerals, calcium and so on. The example was clear."

Marianne's face looked white. "You let them run a spear through you."

"Yes, but by then they were sending me simple chemical messages; a few minutes after a transfer, I would know something I hadn't known before, generally as an image. That convinced me. The transformation was my best chance to make the contact breakthrough before I was gently shoved aside by the expedition bureaucracy and their robots. Unfortunately, the calibration process was not complete when my old body expired. I have probably sacrificed some of myself, but I do not know what, so I do not feel any loss. I have the memory of getting speared, for instance. It was like being hit hard in the stomach at first. The sharp pain came later, but was tolerable."

Next time? Akil felt like a cold wind had just blown through the forest. Olympia? Marianne? Him? What Sharada had lost was her common sense, judgment, whatever tells you not to go making monsters out of people. Steady, he told himself. "How," he asked, "do you know you're you?"

"I feel like me. All the memories feel familiar. How do you know you are you when you wake up in the morning? I'd better let the others know about this." She spoke into her com patch. "Hello everyone, this is Sharada, everything is okay. I have news. The Forest People are not the intelligence here. The Caretaker is. The Caretaker is the mind that inhabits the network of vines that makes up most of the interforest. The Hazians left it to keep their planets from changing too much while they visit a distant galaxy – a round trip journey of about 1.2 billion standard years. The Caretaker thinks slowly by our standards, but it knows what we are and wants to preserve the contact for its masters as long as this can be done without significant change to the twin worlds.

"The Forest People are its automatons. Their behavior is programmed chemically. They do not have a higher form of consciousness because if they did, they would be slaves and that would be cruel. They cull mutations identified by the Caretaker, discourage cross-forest traffic, distribute baseline HTG to preserve the existing ecologies so that Hazians can come home again. Every species is preserved, in approximately the same numbers, doing the same things. Over.

The com patch on Sharada's wrist came alive. "Stavros here. Good to hear from you Sharada. I won't say there's not going to be hell to pay when you get back to the star base, but it's really good to see everyone okay."

"Stavros," Sharada said. "I am not coming back. My body chemistry is now Hazian. My human consciousness is the same, but there is much more. I will do a full report as soon as I get the time, but I must remain here and I am content."

"Hazian?" Stavros asked.

"Biochemically Hazian with the anatomical change that you see."

That got about ten seconds of silence from Stavros. Finally, he said, "Uh, roger. Look, this is all a bit much for people to digest right now. They have to talk about the implications and such, and get back to Richards at the star base before they do anything. It looks like things are stable there for the time being. We've got a good fix. Someone should be up to you in a couple of hours. From what you say, we don't need to worry about technology transfer anymore, so sky cycles shouldn't be a problem. Talk to you later, Stavros over."

Akil didn't know whether to laugh or cry. Hurry, he wanted to yell. But that might just trigger everything.

Sharada nodded. "I want Uma to talk to Olympia before she talks to me. Otherwise, I look forward to seeing you. Sharada out." She turned to Marianne. "Mari, it is time for us to go have a talk."

Every muscle in Akil's body went tense.

"I'm not so sure about that," Marianne said.

"The Caretaker is." Sharada turned and quickly and unabashedly coupled with a Forest Person. Each time she did it, Akil became a little more inured to the function, and this time was able to watch the process with some clinical detachment.

"Maybe in a few days," Marianne replied, as evenly as she could. "This is going to take some getting used to."

"I am very sorry," Sharada said, softly. "But we do not really have a few days. From what Stavros said, it sounds like everyone will be off Haze and Shadow in hours. So please come now? It will be much better for Hazian-human contact if you do not fight it."

As if on cue, some Forest People moved around Marianne and between Akil and Olympia and the other two. Chemical communication was, apparently, very specific once you had the code.

Marianne shuddered, then took a deep breath and looked into Akil's eyes from behind the limbs of a Forest Person.

"Akil. Akil, you've got to take care of Olympia, now. Okay. Just take care of her and *tell* Sharada you two will stay and wait for me? Understand? Just *tell* her that."

Sharada smiled for the first time; it looked artificial. "Marianne is right. There is really nothing to worry about. She will be back as good as new."

A fully human being, he realized, would have caught on. But the new Sharada was missing something, acting too naively. Marianne's ironic tone and body language had meant that they were to do exactly the opposite of what she said. As soon as she was out of sight with the new Sharada, he and Olympia were to run like hell.

Marianne, Akil figured, was going to sacrifice herself to give him and Olympia a chance. If only Stavros had caught on that something was terribly wrong. The rescuers had to be near, Akil thought. Maybe he could delay things until they arrived.

"Marianne," he reached for her, clumsily, hanging onto his vine. Forest People blocked him easily. "Sharada, please, just a minute."

Sharada smiled and brought Marianne over to him. Her eyes warned him against saying anything. He didn't. He just pulled her into his arms and they clung to each other until Sharada said, "Come on, Akil. I knew her before you did. Marianne, let us go now." The hands of Forest People slid onto Marianne's arms and drew her away. There were tears in her eyes. "Remember me," she whispered.

"Uh, Sharada," Akil said, trying for another stall, but a potentially useful one. "Could we have the com patch while you two are having your talk. We've got a lot of catching up to do. I haven't heard much about the eruption and Uma will want to talk to Olympia and, oh, all sorts of things."

Sharada smiled. "Of course. We have to promote good relations as much as possible." She took it off and handed it to him, then led Marianne off.

Marianne looked back once and gave him a brave thumbs up. Then they were gone.

When he figured they were out of ear shot, Akil turned to Olympia and put the com patch on her. "Sharada is not human any more, at least not fully. Do you understand?"

Olympia nodded, trembling.

"I think the Caretaker wants us here as backup specimens, in case it can't transform Marianne correctly either. Or it wants even more Hazian-human hybrids. Are you listening in, Stavros?"

"We copy. We're fifty kilometers out and they're still arguing about sending robots in. What if the Caretaker is hostile and can retroengineer the technology? Similar nonsense. I'm going to do it anyway. Fan cycles with full A.I. enabled. They'll home on your com patch and you can ride them out. 1 hour, copy?"

"Roger. Thanks." Finally! He looked at the dense growth surrounding the clearing. An hour – half that if they could meet him halfway.

"Don't be late. They've pulled the planet side bases, and might leave the system altogether. Some of them feel this puts all of humanity in jeopardy – we don't know what the Caretaker can do or will want to do. So, last call."

"Roger. Uh, let Uma know her daughter will call her as soon as she's free. Akil out."

"Copy. Stavros out."

Haze eclipse was nearing maximum; they should run at first light. "Olympia, you're going to have to climb like the wind. Jump, hard wherever you can. With your Earth muscles, you can move faster than them. But you have to keep going. It's an hour or two to the edge. With the communicator, they'll find you before that."

She nodded. "What about you?"

"I'll be right behind you. But don't wait. Don't slow down. Just go, go, go! Got it? "

Olympia nodded.

"Okay. I'm going to start by throwing you. Step in my hands."

Akil grabbed the bark of the branch to hold himself in a crouch as Olympia put her feet in his hands, pulling her legs up. As he thought they might, the Forest People ignored a posture that probably resembled their normal coupling.

"Now, jump!"

He jumped too, thrusting away from the branch and up with his arms as her long, coltish legs uncoiled with surprising strength. She shot rapidly up and away, vanishing in the foliage above like a human bullet.

Akil drifted up much more slowly, but still fast enough to elude the snatches of the Forest People. He bent his body to glide toward a vine, the only thing that looked to be in reach. The Forest People saw that and rushed for it. There was nothing he could do but hope that he got a handhold before they got to him.

He just made it, and jerked the vine back with as much strength as he had left in him. The mass of the Forest People pulling themselves along the vine actually helped him gain that much more momentum. He vaulted over them, avoided their outstretched hands, and shot out into the gloom of the forest.

There was time for a momentary respite, time to figure out what to do. Marianne was back there having who knew what done to her. His previous life beckoned him from above.

Thinking about it was paralyzing him, he realized. If he was going to try to rescue Marianne, he'd best get going. Same if he was going to try to escape. Forest People started to boil out of the gloom behind him. That decided it. He jumped back toward the clearing and toward where he'd last seen Marianne.

They hadn't been expecting that, and three jumps later when he reached it, it was deserted. He jumped through in the direction Sharada and Marianne had taken. Curiously, despite the effort, he felt better than he had in the last week; the nutrients and the sugar fruit had kicked in. He ricocheted from tree to vine to branch to tree, finding a rhythm.

He overshot, not seeing the spear tip until he was well past it. He turned and, not looking where he was going, crashed full on into the rubbery surface of a huge elephant-ear leaf vine. He was dizzy, terribly dizzy. He grabbed hold and tried to breathe. Gradually his head cleared. Where was it?

There. Above him, as his semicircular canals settled down in the milligee field. The same vine, it followed a curve that led back along his route. He could only see the tip of the stick.

A red globule the size of his fist drifted by.

He groaned and jumped for the stick.

She was there, pinned through her abdomen, apparently unconscious, as the sap from the vine rose slowly around her. He pushed himself over to her and felt her neck. Her heart was still beating. How bad a wound was it, internally? Could he take her with him? Or did he have to find help? How long did he have before the wound, or the vine, killed her?

He'd be surrounded by Forest People in a minute and end up the same way. Or her Hazian doppelgänger would be along to finish the process, whatever that meant. He had to move her, but move her without killing her. If he could break the spear off just above the wound...

He tried to move it, experimentally. It moved easily; but wouldn't pull back at all. Marianne moaned. It wasn't seated well enough to break off, and he didn't dare try to pull it back through her with that resistance; it might be barbed.

What the hell was he to do? If the spear had just gone a little deeper into the vine, it might be set firmly enough to snap it off. That might injure her a little more, but an autodoc could deal with that later. There was another branch above her. He'd have to jump from that right down on the end of the spear and hope the momentum of his body would push it in far enough.

It hurt like hell as the blunt end of the spear slipped through his hand and hit his rib cage, but nothing broke, he thought. He moved the end or the spear, and the result was as stiff as he hoped.

Marianne moaned again, but did not wake.

Trembling, he put his feet beside her, grabbed the spear with the left hand and pushed with the right. It snapped off cleanly above the wound. Now for the hard part.

She moaned and opened her eyes. "Akil, oh, Akil. Get away while you can."

His hand was slippery with her blood. "No way. I'm going to get you out of here."

"It's too late," she whispered. "It's too late." she said so softly that he could barely hear her. "The vine; its tendrils have grown into me; into my body and my head. I can feel them... moving. Tracing my... axons, Sharada says, modeling my brain."

"I'll cut them off. The autodoc will clean them out."

"I, I don't think you should try. Sharada said my other self needs to close loop, or it will be incomplete."

Akil froze, uncertain. "I don't understand."

"There needs to be a..." Marianne gasped and fought for control. "...a calibration of hormonal responses to your thoughts – otherwise the feelings don't come out right. Our minds aren't all synapses. Our chemistry is part of it too; glands, emotions, the whole system. My double needs to sample my blood as we run through memories to get that right."

"To hell with the double."

"No, no." Marianne groaned. "I don't want it to become what Sharada is now, or worse. She can't be completely human or she couldn't have done this to me. The Hazian consciousness doesn't understand this is wrong for us." Marianne gasped and tears ran down her cheeks. "Akil, everyone dies someday and all that matters afterward is: for what? This contact needs someone who's fully human as well as Hazian." Her voice became a whisper. "I have to try."

"No," Akil said. "No way. I'm taking you back, somehow. Now. Stavros says they're going to make a try to pick us up, then pull everything off the planet and maybe out of the system."

"Akil, please. If I die when you try to cut me out, all that will be left of me would be an incomplete monster. Alone with another incomplete monster. I don't want that."

Akil's heart pounded as he fought back tears. There seemed to be no way to win. "Where's Sharada?" he asked. When in doubt, get information.

"Don't know. Maybe she's back at the... replicator, watching. She wants me." Marianne closed her eyes. "Get out of here, Akil," she whispered. "Save yourself."

"The... completion. Will it kill you?"

It took her a while to answer. Finally, very softly, she said, "Don't know. May last quite a while like this. The Hazian... consciousness knew not to hit anything vital this time. My body... sealing off the shaft. Our great genetic engineering."

He looked at her wound; it was clotting already as her body tirelessly fought the intrusion, as it would until death. "Okay, I'll wait until after, then try to cut you free."

She shuddered. "No, run now while you can. Can't tell what's going to happen. If... it doesn't work with me, they might try with you."

She was, he realized, everything he wanted from life. He was not going to let her go. He was not going to endure two such experiences in less than a subjective year.

"No, I'm going to take that chance." He put his hand on her forehead, still free from the sap.

"Thanks," she said, "that helps." She took a deep, ragged, breath. Then she seemed to fall asleep.

This was madness. He would free her, take her and run. Even if she shut down, they'd brought people back after twenty, thirty minutes as he remembered. The sky cycles could be here in less time than that. Contact could come later. He took his obsidian knife and started shaving the fibrous sap away from her. It was tougher than it seemed and there was so little time. He fought despair and hacked away as efficiently as he could.

"No, Akil." Her voice, firm and strong, came from behind him. "That is *my* body."

He turned and there she was, the hermaphrodite version, pulling herself along the vine. He froze, and looked around for Forest People. There were none. Who was this, in Marianne's body?

"What I have to do will not kill the body. I need to make sure this..." she pointed to her head, "...matches that." She pointed at herself pinned to the tree. "I can take the pain away, too. I know how, now. Please do not worry."

"Where's Sharada?"

"I told them to go back when I saw you. They're watching, from a distance. If you do not want to watch, please turn away. I will let you know when we are done, then talk to us."

"Please," Marianne, pinned to the tree, whispered.

He was holding a knife. He could try to kill the doppelgänger immediately. But that might destroy the only hope of life Marianne had left. Could he believe her... it? There are times to act and times not to act; a Buddhist had once said, 'Don't just do something, stand there,' and then Hippocrates, 'First of all, do no harm.'

Unable to trust his voice, he quietly turned away and grabbed the vine with his hand digging his fingers in. In a fit of self-loathing, he let its sap slowly start to envelop his hand. It was almost body temperature and felt almost comforting. But he ripped it away when he felt the subtle stinging of invading tendrils

"Done, Akil," two voices said, in unison.

He turned. The Marianne pinned to the vine smiled at him, seemingly at peace. "It worked," they said grinning.

The Hazian Marianne turned toward him, and sighed. "Do you love me?"

He stared at her, not comprehending.

"What we went through here is the stuff of legend. So if you promise to spend the rest of eternity with me, then you have my permission to shave me off the vine and take me to an autodoc. It might work; the Caretaker doesn't know. It regrets our unhappiness, but Sharada was an imperfect instrument and it didn't understand. Part of me will be left behind and the part that isn't will always wonder. For you, I will bear that suffering.

"But, if it isn't love, and it isn't forever, don't torture me. Let this be. If I have to lose you sometime anyway, it may as well be now. I will still be *me*, made out of Hazian cells, yes, but me much more me than Sharada is Sharada. And I might be able to salvage this contact, being fully human and able to communicate with the Caretaker. So I have to stay."

"You'll be alone. With Sharada."

A tear appeared on the face of Marianne the Hazian. "The stakes are far more important than I am, far more important than my happiness. Things may change in the future. I may be able to fix her. I can endure."

Akil grabbed the hand of the body on the tree. It was cold. Too late, he thought. He thought about Haze and Shadow, the trunk with M&A carved, crazy thoughts about guiding tourists, about watching the volcanoes grow and subside, and about being around when the Hazians came home. He thought about Marianne's uncomplicated, forthright sensuality, and the beautiful, ancient forest around him.

A terrible solution formed in his mind, a way they could still stay together. And it scared the hell out of him that he could even consider it. Then he looked at the Mariannes.

This, he realized, would make a *real* legend. It was a chance to do something that came rarely in even an indefinite lifetime. Legends weren't made by cowards. Perhaps, he thought, if the Hazian consciousness and humans cooperated, maybe what was done could someday be undone.

"Tell me," he asked Marianne, hardly believing his own words, "could I join you this way?"

She opened her mouth, shut it, and finally said. "Yes. Akil, are you sure?

He shuddered. "Don't ask again, let's just do it."

"Akil, you'll need a vagina, or the equivalent, somewhere. Where do you want it?"

Can you handle this, was what she meant. Could he overcome his prejudices and squeamishness. Did he have the guts to go through with it? He felt acute embarrassment, but he had to face this to be with her... "Uh, the usual place is fine. I, look, uh, I've even had fantasies, about reversing roles and having you..."

She grinned. "Me too. Do you want breasts too?" She sounded hopeful.

He shuddered. "Uh... no. This is going to be strange enough. I want to look like myself. Maybe later." Maybe body form would ultimately be no more important to him than clothes had become. "Here?"

"Yes."

Not trusting himself to say anything more, he removed his pouch and floated down beside Marianne's body, the microgravity settling him as gently as a feather against the smooth moist surface. They would become part of the vine, he thought, and their non-Hazian bodies would be found together like this in maybe a hundred million years by some other very confused explorers.

"I'd like to pass on the spear, too," he said, half expecting her to say it was somehow necessary and getting ready to accept the wound.

"Hold my hand," whispered Marianne on the tree.

Had he really heard her? He took the right hand, the one that he had cut free from the vine. Cold now, but there was still the hint of a grip. The Hazian Marianne took his other hand and stretched him between the two of her and held him down so that his back was pressed firmly against the vine. He began to feel wet and sticky. Then there was a stinging in the back of his head, his buttocks, his thighs and his calves. It stung. He gasped.

The Hazian Marianne let go of his hand and floated around to his front. He was firmly stuck, now.

"I will take away the pain," she said, and enveloped him in her arms and legs, caressed him with her lips, and brought him up and into her. There was no pain; he felt only the pressure of her around him. But something warm flowed back through him, something settling and anesthetic.

Then it began.

# STORY NOTES:

This was easily the weirdest thing I've ever written, to me, at least. It was, in part, an effort to deal with, by confrontation, something that affected and bothered me – perhaps more than it should have – as a young reader. That was the fate of one of the characters in Heinlein's *Methuselah's Children*, Mary Sperling, who allows herself to be absorbed by a biological super-being. It's a foray into the milieu of the wet, sticky, plastic, and organic with all the squeamishness that may imply. Whatever else they may be, human reproductive organs are a means of transferring the information encoded in DNA from one being to another. In humans, this is used only for reproduction, but what if that is not the case everywhere? Could we adapt, or be adapted, to that situation?

Haze and Shadow are approximately of Lunar mass; it turned out that they couldn't be much heavier or lighter and be a plausible contact binary planet. If more massive, they would rotate too fast, if less massive, atmosphere retention and volcanism would be more and more difficult to justify. I did the modeling ab initio, independently from Bob Forward's work on *Roche World*, hoping for somewhat larger planets; but ended up very close to his solution. If there are planets with shared atmospheres out there, it seems they will be about this size.

The high atmospheric pressure is important for a couple of reasons. First, it allows the surface to be warmer for a given amount of sunlight (called "insolation"). Second, it makes the atmosphere deep enough that hydrogen-bearing compounds can "freeze out" and fall back before they get above the ozone layer, where ultraviolet light might break molecules apart and make their hydrogen vulnerable to the stellar wind. The graphic below shows the gravitational equipotential surface cross sections (a point mass approximation) for Haze and Shadow, with the approximate atmospheric pressure for that level.

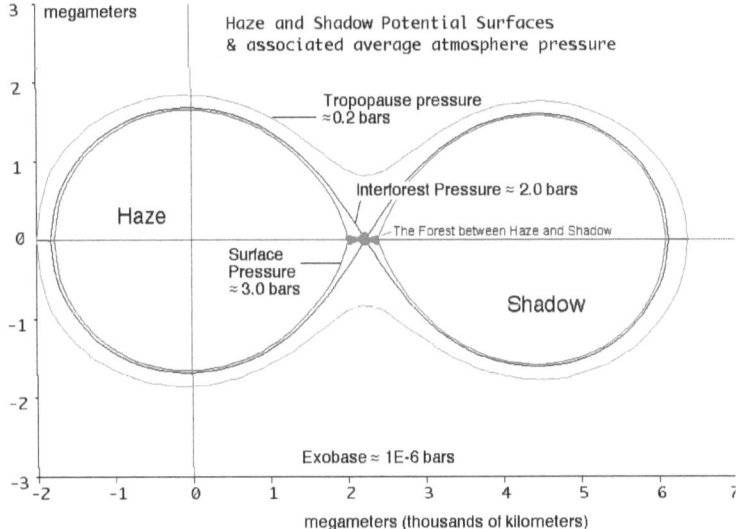

You are looking down on the North Pole; the center of rotation is in the forest, a bit to the right of the center of the forest between the worlds, as Haze is slightly more massive than Shadow.

The modeling was done on a Mac in '98 using the procedure window of a program called TK! Solver, which allows one to write programs in a FORTRAN or Basic like language.

I've obviously left room for a follow-on to this story. Maybe I will be around long enough to get to it.

—GDN Jan. 2014

# THE FOUNTAIN

We were newly arrived on Earth, and all four of our royal feet hurt. But we had a courtyard to cross and then a formal introduction to the Empress of Earth to endure, before we could begin our plea. We would endure this gravity for the sake of the urgent diplomacy involved.

Ignoring the oppressive high gravity, a fountain in the palace courtyard gushed water upwards many times our own four segment height – two meters in local measure – then fell down in curtains blown to our left by a slight breeze. It was a memorial; once before, human beings had gone to the stars to right a wrong, and not all had returned. That had been a tragedy – but it meant our mission was not without hope.

Awful news had poured in from light years away. All projections indicated that within one hundred to three hundred local years, one innocent intelligent race would be exterminated by another, whose intelligence was a matter of debate, but whose technological abilities grew exponentially. Preparations to do something about this would have begun promptly, and they would have to involve this planetary system's resources. There were no others close enough.

A dark sky with roiling clouds overhead promised a sprinkle or two as did the slight ionization of the air sensed by our antennae. The lining of our mouths tasted the subtle tart chemistry of the brightly colored plants around us.

A tall thin human approached, clothed in the same standard dark blue of all the palace staff we had seen. It was a black-haired male, clean shaven, and his decorations indicated a high place in the local hierarchy. As he came nearer, we recognized the Honorable James Omata, the royal coordinator of alien affairs with whom we'd had many conversations during our hive-ship's deceleration from near lightspeed. We read his face through a mask of discipline to indicate curiosity and some excitement at meeting us in person despite our long virtual association.

As cosmic luck would have it, our voices could make the sounds of their speech fairly well, except for the "th" and "ch" sounds, which we approximated with a hard "sh." We turned to our spaceport escorts and said, "We thank you so very much; please enjoy the rest of your day."

The human woman who was their leader smiled and bowed slightly. With that they turned quietly, but with choreographed precision, and walked away from us as Omata approached. This species of individuals, only lightly bound to each other by instinct, evidently enjoyed the pretense of acting as if they had one mind.

"James, it is so good to see you," we said as we came nearer.

"I feel the same way, Your Majesty. Her Majesty is concluding an audience," his eyes rolled up ever so slightly, "with the Crown Princess, and asked me to escort you to the throne room personally. I believe she wanted you and me to have a few moments together."

"And made a virtue of necessity!" Our hive queen laughed, a series of staccato clicks in our species that James knew well. The behavioral eccentricities of the Crown Princess had become well known to us during our three-year long deceleration from near lightspeed.

"Such things are why she is called "Her Wisdom...""

"...but not to her face," we finished his sentence.

He nodded with a smile. "How are you holding up under all this gravity?"

"Our preparations have been excellent. Can you see the antenna stiffeners?"

He looked carefully. "Not at all."

"Our high collar looks natural to you?"

"I would not suspect it of holding up your head."

"Good." Fashion and utility had fortunately converged. The exoskeletal supports beneath our capes cradled our four walking legs so perfectly that we hardly noticed them, and the capes covered the mechanism so well that we seemed to flow along as if on wheels, rather than clatter like metal spiders. The net supporting our lower abdomen seemed perfectly tuned to offset the local pull by six tenths. We nodded to James, a gesture that both recognized his compliment and demonstrated our costume engineering.

We did not mention our feet.

We chatted about the affairs of our coming; human tours of the hive ship, updates of the galactic library, the unfortunate problem of an aggressive new race only two hundred light years away. At length, he touched his head. Unlike ours, their telepathy was biologically engineered and still had signs of being a new addition.

"It appears the Empress is offering a slight change of protocol, should it suit you. Would you be willing to meet the Crown Princess along with Empress Marie today?"

We made some more clicks of laughter. "Tell her we would be delighted."

As we walked by the fountain, the wind shifted and we felt a very slight spray. What a luxury that would have been for our desert-dwelling ancestors, a billion years ago!

The ceremonial room was impressively huge, doubly so, given the gravity of this world. It was ancient by their standards, having once been the place of ritual for a religion, and before that, the local headquarters of a large empire. It once had several floors surrounding an interior courtyard; now it was a huge shell, with crossed wooden beams far overhead, along with, no doubt, as many invisible strengtheners as needed to keep the 5000-year-old structure together.

It had been, we remembered, ten times that amount of time since *we* had last seen our homeworld. Such is the lot of galactic roamers. What must it be like for them, when the universe is new, bright, and full of the yet-to-be experienced? No hive-queen still lived from those days of our race, and records were never quite like experience.

A few dark-blue-clothed humans walked around the periphery, sneaking an occasional look at us, perhaps not realizing that our compound eyes brought everything to us in great clarity except for the half-steradian cone opposite our mouth, and not perhaps realizing that we were entirely comfortable with their curiosity. Our children did much more than look, as they were our extended eyes and ears and their images and sounds flowed seamlessly into our hive-queen. Though the humans were much more their own agents than our children were, their experiences of our entrance would, in their own way, also find their way into what passed as Empress Marie's racial consciousness.

What we would do here was for all time. There are few first things to be had in this ancient galaxy, and our presentation to the human Empress Marie was one of them.

They announced our presence in a formula perhaps as old as the building. Trumpets and drums played and those humans, who looked so alike and moved together in such coordination as to seem like hive children, marched alongside us, then peeled off to the sides of the huge room. Our hive children, as arranged, did likewise.

We drank in this ceremony, and greatly appreciated their staging it despite our aching feet. We were suitably awed, and thrilled by the experience, one of those moments of wonder all too rare in the cosmos. We thought again of their individuality and how difficult it would be to get an equal number of hive queens to behave in such a ritualized, choreographed manner.

Our hive-queen alone walked up to a place before the platform on which sat the throne and stopped. In immense ages past, a hive queen would never have been so alone; ancient emotions rose up and were quieted.

Empress Marie sat on a huge and much-gilded chair. To her right was a simply – even scantily, for them – clad young human female with a somewhat bemused smile on her face. She would be Crown Princess Anne Isabella Masami Windsor Carolina. To her left was a powerful-looking and well-decorated human male holding an ornamented stick of almost our hive-queen's height. He would be the Lord Master of the Staff, the right honorable Thaddeus Zwicky, who led the humans of this palace.

He thumped this staff twice on the wood of the platform and announced us again: "Hive Queen Anathor of the Children of Light accompanied by his most honorable Royal Counselor of Alien Affairs, James Thelvin Krentin Omata."

James had spent many pleasant hours with us concocting a way of representing our title and provenance in their language; as a result, we were the "non-thunderers," a loose translation of our hive queen's enlightenment name.

There was a slight pause as the empress looked from side to side at her courtiers, to make sure, we thought, that it was her turn to speak in this ceremony.

"Our greetings to you and your race, Queen Anathor," Empress Marie said.

"Our greetings to you and yours, Your Royal Highness. May this day be well met in our mutual histories." Those were our lines in this ceremonial play James and Thaddeus had written.

"Hi, Queen."

That was the Princess, clearly off script. It saddened us only in that it would sadden those who had put such work into this once-in-the-history of the galaxy ceremony. The princess was at the age when many of her dozens of predecessors had abdicated, not wanting the duties of her mother. She clearly didn't think much of them, but she had not abdicated, yet.

We nodded to her, which was the best we could do in the way of a smile, and temporized, hoping we would not create a Galactic Incident and endanger the succession nor our mission, "Our greetings to you as well, Your Highness."

We heard James let out a slight sigh, probably of relief and probably not audible to those of his race. Thaddeus' face was immobile, but his eyes had begun to water slightly and his grip on the staff seemed very tight. Our antennae are quite sensitive across a variety of senses, and we realized we would need to bring all of them into play at this point.

We made a conscious effort to control the flutterings of our antennae and keep our posture straight. James, at least, would have recognized the signs of stress in our species, and some other humans may have put in the study effort, too. They were likely having quite a chit-chat about us on their net and while none of the individuals would match our organic brainpower, they would exceed it collectively. Anyway, organic brainpower was beside the point; their "Earthmind," an orbital cybernetic repository for generations who had given up physical form, would certainly be involved. Not that any of this vast assembly of brainpower could do much about the behavior of a young human female who was a hive-queen onto herself.

"You can call me Annie when this is over," she said. "Hey, we have the same name! Who would have thought that?"

She was looking right at James, who held his face rigid. But one did not have to be a well-sensed hive queen with several years of studying human beings to tell that the man was extremely upset at this turn of events and would so much rather be somewhere else. We saw a slight frown on the Empress Marie's face. Not good.

Well, we are not for nothing a starfaring hive with twelve-hundred-and thirty-four first contacts behind our myriad lenses.

"We fear that we did, Your Highness. Many things went into selecting a name for us in your language, and the likeness of this one to your own pleased us greatly, even if our dear friend the honorable Counselor had reservations. If it does not please you, Your Highness, it is not a word of our language and it would be a small matter for us to make adjustments."

"It pleases *us*," Empress Marie said quickly and somewhat severely. "It pleases us greatly. We are honored by your presence among the worlds of humanity and at our court."

She was back on script, and that was our cue. "And we are honored to be here."

"Let this be the beginning of a long and fruitful relationship between our races."

The princess laughed. "Fruitful? Fruitful?" She laughed again, then put a hand in front of her mouth in a belated gesture of decorum.

Empress Marie shut her eyes briefly and her lips tightened. James sagged. Thaddeus gripped the staff even more tightly if that were possible.

"So shall it be," we added, hoping we did not offend the princess too badly by ignoring her remark.

The empress spoke to James. "We entrust our visitors to your care." Then she turned to our hive queen. "Our world is your world, our house is your house."

"Maybe they'll put it on the market?" The princess giggled again, for the benefit of an audience that would eventually span the galaxy and beyond.

"By your leave, Your Majesty," James said, ignoring the princess completely.

"You may leave," the empress said in a formal, controlled voice.

The humans and our children bowed to the empress. We nodded to her, and she back to us, not that we were her equal but that what we represented put us on equal standing. It was somewhat a condescending act to the representative of a ten-billion-year-old galactic civilization of twenty-eight thousand races and over a million inhabited star systems, and James had worried about that, but we had insisted.

We were here to ask a horrible thing of this bright new collection of worlds and its peoples, whose bad luck it was to drift through the wrong part of space at the wrong time.

Trumpets sounded. Then, to the sounds of horns and drums, we backed away from the throne about twenty meters, turned, and as our retinues flowed in behind us in stately choreography, walked slowly in recession from the throne room.

"Well, that's over," James said as massive doors closed behind us. It was clear he had no love of such ceremony. The showers had come and gone while we were inside and the air tasted of fresh and alien scents.

We stepped out of the anteroom into what had become a clear day, filled with the intense radiation of their star. We had taken effective measures of protection, but the light still had a sting to it.

"The ceremony was very beautiful, moving, and interesting." we replied. "In more ways than one, as it happened. We would greatly appreciate it if you would convey our personal gratitude to Thaddeus, and our appreciation of his preparations and steadfastness."

James smiled. "I'll be very happy to do so, but if you would like to meet him personally, I can make some time in the schedule?"

Though James had not met us physically until today, we had worked together so long, he had developed an intuitive understanding of us.

We nodded. "Thank you, so much. We have another thought, concerning the banquet seating arrangements?"

"Uh, yes. What I imagine discomforts you is the potential discomfort of those around you, am I correct?"

It is a wonder how this alien appears to read our minds. We rested a pincer on his shoulder, which we know to be a gesture of comfort and camaraderie among humans.

"You are thinking of changing them, given what happened in the throne room. But given that the integrity of the ceremony is likely to be altered, one way or another, and we regret this as much as you, we would find it most interesting and entirely comfortable if the princess remains as placed. In such case, any alteration would be entirely *her* doing, and not *ours* in fear of what she might do. We would not want to give or appear to take offense to anyone. But, of course, the comfort of the empress would be the overriding concern."

He nodded. "Then we won't alter the seating arrangement on your account. Despite her discomfort, Empress Marie sees these things as part of her heir's education. She does not give up hope easily."

We knew the history of the empress' efforts at succession and patted James' shoulder again. If we could be of some assistance, we would.

He smiled. "Well, let us go to your quarters." He gestured to a large cylindrical structure that had been set up in the center of an athletic field. In its core would be a room of a few meters diameter in which a magnetic field gradient would thrust the water molecules of our bodies upward, and so cancel much of the awful gravity of this planet. We would have three hours to rest our feet before the ceremonial banquet.

But not our mind. The grumpy empress was beloved, and while she had no legislative power, we thought her assent or opposition would determine what the humans would do. How would her difficult daughter affect that? And was there anything we could do about it?

The banquet was a traditional human ceremony in which we had wanted to participate, despite our very different sustenance procedures. It preserves, in a way, much of this race's antecontact culture. It is the rare alien art form that our race can appreciate in its symmetry, it choreography, and its orchestration of a wide variety of senses. The underlying purpose of all this runs slightly afoul of a difference in our biology, but that is beside the point.

Our royalty sat together with theirs at the head of the table. While the placement and service were formal, there were no conversational scripts.

"Nine hundred and seventy-eight million years, with no meaningful change?" Empress Marie asked. "How does that feel?"

We clicked and nodded. She knew how to interpret that. "We have personally experienced only a hundred thousand or so of that, allowing for frame of reference changes and hibernation. And much of that time is filled with experiences like this, which are a feast for the appetite of curiosity."

We shall forgive ourselves for our cleverness in constructing a human metaphor.

She smiled, "I'm happy you are pleased. Our staff lives for such ceremonies, and takes these anachronisms very seriously. It is quite an art form for them. I am a constant part of this, like the walls of this building," she sighed, "but the staff change every fifteen or twenty years, to give others a chance, and so the creativity is always fresh."

We studied her. Human biological science had long since arrested their physical development at what was approximately thirty-four years of age. But while their bodies renewed themselves, their minds continued to accumulate experience. And this showed for those who have studied their faces and body language.

"You have done many of these," we observed.

She hesitated a moment, likely to query some data base.

"Thirty-three thousand seven hundred and twenty-eight state banquets." She shrugged her shoulders. "With the help of Earthmind, of course, I can remember each of them in every detail. Seven hundred twenty-three years ago, a server tripped and spilled seven main courses when we entertained a Kleth ambassador at our Martian estate." She smiled. "I was quite amused, but, of course, didn't let on. I'm afraid I'm less of a poker face now."

"Oh, mom's still pretty good at it," Princess Anne injected.

It was a fact we had not thought to research. The one thousand one hundred and thirty-eight years she had been Empress is a trivial star-frame time interval for a space-hive queen. But it was now clear to us how much of an endurance test this might be for a human. Empress Marie was weary. She alternated between moments of arch perkiness and stoic passivity.

"This isn't how you normally dine, is it?" a young woman next to the princess asked us, sounding casual.

Our antennae stiffened. This was a potential disaster. Intelligence flowed into us. The speaker was a Lady Linda Sanchez. She was a lady in waiting and friend of Princess Anne. She was connected to... Chaos! Her great, great uncle was a populist xenophobe.

As this information flowed into us, we felt the touch of James on our left rear leg. James was the only human we had told about royal feeding. Human beings were not universally sophisticated and the majority still thought of their own species' instincts as moral laws of the universe. It had been James' judgment, and ours, that it would be very difficult to obtain the support we needed if royal feeding became common knowledge.

Of course, if we had not been so clever as to advise James on how to handle the banquet seating, this situation would not have arisen. Well, we had made our hive and now we had to lay our eggs in it.

"There are differences, of course. We have a grazing area with fruits and seed plants. We pick what we choose to eat, cut it into quite small pieces, and inhale it, the solid substances being diverted to our digestive system by a sort of screen. The details of our anatomy are in our cultural exchange data if you wish to know more."

"I do," Lady Sanchez said. "You eat your children, don't you."

"Lady Sanchez," James said. "This is not appropriate for this time and place."

Empress Marie seemed frozen.

"I won't be corrected by a bug lover. Anathor, will you answer the question or will you continue your concealment?"

"Linda!" Princess Anne exclaimed, "not now!"

"Are you one of them too?" Sanchez asked. "My mistake. We the people of Earth and its worlds need to know the truth about these monsters."

"Linda! I'm your friend."

"Anne," Empress Marie spoke at last. "You were used." She hesitated, then sighed. "We don't get to have friends."

"We?" Anne said. "We?"

James looked at the Empress and we followed his gaze. Her shoulders sagged, her head lowered, she seemed infinitely tired.

Had the only concern been the relations between the humans and the Children of Light, I would have answered the question in detail; indeed we would not have omitted the information in the first place and likely have had our meetings in some distant place of no concern to xenophobes. But there was much more at stake here.

Somehow information had gotten out. If not from James, where? The galactic library node at Proteus? That had been informed before our visit and its caretaker mind had agreed on discretion. There had been no previous queries about our species.

We looked around. The man seated next to Lady Sanchez was deep in conversation with the woman next to him, and appeared not to have heard anything we were saying. Ms. Omata, seated next to her grandfather James, could be trusted.

"Lady Sanchez," we started, "in our prehistory, we evolved a far more collective existence than your race has. We share our sense data and thoughts more readily through the electric organs we evolved. Our sense of individuality is much different..."

"Queen Anathor, you do not have to answer this... impertinent question," Empress Marie said, imperial ice in her voice. "Lady Sanchez is no longer part of the royal household and it is our pleasure that she be escorted to the entrance without delay."

"Mom!"

"I'll scream!" Linda Sanchez said as dark blue-dressed men approached her.

One of the men behind her held up a soft ball on a stick and nodded to James. A sound canceler; no such scream would be heard more than a few meters away.

"Princess Anne," we said. "The possibility seems very great that Lady Sanchez' friendship with you was not sincere. She is of a family with a great dislike for non-humans, and her loyalty to that family is great."

"My loyalty to *humanity* is great, Anathor. Why don't you show us this feeding? Let people see what you really are! Will you answer the question or will we answer it for you?"

Empress Marie gestured to the men in dark blue. They moved forward. What would this scene would look like to billions of human viewers?

"I beg your peace, Your Royal Highness," we said quickly, "but those do appear to be the choices. We do not ask that you tolerate this, but only that you delay what you must do for a few minutes, for the sake of appearances."

Taking a few moments of shocked silence as assent, we flew on. "Our social evolution preceded the evolution of tool use and the expansion of our minds to comprehend the universe. Our brains are given very strong rewards for following these presentient instincts; and those of us who choose to maintain a corporal existence, for tradition's sake, also choose to tamper with these instincts in only very limited ways, for our intention is to be who we are. The royal feeding is part of that inheritance."

Everyone froze, including the escorts who had come up behind Lady Sanchez.

"We are neither like your hive animals, nor like your human communities, but are somewhere between. Our children, with whom you have been eating and conversing, have few individual goals. They are not robots, and they are not simply parts of our collective body, but they are not as independently motivated individuals as you are. You have no analog to this among your life forms or, we understand, nor any you have encountered. We ask that you set aside such analogies as you can and take us for what we are.

"Only one of us is female, and lays eggs. The hive queen is strongly protected. The hive, in presentient days, did not allow her to leave the hive to forage on her own. Over millions of your years, the hives evolved a simple system to feed the queen and fertilize her eggs. One of their members would gorge himself, then offer his fattened body to the hive queen. The urge to do so was very strong, and the reward during the process was also very strong, perhaps similar to what you feel in your mating act."

Princess Anne suppressed a giggle and the color of Lady Sanchez' face reddened substantially. We had, by accident, touched on something meaningful to them.

"In a space-hive, with a constant population, and no reasons for the hive queen to not forage on her own, the question of royal feeding does not arise."

In this, we were being disingenuous. Our hive did not spend all its time in space, and there were needs for replacements from time to time. Nor, when our biochemistry decided it was time, would a hive queen deny to any of her children so anointed the one great individual joy of their existence. But we were truthful enough about this hive queen's recent history.

Lady Sanchez' glistening eyes locked onto us. We could taste her hatred in the air around us, emotion having caused a sweat that overpowered whatever inhibitors she wore. It was an incongruously lovely taste.

"Tell us how you do it. Or if not you, as you say, your other hive queens do it. Tell us. You bite your children open and suck them dry. That's what you do, isn't it?"

"In so many words. The bite of the hive queen is accompanied by fluids that produce euphoria, anesthetize, and digest the organs of the chosen, except for the nerves and brain, which experiences the euphoria, and the seminal cells.

"The hive child's head remains conscious for several minutes, communicating the joy it feels." The hive experiences what we suppose, in human terms, a group orgasm would feel like. But we did not describe this in our literature; there is something to be said for an economy of information under such circumstances.

"And if you don't have a fattened hive child handy, you'll take something else," Lady Sanchez snapped.

"That is not biologically possible," we said. "What made you think that?"

Lady Sanchez looked distracted and confused.

"Records have been found on other worlds. Your censored galactic library does not have a monopoly on information."

So *that* was the source of their information; propaganda from a race of conquerors our ancestors pacified a billion years ago, one that was unfortunately more like humans than us.

James sighed. "Milady perhaps is receiving information, from sources she trusts, that it is indeed not biologically possible."

"Do you have any more questions, Lady Sanchez?" we asked.

She shook her head and rose to be escorted out, but with a look back at a shocked Princess Anne that said their relationship was not entirely a hoax Perhaps it had been sacrificed for too little. So we hoped.

Empress Marie laughed, a deep, cynical, bitter laugh. "Now you all should have a very good idea of what 'figurehead' means. If I command that you now finish your meal and make pleasant conversation, will everyone get up and go? Or, if I command you to get up and go, will that then ensure that everyone finish what our culinary artists have tried so hard to make and which is now no longer so fresh?"

"Mother!" Princess Anne exclaimed.

"As you wish, Your Majesty," we said, forked a small morsel of fish, placed it in our mouth, and sucked it down.

Princess Anne laughed, James laughed, and soon Empress Marie was unable to help herself. So the banquet resumed in a nervous semblance of good cheer.

This was well needed, for the real hard part lay ahead.

"Your Majesty," James said to us as we left the banquet table for our quarters, where the substantive discussions were to occur. "That was well played."

"We did what we could, under the circumstances."

"Empress Marie..."

"...did, we think, no more than what she had to do. Thus, she did no harm. She could so easily, and so understandably have made the situation much worse."

"She has been empress for a very long time."

The night had grown clear and the temperature had come almost down to what was normal for us. The brightest stars shone down on us past the lamp glow. It was beautiful, but we looked forward to releasing our bodies from the force of this gravity. We'd had some thought of touring the planet and seeing firsthand the relics of the ascent of its people. We pruned our list of such things with every step our mechanical frame took.

"Whatever happens this evening, would it be possible for us to have some words alone with her?"

"Queen to queen?" James smiled. "My guess is that she would like that. She has nobody of her station to talk to. You may do."

"I have one other request, which you may find strange. Could the Princess Anne attend our session this evening?"

James stopped. This clearly surprised him. Then he nodded. "You think she should understand what's at stake."

"We do."

"You think Empress Marie thinks so as well."

"We do."

"If you will permit an impertinence, you may both put too much hope in that young woman."

"Your people play a game called contract bridge,"

James nodded. "Yes?"

"Princess Anne is the key to what is left of Empress Marie's..." we searched for a word that meant willingness to strive, to try, to lead, "...heart. When there is only one distribution of cards that will allow you to win, you play the hand as if that were the distribution."

James nodded.

The magnetically generated release from gravity was even more welcome the second time than the first. The dome overhead showed the stars as if it were transparent, and decorated paper screens covered the massive coil walls of the room.

It was room enough for eight; our children rested their bodies in a nearby pool, which was equally effective, but less conference-like.

James and our Hive Queen were joined by an Admiral Sun Zhao-Li and his aide, a diminutive dark woman called "Commander Jai." Prime Minister Eisen and the Uniformed Services Secretary, Jacques de la Soire came during our introductions.

Then we all stood for Empress Marie, who immediately waved us down.

"Be about your business. If I have to say something, I will. Otherwise, just ignore the old bag."

Prime Minister Eisen suddenly turned bright red; a very obvious display to our infrared-sensitive vision.

"The walls have ears, Hans. Don't bother with an apology, I am an old bag."

Princess Anne walked in then.

"You came," Empress Marie said, sounding somewhat surprised.

Princess Anne nodded. "I came." Some redness surrounded her eyes. "If you're going to destroy the universe or something, I may as well be in on it."

We clicked and motioned her to a human chair. We were the hosts here, in a temporary simulation of a home thirty thousand light years distant.

"Princess Anne," we said, "the destruction of universal civilization is actually in play, should we fail badly enough, but only as a very low order of probability."

"That is a gross overblowing of fact, yes?" Eisen said.

"But it does get one's attention," Admiral Sun said.

We nodded. "We are at least ninety-seven percent certain that, even in the worst case, the outbreak would be contained within about twenty-five hundred light years by other forces being assembled. You all have the brief?"

"Annie come lately, I'm afraid." Princess Anne said.

"If you touch the net, Your Highness," Commander Jai, said, "it should now be there for you."

"We shall summarize," we said. "A very rare event has occurred; the breakout of an exponentially expanding technological species which resists efforts of communication and may not even be conscious, as most of the universe understands awareness.

"They are percolating outward at an average of a tenth of a light year per year, but very unevenly; almost half the speed of light in some directions. They are now about one hundred light years away, in the direction of your constellation of Canis Major. For convenience, we can call them the Canids.

"There is another proto-technological amphibious species on a world around a red dwarf about forty-eight light years away from here, and more toward Orion. They make music, poetry, and some crude pottery. For convenience, we can call them the Oriona.

"The Canids reform the surfaces of the planets they encounter to suit their own parameters, destroying all surface and oceanic life in the process, so this second species is at great risk. They have reformed fourteen life-bearing worlds and probably many more in the time the information has taken to reach us."

"So for us, it's about twenty-five hundred years before the cavalry arrives, about five hundred years late, give or take a millennium?" Empress Marie asked, with not a little irony in her voice.

A slight exaggeration, but we nodded.

"That all must be verified," Eisen said.

"I have not been complacent since receiving Anathor's data," Admiral Sun said. "It is consistent with everything we know. For example, there has been a recent sixty percent decrease of oxygen pressure in the atmosphere of a world sixteen light years from the outbreak world. It is down to eleven percent. Another fifteen worlds show similar changes of lesser magnitude."

That was about half of Earth's oxygen, and a quarter of ours. We looked at the Crown Princess, whose eyes were wide and mouth slightly open. She knew the significance of that number. The information was new to her, and she was still in a slight state of shock from last night; she had said nothing since the summary started.

Though it was not necessary with our compound eyes, it was useful in the way of human body language to turn our head to each of the conference participants. "What we suggest is that we spend the next two decades converting about ten percent of the mass of your asteroid belt into a fleet sufficient to provide an overwhelming numerical advantage over whatever forces they are sending toward the Oriona world."

"A tenth!" Eisen shouted. "You can't be serious! The bodies of the Solar System are the common heritage of all humanity. Most of the larger ones are settled, with families, communities on them. This is outrageous!"

"Are you sure a tenth will be enough," Admiral Sun asked quietly, "to end this, if the show of overwhelming force is not sufficient?"

"End this?" Princess Anne asked.

Empress Marie looked at her daughter. "A final solution, my daughter." She turned to us, her visage grim. "We are asked to contemplate genocide, are we not?"

Her two dark pupils focused on us, boring into us in a way no compound eye could communicate. She was, of course, linked to their Earthmind and the whole of the heritage of this species from the time they were able to transcend biology, and even before, by cruder means of recall. Their parallel collective experience dwarfed even that of our billion-year star hive.

She continued. "Queen Anathor, this ramshackle galactic civilization, with its library nodes scattered here and there, with its relative handful of anachronistic wanderers flitting randomly from this star to that, this galactic civilization so wise and so hands-off that it can't respond to genocidal evil in less than a couple of millennia, this galactic civilization wants *us*, the newest kids on the starfaring block, to do its dirty work for it. That's where we are at, isn't it?"

Despite our vast seniority, we did not feel very superior at that moment. But we did know better than to prevaricate. "Yes. We should mention that in the process, you would be saving yourselves."

"Oh? Admiral Sun, if we just sat still and built weapons, we could handle these vermin when they get to us, couldn't we?"

"If! Not when!" Eisen said. "You are being too credulous!"

The Admiral ignored that and spoke to his empress. "Your Majesty, a prepared defense has a great advantage over any offense, but I have no way of knowing what our opponents' strength would be at that point."

Eisen harrumphed. "In such a preposterous event, the political problem would belong to someone else; we all will have passed from the scene," he said, then caught himself, "except Your Majesty, of course."

We tried to put our pincer claws into the notion that the possible extinction of one's species was a 'political problem,' and noted that this remark brought an even greater tightness to Empress Marie's face, and that she had, unconsciously perhaps, formed a fist with her left hand. As had James.

"Your Excellency," we addressed Eisen, "another intelligent species, as well as countless worlds that may sometime develop thinking beings, are also at risk."

He snorted. "About that, my voters are not likely to much care."

"And you, Hans?" Princess Anne asked. "Do you give a fart?"

A brief smile touched Empress Marie's face, even as she shook her head at her daughter.

"I represent the people of the solar system and beyond. Myself, not."

"With your leave, Admiral," Jai said.

Sun nodded

"Perhaps we could follow both courses of action, even though it might cost us *two* tenths of the asteroid belt, or the equivalent excavation of Mercury. If we simply wait here, we would put all our hopes on one battle. Perhaps we should give ourselves two chances."

Sun smiled, and nodded. "My student."

Jai bowed to him.

They are beginning to take ownership of this calamity, we noted. That was a good sign. We also wondered that this loose non-hive of associated individuals had a warrior class, whereas our hives had not evolved one. A primitive feature, perhaps, but for now, a useful one.

"It's late," Empress Marie said. "We'll all want to consult, study, and think a bit more. Tomorrow afternoon, here, Queen Anathor?"

"We are at your disposal, Your Royal Highness."

"We as well," Admiral Sun said.

"More talk," Eisen said. "Ach! Very well. Better than starting a war over fish today."

"The Oriona are amphibians, Hans," Princess Anne said, "like frogs. If we save them, maybe I'll get to kiss one someday."

Eisen grunted, while Jai put a hand in front of her mouth to hide a smile. Empress Marie sighed very slightly. Admiral Sun stood and bowed to us and his empress in turn. "Your Majesty," he said softly and walked from the room, Jai trailing.

Eisen pushed himself up, nodded curtly to the Empress and left.

Empress Marie looked at her daughter. "I just don't know what..." and then was overcome with laughter. "I just don't know what to do with you. Queen Anathor, you wouldn't know, but the frog kissing remark was a comment on my efforts to produce an heir who would actually want this job. I've been through thirty-seven consorts."

"And fifty-six crown princes and princesses, counting me," the crown princess added. "But you've had a lot more children than that, haven't you, Queen Anathor?"

"This queen has laid 573,835 eggs in her lifetime, but that is an ordinary, even a small number for a hive queen of our species, whereas your mother's fifty-six is a very impressive number for one of yours."

Empress Marie rolled her eyes up and laughed a bit, but the laugh died quickly.

"Your species normally mates for life, we realize," we added.

She waved a hand, "When a lifetime was fifty years or so."

"There would have been a cost," we said, knowing human beings perhaps better than most knew themselves, "to every marriage, to every separation, to every child who rejected this heritage." It was very clear to us why Empress Marie was so tolerant of Princess Anne's disrespect of form and tradition. In spite of all evidence, she still had hope. "And you have borne all this for the sake of your people."

This would not be something that was of any news to Empress Marie, but we wanted the crown princess to hear it.

"I should just abdicate. A robot could do this."

"Mother! Queen Anathor, she has never carried through on that and I'm sure she's been saying it for a thousand years."

We clicked. "We have had similar thoughts ourselves, for a thousand thousand times your mother's thousand years."

"Hive queens abdicate? That wasn't in the background material."

"It is a variant of Royal feeding. Two queen eggs are laid, and when the larva have drunk in all the knowledge of the hive, and emerge from their final molt, the old queen feeds them her body. It is the greatest and final joy of her life. It is a joy such tasks as this mission make seem very attractive."

"But the galaxy has a cancer in it, and we must not think of ourselves," Empress Marie said.

"Exactly," we replied, and turned to the crown princess.

"Well," she said, "I'm going to think of myself at least just a bit longer and get some sleep. G'night, Queens."

But in contrast to her brash language, she touched each of us, gently, then turned and left.

Empress Marie turned to us. "I hope she hasn't irritated you, Queen Anathor. Though it seems nothing much does; you're an inhumanly good diplomat."

We clicked. "We are, of course, not human. But, Your Majesty, we can be irritated. 520,000 years ago, we encountered another breakout such as this. They had powerful religious instincts, and their leaders found themselves physiologically bound by their religious duty to their priest caste to carry out exterminations of nonbelievers. Yet they realized the logical wrongness of this in the real universe. So they contrived a frontal attack on our overwhelming numbers and would not stop until we were forced to change their genome; what survived was no longer them. It was a racial version of what humans called 'suicide by cop.' Being forced into *that* irritated us."

"I see."

We waved our pincers in mimicry of the human gesture of helplessness. "It wasn't as clear as it is in this case; there were negotiations, deceptions, minor conflicts, and then a crisis. We had to act. The propaganda your xenophobes found was left over from that encounter."

We sat silent for what seemed several minutes.

"And still you roam the galaxy?"

"Some must. Most roamers are cybernetic beings, of course. So, we are a bit old fashioned. It helps in contacts with young races. But, we, too can be replaced by robots."

Then Empress Marie laughed and said, "By Chaos, we can feel sorry for ourselves! I should be doing a better sales job on Anne, or I'm looking for number thirty-eight and number fifty-seven. If I can. Or maybe Hans will just change the constitution and make himself president, chancellor, or dictator or something."

"We are new here, of course, but would think that in this crisis, your people, and the Oriona, and the galaxy, and perhaps even the Canids are much better off with you leading your hive."

Empress Marie sat down, no, she fell into the chair as if exhausted, as if weighed down by a mass that even the low gravity of our quarters could not ameliorate. We pulled our stool over to her side and sat with her.

"I'm really just a figurehead," she said, "a romantic, royal, ceremonial prop. We never went as far down the road of collectivity as your species has, but we still have our own hierarchical instincts. So, someone needs to look like they're at the top. People are more comfortable that way, regardless of reality. I have no real authority. Hans can do whatever he gets the votes for and I have to go along with it unless it becomes an Earthmind issue, in which case I have to go along with what Earthmind wants. Oh, of course, when nobody knows what to do, I'm the royal executive flipping decision-maker. Throw me up in the air and see if I land flat on my face or my butt."

We gave that the clicks that would be expected, though she didn't sound humorous at all.

"You've had to go to war before," we noted.

"I have. Over three thousand people died because of it. That fountain outside is their memorial. Queen Anathor, that was three thousand individual, unique consciousness. Imagine three thousand hive queens."

There had never, to the best of our knowledge, been as many as three thousand hive queens in our species at one time. We, of course, knew of the war she had then felt she had to support. Parliaments and politicians aside, if she had chosen to publicly oppose it, that fleet would not have gone.

"I have done this before, and now I've hung around so long I get to do it again." She held up her hands and looked at them. "They don't come clean, do they. So what's another sanguinary bath?"

"You would not tolerate evil done by your own species, even at so great a sacrifice. You did not know it then, but you have gained the respect of all the dozens of civilizations that are in the light cone of that event. It was part of why we have turned to you in hope."

"Have you? I'm not the woman I once was."

We sat silent. So much hinged on the hope that she was still that woman. But somewhere inside, she had to realize it.

"She came to the meeting, didn't she?"

She meant the princess, of course, conjured in her mind by the hope of laying her burdens down.

"She did." Anne's presence, her interest, premolting behavior aside, was the hope that sustained her.

Empress Marie nodded and took a deep breath. "A long day tomorrow. I shall call my escort."

We accompanied her out to the great stone square and felt the mist blown from the great fountain again. A car came and whisked her away. We looked up and saw maybe a handful of stars. Our eyes, like human eyes, limit the amount of light they admit, and the courtyard was well let. A woman came toward us; the crown princess, our children told the hive queen.

"You want to see the stars, Queen Anathor?" she asked.

"We do. But the lighting is too..."

Princess Anne raised a hand to her head, "Zwicky will take care of it."

The lights vanished and a million stars burst forth. The high gravity of Earth needed only a thin layer of air for its atmospheric pressure, and the stars shone down with almost the clarity of space. Our ancestral soup of an atmosphere was almost three times as thick overhead and hardly ever cloudless.

The princess produced a light that shined up into the sky as if to infinity. "The three bright stars in a row are the belt of Orion."

Seeing alien star maps is vastly different from having their stars shown to us in their natural depth. Our eyes now traced the imaginary lines in the sky and saw the figure humans saw at the dawn of their civilization.

"They sort of point to that very bright blue-white star, Sirius."

We nodded. "So, our fate lies between those stars."

"Hard to tell who all you mean to include with that 'our,' Queen Anathor."

A grammatical ambiguity that worked in our favor! We clicked softly.

"We are surprised to find you still awake, Your Highness."

"Oh, no, you don't. Anne. Just Anne."

We said nothing.

"I couldn't sleep. Too much to think about. I think better walking around."

"Your mother thought well of you, this evening. We did too."

She shrugged. "I haven't abdicated yet. Until I do, I should keep up with things. You never know. At any moment..."

"Your mother's inner strength is greater than she knows."

Another long period of silence followed, filled with the tastes of flowers, the mist of the fountain, and the hard bright stars above.

"Why does she do it?" Anne asked.

"Have you ever read the stories of Robert Heinlein," we asked, "from the days when your species first dreamed of leaving their planet, and then, finally, haltingly, did?"

"The story *Double Star* gets given to anybody with royal blood. *Glory Road* as well. Not necessarily by our parents, or the palace staff, however."

"Then you know about paying it forward."

"Yes. Mom has a debt she wishes to pay forward? It must be some debt."

We nodded. "Twenty thousand years ago, your species might well have perished in the ice ages. It was not us, but some other wanderers. It is all in the library."

"If you ask the right question! Chaos!"

"Your mother has spent a lot of time with the library records. Only a few of each species choose to lift their kind. Only a few are such heroes."

"Mom?"

"You know she is. And you know what it costs her."

"Yeah, well the reason I'm going to abdicate is that I'm not up to that kind of thing."

We didn't answer.

"Well, I'm not. Sorry to disappoint."

We touched a claw to her shoulder.

"I'm twenty-two years old. You and mother are trying to get me to think in terms of centuries, millennia, eons. It's too much. I have no reference. I'm just not..." She looked up at the stars.

"You're not, perhaps, getting the sleep your species needs." We knew all about protesting too much.

She laughed. "You've got that right, Queen Anathor. I'd better get in now. It's getting chilly." She gave us a wan smile and left.

The temperature seemed just fine to us, of course.

When the next day's conference started, Princess Anne was last in again, but only because the prime minister, somewhat late himself, bulled his way past her as if she weren't there. She was dressed differently today; in severe gray pants and a tunic with a high collar and a small blue gem at its clasp. Her hair was back and tight.

We went over everything again, and the prime minister still resisted doing anything.

James, who had said almost nothing yesterday, finally turned to Eisen. "Is there anything that the Children of Light have presented which you question in any way?"

Eisen sighed. "Omata, what *I* question, or do not, depends on what the voters believe, and that changes daily."

"Facts mean nothing, then?" James asked.

"In terms of what decisions I make, what I decide to do, to put it bluntly, no, they themselves are not important. I must work with what voters *believe* are the facts. Though I must say we have here not facts as much as probabilities and judgments. Most are very disputable and are so disputed."

"One," James said, "the Canids exist, sterilize worlds, and are expanding. Two, the rest of the galactic civilization cannot get here before they do in another inhabited world. Three, we can meet them half way, or wait until they get here."

The prime minister shook his head. "Or we can meet them two-thirds of their way here. Or they may self-destruct before they reach anything else. They may already have self-destructed. Or they may not come here and expand in some other direction. If, and I say 'if' advisedly, we must do something to antagonize them, we can do that when the public is fully on board with it."

"What if that's too late, Hans?" Princess Anne said, speaking for the first time.

"What if, what if, what if. The *what ifs* can be someone else's problem."

Empress Marie spoke. "Queen Anathor, if we do nothing, what will you do?"

"Head for the Oriona system."

"With one ship?" Admiral Sun asked.

"Their Sun has an asteroid belt. With fortune, there would be many more than one ship before the Canids arrive. As the Prime Minister has pointed out, there are many what-ifs in this situation. Some of those would allow for our success."

"Most would not," Admiral Sun said.

"To guard against that, we would create an Oriona arc and send it outward toward the converging galactic forces. Even if the defense fails, their escape would be success of a sort."

"Your Highnesses," Admiral Sun said. "There would be at least two ships headed toward Orion. Whatever is written of the history of my kind, it will not be said that I was a coward or turned away from such duty."

"You will not act against the orders of the minister of conflict resolution," Eisen said.

Admiral Sun smiled and bowed slightly toward him. "I would not then be part of the ministry, of course, Your Excellency." Then he turned to us. "At *least* two ships."

"A suicidal fools' errand," Eisen said.

"I'll go with them," the crown princess said with a shrug.

That stunned all of us into a silence.

"Nonsense. Overblown nonsense," Eisen blustered. "Consider your duties."

"I am. I need to see more of this galaxy while Mother's still around."

"Your Highness," James said, great worry on his face.

Empress Marie reached over to touch James. We marveled at the complexity of the interactions between the humans compared to the simplicity of our own.

Empress Marie turned to the prime minister. "Hans, your problem is perceived political backing. Very well, I will make a speech."

"Your Majesty, the government has not yet decided that there should be a public airing of this, nor what the form would be, nor that it should have any advocacy, and particularly not from the head of state."

"I will make a speech, and then you will have new political realities to deal with."

"That is not your role as a constitutional monarch."

"Then fire me. It appears I have a successor."

The prime minister sat silent for a moment, then said, "There are bills for constitutional change presented at every session."

"Hans," Princess Anne said, "the sessions have been an average of ten years apart."

"I could call one."

"It would be a vote of no confidence," Princess Anne said. "Touch the net, do the numbers. You won't beat Mom."

James laughed, "Of course, Your Excellency, then it *would* be someone else's problem."

"Do not patronize me, Omata. At least, Your Royal Highness, allow the government to draft the address."

The way he said 'Your Royal Highness' tasted of contempt, and the resulting smile on the empress' face reminded us of the baring of fangs by one of this planet's carnivores.

"I will draft it, with James' assistance."

"One of your former consorts?"

A quick check showed that James had been consort number twenty-five, but had never totally left the empress' life, a factor that was rumored to have been a factor in the departure of number thirty-seven, who, we now suspected, may not have been Anne's biological father. With human leadership there are often two stories, the official and the real. We struggle to keep up.

"...and that of Earthmind, of course," Empress Marie continued with ice in her voice. "We will give you an advance copy."

"Earthmind," Eisen spat the word out. "The dead cannot rule the affairs of the living."

"Your Excellency, the survival of the human race, and the survival of Earthmind is their business as well," James said.

The prime minister sat silent, bent over with his face in his hands. Nobody said anything.

"If it matters," we said, "even the first ones tell us the greatest lesson is that what the universe lays on us pays little heed to the wills of minds within it."

"Not my will but thine be done," James whispered. It was a quote from a human religion that lived on in their culture. Wisdom is wisdom, wherever found.

"Hans," said Empress Marie, in a softer voice, "we will make no mention of what has happened here. For those outside, it will be as it always has been."

He sat up and shook his head. "No. I am no war leader, and I have clearly lost the confidence of Your Majesty. I must consult the others of my party first, but you shall have my resignation within days." He stood up. "We haven't had elections in over a hundred years. Perhaps it is time. At any rate, you will do what you will do and my presence here serves no further useful purpose. By your leave, Your Majesty."

Empress Marie nodded and he left. We never saw him again.

"The casualties have begun," she said into the silence that followed the Prime Minister's departure. "I have a speech to write."

With all the others gone, we walked out into the gravity with James and Anne, into the great plaza to watch the droplets of the great fountain ascend to the stars and fall back in their endless cycle. There was not much more to say.

The next twenty-three revolutions of their planet about their sun brought more change in both them and us than the previous thousand. The star became almost ringed with machines to absorb its power and send it to the growing fleet. For ourselves, we laid another thousand and twenty-four eggs. There were no royal feedings; we needed every hive queen we could produce. We could wait. Interestingly, we had now become "Empress" Anathor in human language, a queen of queens.

When the day came, we joined the human dignitaries. In deference to our feet, we met on the deck of the Mars gravity level of Fiji Tower. Prime Minister Thaddeus Zwicky personally escorted us to Empress Marie, Prince Consort James, and Admiral Jai of the home guard.

All but Thaddeus wore some version of their military uniform, a show of solidarity with the thousands that would soon follow Admiral Sun and Princess Anne towards Orion.

James motioned us to our place and waved to the stars above us. "The light from propulsion beams reaching the first wave should arrive at any moment," he said.

Almost before he stopped speaking, a thousand new stars ignited above us, then grew tails that flowed back toward us like contrary comets bound away from the Sun. Two hundred and six of those were hive-ships of our hive's daughter queens.

"Farewell, our sons and daughters," Empress Marie said.

They did fare well; the Canid hive, in fact, recognized overwhelming superiority and the most awful deed contemplated proved unneeded. They retreated to their home system without violence. Three hundred years later we, the Children of Light, left Empress Anne, and the human stars for another story. Marie sent her farewell from Earthmind.

The Orionas, blissfully unaware of any of these events, continue to make their pottery, their poetry, and their music. Perhaps, in another turn of the galactic wheel, they will also pay it forward.

# STORY NOTES:

What will biological immortality be like? And what will be the place of those who decide to go a non-biological route? Is there a scenario for extraterrestrial intelligence that makes sense other than nonexistence? As the vast majority of people become tired of politics, what will governance be like? Will ancient human values still have meaning, and, if so, which ones?

This story was my last magazine sale as of this writing, more of an accidental circumstance than by intention. Thinking about "big issues" seems to lead to larger works, but at least this one did not turn out too badly. There are millions of possibilities for the future (a testament to our ignorance of so many things) but the wave function has to collapse when you tell a story. You make your choices and start typing.

I'm perhaps more comfortable with the extraterrestrial intelligence scenario, despite Fermi's question of "Where are they?" The "great silence" becomes a bit more understandable when you consider time as well as distance in the distribution of ETI. Someone once remarked that the search for extraterrestrial intelligence was really the search for extraterrestrial us. But we will not be "us" that much longer. Whether something resembling the Vingean singularity is just around the corner, or will take another century or two does not inform the larger view.

From radio to as much of a Dyson sphere as we wish to build looks to be a period of something less than a thousand years. That's 500 light years round trip. The Roman Basilica used for the welcoming ceremony is modeled on one in Trier, about 2,000 years old. Homo Sapiens had been around for about a hundred times that, or 200,000 years. The average age difference between the Sun and the nearby stars is about 10,000 times that interval, i.e., two billion years.

The starry part of this galaxy is something like 150,000 light years across. At light speed, that's about the length of one trip across the galaxy, or to the Magellanic clouds. Allowing 4.5 billion years for some fraction of the first planets to start generating intelligences, there's a nine billion year trace through time available. That's room to fit a lot of 4x500 bubbles without any of them touching each other. Of course there may be a lot of post-singularity contacts, but they wouldn't be ET-us, except perhaps for remnant populations that for reasons of their own have decide not to go to the next level, but roam the galaxy pretty much as they were when they started to do so.

What I've envisioned here is a very loose-knit web of post singularity ETI, billions of years old, whose doings are limited only by the laws of physics, their own proclivities, and perhaps the evolved sensibilities of the ancients. Carl Sagan is credited with the idea that intelligent life may be how the universe becomes conscious. If such a consciousness exists, it must be very slow-paced, with "thoughts" evolving back and forth across the galaxy on a timescale that dwarfs that of the existence of our species. What we know about it, mainly, is that it has had very little to do with us, overtly anyway. But this vast, remote, galactic body may have need, from time to time, of something that metaphorically resembles white blood cells; perhaps drafted from the newer recruits to the fellowship of intelligence.

# THE TOUCH

**S**ani moaned in a high-pitched airy whistle and Modani rushed back to the screened-off alcove in the mud brick hut after showing a comforting fluff of featherfur to the children. That was the way Sani wanted it; the young ones would have to deal with her final crisis soon enough.

"Apologies, my love," Sani whispered. "For a moment the pain was too much, and I lost control."

Modani made no sound, but with a fluff showed his deep concern. Softly, with all three fingers of his left hand, he groomed his dying mate, a gesture that at one time might have led to ovulation, but now only recalled fond memories. Though she had become thin, Sani looked no worse for the immobilizing cancer. The small lump on her neck was hardly noticeable, but their local crest-pruner said it went down into her spine, and to cut it out would likely kill her immediately.

"I will get more painkiller from the chemist, my love." Modani whistled and they touched beaks in a gentle reminder of their mating dance so many years ago.

A hundred thousand years before Sani's cancer took hold, the great blue disk and ultraviolet arms of the majestic Whirlpool galaxy filled

David Martin's field of view. He scanned for polarization by strong, extensive magnetic fields. There! An evolved neutron star... not a lopsided pulsar with a bumpy field whipping around, but a near-classic dipole with an ion wind streaming out of its poles. The field should, he determined, be well organized, with hundreds of Tesla out to megameters from the relatively tiny thirty-kilometer sphere at its center; a featherbed entry.

Orienting the superconducting loops in every nanocell of his body, he tacked against the faint plasma breeze of the galaxy's central black hole, gradually bending his path toward his chosen decelerator.

His pattern recognition codes latched onto a memory of air pillow diving with Ellen from a hundred million years ago, and he re-experienced the undiminished thrill of defying his youthful fear of heights. Ten thousand light years out from the star he woke his wife, and suggested a reprise.

She gleefully concurred, so they willed their nanocells to take human form again, for the first time in ten million years. Trillions of submicroscopic hexagonal toroids arranged themselves to emulate skin, hair, flesh and bone; optical data links carefully arranged themselves to simulate nerves and glands. Most of a billion years of experience was set carefully aside from conscious thought so that they could enjoy real-universe sensation again.

Ellen laughed joyfully, surrounding him with legs and arms, devouring him with kisses as they tumbled through the void, delighting to join one another as if they had not been one undifferentiated physical being just a few moments before.

For Modani, the trip to the village would not be the simple thing it had been as a youngster. There were too many angry people out there, would-be tribal leaders whose superstitions and egos had been bypassed by the new, Ixoran-style civil service. The desperate and the lazy had been known to waylay travelers. *I should not go alone,* he thought. *If anything happens to me, it will be a far worse tragedy for the children than Sani's pain.*

He stuck his head out of the door, smelled the freshly mown reeds he kept around the border of his land and listened. They lay on top of older dry reeds because this allowed air circulation which hastened drying. But this also let the unwary think they could place a silent foot on the soft new reeds — and then the snap when the dry, brittle, reeds below broke would betray their approach.

He thought he heard such a snap, then silence.

The silence continued. An animal?

He almost turned back, but then thought of his poor mate's agony. Convincing himself that he would probably get away with it, he donned a leather greatcape and bid his oldest to care for Sani. He resolved to buy as much medicine as he could to reduce the number of such trips alone. Half their family's savings were in his purse; he would have taken it all except for the threat of robbery.

Then Modani headed across his fields toward Omphan Village at several body lengths in a heartbeat, his four sleek thin legs still whipcord strong, galloping at the pace of urgency. He felt guilty about his own good health.

The neutron star lay in a medium-age open cluster, still brilliant with new blue-white stars and set off by a garnet-tinted supergiant here and there, but already penetrated by the older stars of the arm and of the halo. David and Ellen hit its magnetic pillow holding hands in a flat spin like a pair of skydivers, and bounced away at half of lightspeed, having raised the general temperature of the plasma around their impact point a femtokelvin or so. They tingled as their nanocells repaired radiation damage as fast as it happened.

As they left the region, they reformed themselves into a thousand telescopes, which they spread into a globular constellation a hundred million kilometers across; a giant's eye to examine their surroundings in detail, sending everything to the small remaining central coordinating sphere. Their conscious time sense slowed. Thoughts that used to take microseconds now took hours as their data links stretched over light minutes, but to them it was as if the galaxy around them had contracted and accelerated its motion.

The view exhilarated them. Indeed, David reflected, by their self-chosen logical structure, it was one of those fuzzy patterns that *defined* exhilaration; the feeling of speed.

There! A white and a yellow giant were distended into nearly touching eggs of light, spinning madly around each other, almost ready to coalesce.

There! Orbiting a brand new white dwarf, they found a brown dwarf with glowing bands under a magnificent multihued ring system, all still encased in the nebula of the white dwarf's final mass expulsion. A secondary planetary system was forming.

There! An old ruddy, overinflated windbag of a star circled a white dwarf grown heavy from the giant's effluvia. If it grew heavy enough, it would collapse and explode as a supernova. Though such things were always hard to predict, they might be in time for the show.

And there! Not a thousand astronomical units from the red and white pair was an older interloper, its spectrum tinged with orange. Its passage was distant and gentle enough that its planetary system was undisturbed — and this planetary system included a rare, tiny, blue and white marble not so different from far away Earth.

Ellen turned all their thousand eyes in that direction. It was her initiative, but there was no conflict — such design problems had been well worked out even before they had moved out of the Mind of Mars to seek adventure in the real cosmos with nanocell bodies. This blue-green world they saw was teaming with life by virtue of the oxygen in its spectrum, but had it evolved intelligence?

Close enough to the orange star for heavy tides, it had a large moon locked in synchronous orbit of about a day and a half. The star's gravity tried to stretch the system, adding orbital energy which the tides in the planet's ocean tried to take away, pounding on its continents — neither, David thought, would win their argument in the lifetime of the orange-tinted star.

*Remarkable, Ellen, to chance upon such a world so soon in our exploration of the Whirlpool.*

*But, David, what a dangerous place indeed for it to be!*

David agreed. That incipient supernova should soon reset any biological evolutionary clocks in the area. The white dwarf had already grown to an almost unstable 1.44 solar masses, and the giant's atmosphere continued to slosh out of its Roche lobe, adding more and more mass.

Collapse was inevitable, but when? The model was too sensitive to a myriad of conditions and the supernova might have already happened, or it might not happen for another hundred thousand years.

In one of her earliest memories, the ones you never throw away or store elsewhere, Ellen had been a ranger at Mt. Hood and rescued an orphaned bear cub. Despite geological warnings that an eruption was about to occur, she had been told to return it to its environment. After the eruption, she found its charred body with the beacon still operating. What choice would it have made if it could have understood? "Let nature take its course" was the rule then and wisdom now; but sadness still held her.

David, not snooping, but aware of her as always, prodded her to reduce the output multiplier of her emotive subroutines. *Silly*, she thought, she had left it on high from the lovemaking. She imagined a strong cup of coffee, and that chased the blues away. Contentment returned.

Long ago, unable to resolve the problem logically, they had simply decided that their place in things was to let the universe unfold *its* will and watch. But since it was their rule, and they were a hundred million years away from any human critics, they could make exceptions.

Curious, David and Ellen reconfigured themselves into a great conducting loop and soared in the plasma currents of the cluster, gently bending their path in an arc many billions of kilometers in radius toward the golden sun of the little blue world.

The data they gathered confirmed early hopes and fears; the world was inhabited. A race of gracile, vaguely avian centauroids lived in a metastable system of low-technology tribal cultures that, from the ruins they could see, had lasted for thousands of years. Cycles of conquest, decay, and rebirth would allow little progress toward the technology those beings would need to survive.

Reaching the star, they parachuted through its ionic wind, slowed to a planetary pace, and drank in the light of the star, giving trillions of trillions of tiny flywheels their fill. They felt powerful.

Then they sailed to a chance comet and devoured it as it bulled its way through the starwind back to its cryogenic lair. A year later, the comet was a shining sphere, composed almost entirely of their nanocell dopplegangers, and went off to convert some of its fellow comets to their purposes.

Thus, they built a great telescope system at the edge of the planetary system, to observe everything from gamma rays to quasistatic currents. Soon, the vast storehouse of memory that had followed them as photons would be collected again, augmented by news of home and beyond. And thirty million years from now, the great eyes and ears of the Milky Way would learn of their adventures and spread the word to the minds of a hundred billion worlds.

But that would have to wait. The nuclear weather inside the nearby massive star was as chaotic and unpredictable as rainy days in the Minnesota Augusts of David's childhood. If there was to be any data from the blue green world, they'd best get it with what they had while it was still alive.

With a fountain of ions, their machine pushed them toward the golden sun, and they curved through its solar wind to reach the life-world.

Modani saw the ruffians before they saw him, and had a bolt on his bow in the flick of a crest. Nonetheless, they continued to shadow him, racing along in the brush parallel to the road. *They could not keep that up and remain quiet*, he thought, and he broke into a light trot.

An arrow whistled by him, with the black and red feathers of Drua's cult. Superstitious mystics! Fear tugged at him. That group preached the strong should rule the weak, and resented the increasing influence of technicians. Which meant they would resent Modani, if they knew him.

*No*, he thought, *it was not so romantic when one who ground glass well stood equal with powerful warriors*. But most people were not warriors, and bit by bit, through the central council, the guilds had a crest-standing strength of their own.

Another arrow brought him back to reality; no guild help today! Enough of philosophy; more likely these hoodlums merely thought they had a right to his purse if they could take it. He'd been a racer in his youth and had kept up with it after a fashion on the odd rest day. The young ruffians would be surprised to see an oldster pick up the pace so!

As he did, they broke cover and scrambled after him. Indeed, they were mottle-crested young — but heavy with the indulgence of the undisciplined strong. He increased his distance, gauging his own endurance carefully. He could not, nor would he, run forever, so he looked for opportunities.

After a bend in the road, he spotted a large Athota plant circle — one of the trunks was down, making a door, and there were gaps between the trunks for shooting arrows. Excited by danger and angry with the degenerates, he dove into this natural blind before they rounded the bend and plotted his ambush.

They galloped along in clouds of dust, puffing with fatigue. They wheeled and reared, confused at his absence. Then they saw the Athota circle, but too late. He put a bolt into the flank of one of them and the neck of the other. *Maybe they would respect that!* he thought. At least they fled squawking, in pain.

Still nervous, but urgent in his errand, Modani left the Athota plant circle and continued down the road for Omphan in the fastest cursorial trot that he could sustain.

"Look," Ellen exclaimed. In the form of a flock of local avian life, their eyes turned to a fertile valley just north of the south polar glaciers, between two dramatic mountain ranges, one folded, the other volcanic, and they wheeled in the sky as one, descending to spy on its villages and farms. They drank in the smells and sights, the culture and language, the sounds and music. David dipped into his memory and relived the wonder of one who had seen thousands of crystal blue lakes ringed by great white pine trees in his youth, and could spend hours in contemplation of yet another.

While their conscious minds wondered, their myriads of subroutines were busy with the data coming in. Flying insects gave them the key to the biology of the land below, and samples of the blood of its dominant vertebrates. They saw a great stone temple with handwritten scrolls, and learned the world was called Li and the people, Tha-Li. They perched for days in the marketplace and the temple to learn its brand of wisdom. Then the flock that was David and Ellen flew out along an uncrowded path to the countryside, took the form of the visitors from a different part of Li and began walking back to the village.

Preoccupied with Sani and his burden of painkilling medicine — which some of Drua's cult might mistake for wealth to be plundered by the right of might — Modani had trotted well past a finely dressed Ixoran couple before he realized something was wrong. After a moment of indecision, he quickly retraced a few strides back to them: a silvercrest and a gold, decked out in folly. He would not have their blood on his conscience.

"Forgive me, Gentles, but you should not be seen out here like that. There are those around who would kill you for it!"

The couple clicked their beaks in surprise.

"Our apologies for whatever offense we have given, Gentleone," the silvercrest intoned. "We are new in this land, so please educate us to our danger, whoever you are."

It was Modani's turn to click in surprise at hearing such a natural Thocan accent from Ixorans. "I am called Modani, Gentles. But, the eastern cape you wear, with its high collar and cuts at each hip! And you are weaponless! Do not think your people's conquests have been forgiven by the followers of Drua's cult in these parts."

"We heard little of this in the town," the silvercrest said. "We came to study your people and thought we would most easily fit in as eastern visitors, whose questions would not seem too ignorant. This Drua is news to us. Do you credit his views yourself, Gentleone?"

"No," Modani replied softly, "I put my faith in chemists and in the school of experience. I think the change you easterners brought was healthy, but I am quiet about such views in the Thocan countryside! The livelihood of priests is threatened and their ambitions are not kept in check by fear of their own lies." He snorted in contempt. "But take no greater comfort in the fanatics who actually believe their cant; for, if anything, they are even more dangerous. Even I was pursued today, by bandits associated with Drua. Please disguise yourselves or you, and I, may be killed!"

Their crests rose in mild surprise. He blinked hard at such ignorance and flipped his own in condescension. Despite the cold, the couple shed their cloaks immediately, revealing fine linen shifts and rich woven back blankets with elegantly restrained silver embroidery, still a rich attractive nuisance, but not so obviously foreign. Something seemed to go between them as they momentarily touched hands, and this made Modani think poignantly of Sani.

He flicked his crest in an approving farewell and said, "Now Gentles, you must excuse me. I would talk, but my mate is deathly ill and I am bringing medicine," then turned to resume his journey.

Though David and Ellen, with the wisdom of ages at their disposal, discussed billions of options through parallel optical channels at near lightspeed, the question was simple:

*Would it bother the dance of the cosmos if we help?* Ellen asked. *Modani has befriended us, with no interference on our part, for a perfectly moral and sentient reason. That makes it different; a friend is not a specimen. This matters to me!*

*But the supernova!* David replied. *Why save someone now, only to have them die even more painfully of radiation poisoning? Or do we try to stop a supernova, too, and alter the evolution of an entire galaxy?*

*David, this galaxy will evolve anyway. Maybe not the same way, but so what? Anyway, by the laws of chaos, even the littlest conscious thing we do might eventually change things more than a supernova. Besides, delaying a supernova would be an interesting project. I'm not sure even we could do that!*

*There might be another way to handle the Supernova,* David replied, *but Modani and his people would have to be mentally strong enough to learn, very quickly, that the universe is much different than it has always been to them. We may have to destroy their culture to save their lives.*

*Perhaps not. The first step is Sani's illness. Let the new patterns form from there.*

"Pardon us, Gentle Modani. I am Daiffidi and my mate, Ellani," the silvercrest gestured to his companion, "is a physician of some ability, and I know a thing or two as well. Perhaps we could help you, who have been generous with your advice for us."

The gold moved her hands and produced a seaflyer by some conjurer's trick. Modani thought momentarily that these people were just the type of charlatans that should be avoided at all costs. But then the seaflyer quietly and purposefully flew on toward the hut. What conjurer could make it do that? Despite his rational philosophy, he did not dismiss the gods entirely; he had only a lack of evidence. But here might be evidence! He pranced nervously.

The one called Ellani read this tension and sang the song of jest. "Forgive my theatrics, Gentleone, but that bird was, well, part of me. It will look in on Sani to see if we need to make haste. Please don't worry; it only looks like magic. We have much to tell you, friend."

They claimed no magic, but what art could do that! "Much indeed!" he stammered, "But we should hurry."

Ellani only fluffed comfortingly. "Sani is asleep and does not suffer now."

*How could she know?* Modani wondered. But he led them at a normal pace.

Once at the hut, Daiffidi took up immediately with the young ones. Modani and Ellani went behind the rude curtain, where the gull perched on the rim of the sleep basket in which Sani curled. Ellani held out a hand. "Your lessons begin now, Gentleone."

Ellani displayed a posture of simplicity to him, and the bird flew to her hand.

It dissolved into a sphere of white and melted into her hand, which became empty as if the bird had never existed. It was too much.

Modani fell upon the floor and wailed in the minor key of abjection, his mental universe crashing down around him as he uttered the formulas he had learned as a youth. "Forgive my unbelief, I pray. Forgive my lack of sacrifices. It is my fault, not Sani's. Curse me, not the one who is faultless."

But the presumed god, Ellani, fluffed in disappointment and frustration, crest down in despair at his obeisance.

"No, no," she protested. "We are just very ancient people who have learned a few wonderful tricks through the ages."

Modani looked up, crest splayed in embarrassment.

Ellani smoothed it as a parent would a nestling's.

A thousand astronomical units away in the heart of the distended red star, nuclei roared from collision to collision like lions caged in desperately little space. The worst of these rattlings made their torturous way through dense stagnant plasma to the outer layers of the star. Free of the compressed core, the eruption burst forth and roiled the great distended atmosphere. Gas slopped gas over its gravitational border and spiraled onto its dying white dwarf companion.

A lesser star might have gone nova and blown off the excess in a self-extinguishing spasm, but this white dwarf was heavy and drank deep from its companion; the infalling hydrogen and helium sustained a stellar atmosphere thick enough for a gently pulsing fusion reaction. A few kilometers deeper, the helium ash of this fusion, fused into carbon, nitrogen, oxygen, and neon. Below that, the core of the white dwarf, already dangerously massive and degenerate, grew even heavier.

David and Ellen's telescopes noted the flickering, and updated their model. It could not be too long now — a billion seconds, perhaps.

Ellen saw Sani stir from her fog of pain. A brief ripple of uncertainty went through Sani's crest and Ellen took her hand from Modani's crest. "I'm afraid I've disturbed your mate."

The Tha-Li woman made a gesture of unconcern. "My pardon, Gentleone, but what did you do?"

Crest and featherfur rising in hopeful anticipation, Ellani produced and absorbed the seaflyer.

"Marvelous!" Sani even managed a chirp of delight. "How did you do it?"

A volume of infrared communication passed between Ellen and David in a millisecond; it was review — they had already made their decision.

"First," Ellen said, "we must be the greatest secret of your lives, because what we are and what we have would change the pattern of your race. So please hold all this down the gut. Understood?"

Modani nodded, but Sani's crest rose a bit.

"Would that be so awful? I knit, but while I dream of many patterns, only a few get finished. The children need to eat," she clicked apologetically. "I think what our culture might become on its own is like some big pattern in the future, which we may or may not finish. Is so abstract a thing worth the hunger of even one child?"

"It is a hard choice, Sani," Ellani agreed. "Yes, some pattern will develop regardless. But think of the millions of lives that have been spent through your history to get you this far. And look at your priests and kings; some are good men, no doubt, but would you trust most of their lot with the abilities we have? Or would you have us reign like gods, picking, choosing, disciplining and inevitably remaking you into our image?"

Sani's crest fell back. After a long silence, she said. "I understand. But I ask you, whatever you are, to pity the children who may die."

Ellani nodded gravely. "We promised we would save Sani, and that means save your world as well. It's a somewhat bigger project than you can now understand, but, Modani, if you and your family will keep our secret, we will do it."

Modani held still for several heartbeats to show contemplation, then flicked his crest in agreement.

Ellani's featherfur suggested motherly understanding. "And yes, Sani, we pity all those who suffer and die. We were once flesh and blood, just as you are..."

Everyone watched the operation, magnified and displayed on a large flat screen grown by David, who narrated for the wide-eyed tall-crested young ones.

Ellen laid a finger on Sani's tumor, and sent some of her nanocells in through the pores under Sani's featherfur. Using ultrasound, she found the nerves and blood vessels that served the tumor. At incredible speeds, her nanocell constructs severed and cauterized the vessels, starving the tumor. She found where the tumor was pressing Sani's spine, and busily ate it away, sending the debris into the waste removal vessels. Normal cells began dividing immediately to replace the tumor.

*Something in their past evolution prepared the Tha-Li for massive cell replacement.* David noted.

*Li is passing through a spiral arm and has drifted through young star clusters for millions of years*, she replied. *More than one supernova may have helped select survivors.*

Ellen made a special nanocell that included a diamond stylus to serve as her tool, and then, atom by atom, she charted the proteins of a cancer cell and found out how it was fooling Sani's immune system. She sent nanocells to the organ, which ran Sani's immunological defenses and made a few slight improvements. With their chemical blindfolds removed, Sani's own scavenger cells attacked the cancer cells with impressive efficiency.

Job done, Ellen's nanocells rushed back to her finger, and her host's beaks clicked with surprise and happiness.

"What," Sani inquired following all the congratulations, "is it like to have such powers?"

"It is," David answered, "like having an almost infinite set of choices and trying to decide what to do, or not do with them. You worry about the non-choices forever."

Sani's crest fell a bit. "You don't sound entirely happy," she clucked.

Ellen gently stroked the featherfur on Sani's forehead, and cooed. "Don't worry. We can tell ourselves to be happy, or even tell ourselves to just not think about it. Then everything is fine."

A thousand astronomical units away, another David and Ellen reformed themselves in the cells of their communications base. They shared anticipation. The best part of splitting themselves this way would be the thrill of discovery when they rejoined the selves still on Li. Being two places at once was nothing particularly new to them, but this would be a significant separation in distance.

They expanded the communications base's thermonuclear powerplant and diverted work to an ultra-efficient microwave transmitter with the capacity of thousands of terawatts. When it was done, David and Ellen formed themselves into netlike fabric, spread themselves in front of the beam and were thrown toward the incipient supernova by a blast of microwaves too big to pass through the tiny holes of their net.

The universe contracted all around, and the great angry red star, now blue-shifted into the x-ray spectrum, rushed toward them as their own tiny microscopic lasers twinkled, acting in unison to urge the odd atom or dust mote out of their way.

Even a hundred astronomical units out, David and Ellen saw that the space around the red giant was rich in matter. Approaching from the white dwarf side, the accretion disk looked like a dark line against the surface of the reddish giant star, except where it was closest to the white dwarf and hottest. To sensors shielded from the direct light of the stars, space was filled with the reddish glow of discarded atoms.

Many of these atoms were already ionized by the ultraviolet part of the white dwarf's spectrum, so, to their magnetic field, it was like falling into another pillow, or diving into molasses.

*It's going to be very, very close, David.*

*Yes; there is perhaps already enough mass in the accretion disk.*

*But not on the star itself. It's still below Chandrasekhar's Limit. If we were to ignite it now, in a nova, it would blow the disk and some of the companion's atmosphere away.*

*And there'd be a little time even after it passes the limit?*

*Maybe, Ellen. But the timing depends on things inside the white dwarf we cannot possibly know. We'll have to control things in real time.*

*Leave a relay?*

*Maybe...*

*I am not afraid,* they told each other.

The fall through the giant's hot sticky plasma breath toward their ticking cosmic time bomb would take years, but there was no help for that. It was, in fact, enough time for even their long lives to pass before them in detail.

Modani's crest stayed rigidly poised between up and down as Daiffidi explained the danger from the tiny red disk in the sky that did not move. The telescope made it easier, but still, it was a stretch of comprehension. What he grasped was that stars could explode in big ways and small ways, and that the tiny white speck next to the disk that did not move could explode in either way. It was particularly hard to understand that that tiny point was heavier than the huge red egg.

But he had no basis for questioning his benefactors as Daiffidi told them how to build shelters that would protect them if the star exploded in the small way. They would need to live underground as a separate sun scorched the land for a few weeks.

"We should survive that," Sani remarked, full of the confidence of restored health. "Especially if we take seed stock into the shelters with us."

Modani touched her bill with his. "I think there is more. Daiffidi, there is no guarantee, is there, that such preparations will be sufficient? In the worst case, if the star explodes the large way, what will it be like?"

For one of the few times in the year Modani had known him, Daiffidi hesitated. "There will be burning," he finally said. "The neutrinos themselves won't quite kill you this far away, but some of the atoms throughout your world will become radioactive. A gravitational wave will flex the planet. The temperature of your planet's mantle will increase a degree or so, almost instantly. Magma will start moving.

"A few days later, a blast will reach you. X-rays and Gamma rays will cascade into your upper atmosphere and it will appear to burn. A blast of photons will scorch your planet's surface. But no one will be here. In the far reaches of your planetary system, we are preparing a fleet to take you to a new world before that happens. You'll have a badly shocked culture, but better that then none at all."

But Modani resisted that thought. "What would happen if we stay with our ancestors?"

Daiffidi showed discomfort. "Things will seem to back off for a bit, but silent invisible and lethal particles will sweep through as the star dims to merely the brightness of another sun in your sky. Within a week of that the star will become a visible hairy globe that will increase in brightness again until, for several weeks, it floods you with a million times your own sun's brilliance. The deep sea shelters will last the longest, but we think the oceans may boil away, eventually. It will take years to dim; the planet's surface will be cleansed of everything."

So they would all become Daiffidi and Ellani's foundlings, shorn of their world, their history rendered quaint and meaningless. A great emptiness came over Modani.

"Don't give up hope yet," Ellani said.

David and Ellen fell on the moon of a subgiant planet in a delicate resonance orbit that skirted the edge of the red hot vacuum disk around the two stars. They began immediately to devour the moon. In an hour, their two hundred kilograms of nanocells became four hundred. In three days, they became as massive as a small moon themselves. They spread themselves out in a great sheet of matter, balancing between gravity and photons, shielding the planet from the glare of the star, drinking in the wind from the disk and channeled it down to the planet, using the energy of its fall to the surface to run a vast refrigerator, pumping heat out the other side.

In a month, the planet had gained enough mass to affect its orbit. In two months, the resonance was broken and it was on a trajectory that would take it first through the outer layers of the red giant and then onward toward the white dwarf.

On a crisp clear night, Modani watched the star and tried to imagine what was happening. He felt a confusion of feelings. Yes, he felt pride in the telescopes he had built that had shown exploding stars and discredited the cult of Drua, but that had been Daiffidi and

Ellani's knowledge. And he felt pride in the shelters built in caves and in great tubes on the sea floor. But he and Sani were too healthy and active for their age, something that had begun to attract notice as their friends passed on. Little by little, they had withdrawn and now kept to themselves and their small fields. Thus it was a surprise to have folk approach from out of the night. But caution turned to happiness when Daiffidi, Ellani, and Dosni identified themselves.

"The years treat you well, Gentleones," he greeted them, touching beaks with all.

"Ah, years ignore us, but you have fought them well. And Sani?"

"Still in the race, thanks to you. But we both see the finish line."

He brought them in, and helped Sani up off her blanket to let her touch beaks with neck unbent.

"We understand. That is what we've come to talk to you about. We think Dosni is well prepared to take over your duties. And we have a promise to keep."

"Ah, elders," Dosni said, "To speak of promises reminds me of my mate at home. But before I go, I have a request. You have told us you were once flesh and blood, like us. What did you look like?" Dosni's eyes reflected the sunset from the hut's single window, and so seemed to glow with curiosity. Modani flicked his crest in amusement at his son's insatiable thirst for the new.

"Do you promise not to be afraid?" Ellani replied — part in jest, Modani thought.

The young one's featherfur ruffled down in embarrassed assent.

"You too, Modani?" Ellani asked. He nodded. *What had he to fear?*

But, before his eyes, their perfect Li bodies melted into a hairless, fleshy-lipped, biped half again his size, with a bulging skull and odd flesh protuberances. He was prepared, intellectually, for the difference, the alienness. But he had been thoroughly imprinted with the old fears of devils, monsters and jealous gods as a young Li, and his featherfur fluffed out involuntarily, embarrassing him. In spite of himself, he backed away.

Dosni's crest was relaxed, however, and his eyes were bright and curious. He asked Daiffidi and Ellani many questions, which they answered without embarrassment, which Modani had always been too deferential to pose. But Modani made no effort to stay his son. His own reluctance to ask personal questions was the imprint of a more cautious time and a more stern upbringing.

"Father, I need to go back to my own house, now," Dosni said at last, long toward midnight. Modani nodded in assent. Dosni lived with his young mate a short trot down the trail, not a dangerous journey even in these times, and there was work to be done tomorrow.

So, to Modani's relief, Daiffidi and Ellani resumed their Li form and they all made farewells to Dosni. Afterwards, the four remaining friends went into Modani's house and settled down and pushed sucking needles through the skins of fermented tholfruit.

"What promise did you mean," Modani finally asked, slightly less inhibited and still unclear as to what Daiffidi's greeting statement had meant.

"We promised to save Sani's life," he answered, simply.

"But you did!" Sani chirped.

"For the tissue-thin slice of a world line. We can do much better than that, but there is a cost to an indefinite life span, which is very hard to explain. You must imagine yourselves going on without end, and ask yourselves if that is what you really want."

"I think I understand," Sani chirped in low, thoughtful tones, "that to live in such a manner is both its own blessing and its own curse. I know the blessing, but what is the curse?"

"There is," Ellen added softly, "some wisdom in your myth of a musician who wished for wings, and, having her wish granted, loved flying so much that she never used her hands again..."

"...and so became the mother of all flying things," Modani added. "I think I understand the dilemma. In fact, by just making the offer you have put us in it, have you not? For if we refuse now, our end becomes not simply an inevitability, but a form of suicide."

"My mate!" Sani interjected. "That's not fair to our friends. Daiffidi, we have suspected for some time that you could do this for us," her crest made an ironic half rise and settled, "or to us. And we have not asked. Someone could call that a form of suicide — being too polite to ask for our lives. Well, I am curious and want to know more than I have life in which to learn. How is it with you? What is the problem?"

"We all exist," Daiffidi said, "as patterns of data and logic, systems of input and output which can include biological parts or not. It doesn't matter as long as the same sensory input leads to the same conscious image. We can exist in any calculating machine that is large enough, and for Ellani and me, these assemblages of nanocells give us the greatest independent physical capability.

"We worry about why we keep going, whether our existence serves any significant purpose. Can anything in an infinite cosmos claim to be significant? We accumulate knowledge, but it all falls within known bounds — it is like numbering all the points on a line. But however pointless existence is, there never seems sufficient reason to *stop* existing." He flipped his crest in a yes-and-no gesture. "So we go on."

"It's a logical trap, really, but I doubt it is possible to appreciate the full complexity of it without having the logical resources we have."

"We shouldn't be too discouraging," Ellani added. "We don't worry when we don't want to worry, we don't feel sad if it isn't convenient, and we've had an awful lot of fun. This living forever isn't bad at all, but it is a decision you need to make, and, in our experience, it's a decision that doesn't get unmade."

Sani closed her eyes completely, then opened them again. "I'm not sure."

Modani's featherfur bristled again with memories of village stories about immortal ghouls that sucked life fluids from the living like juice from a tholfruit. "Gentleones," he said, "I am overcome. Forgive me if I absent myself a moment for nature and to find the rightful place for my featherfur."

Everyone nodded at him and he left the group to be alone in his garden for a few moments, fertilizing this and that. He told himself over and over that this strange offer was from his dearest friends. Sani and he could live forever. But at a price — a price that would clearly mean giving up much of what he thought he knew about life. Could he do that? Could he embrace such a strange future?

The larger moon hung low in the east, a bright crescent the size of a child's kicking ball held at arm's length; they had stayed up late and the sun would soon rise. Modani had no trouble in seeing the craters and mountains on the back side, nor the minuscule disks of the nearer wanderers; it was as if there was more light. His hindquarters shifted involuntarily and his crest rose.

Slowly he looked up. The tiny red disk which did not move was now a brilliant beacon, a searing point of light in the west that cast its own shadow.

Keeping himself as calm as he could, he turned toward the house and called out.

"Sani. Gentleones, it has started..."

A white dwarf is a small target. Tides stretched the planet one way and squeezed in another. Great magnetic fields formed and whipped up an uncontrollable magnetic storm. Radiation from both sides lanced through David and Ellen faster than they could repair themselves. Still they fought to keep it on course.

The dwarf flared and the planet broke, disrupted as billions of atmospheres of pressure blasted through its ends. All became plasma, trapped in fields beyond any control. There would be no escape. To preserve themselves for a few more moments, they contracted to an essential core and used the mass and energy of their dying outer layers to cool the inner layers.

*Have we succeeded, David?*

*I think so, but it all depends on how advanced the dwarf's core is, and how much matter we will blow away from it.* Thoughts were harder now, as cells struggled to contain damage and redundant pathways were lost.

*We are evaporating*, Ellen observed. *It seems strange. I wish we could send this experience to the other David and Ellen.*

*If we could, we would send ourselves. Since we can't, the logic is that we accept what must happen, and enjoy it. I think they will understand and be happy for us. Since we are them, we would understand in their place. That is all they need to know; that it can be done. They will know that... that last logical barrier to will can be broken.*

*David, I'm losing memories. I'll hold onto you until the last.*

*And I will hold onto you. So, after a hundred million years, to end. I am at peace. And free. Free... Farewell.*

*Farewell.*

Photons ran rampant inside the white dwarf, chipping off pieces of nuclei here and there, which were gobbled up by larger, more stable nuclei. Here, a neon nucleus collided with a helium nucleus head on, and before they could disentangle themselves, a neutron stole away with their excess energy, and a magnesium nucleus was born.

An iron core started to form, the harbinger of catastrophe imminent. Iron had no excess energy to give in support of the hungry masses pressing upon it. The star began to shrink, compress, and burn hotter. Soon the remaining nuclear fuel would detonate. Immediately. Devastatingly.

But on the surface, triggered by the disintegrating planet with far more hydrogen and helium than the white dwarf could digest in its usual incremental manner, another explosion was already in progress, throwing matter out and away. A glowing cloud, bright as a million suns, fled out from the white dwarf. The influx stopped. The star stopped growing, poised on the brink of disaster.

On Tha-Li, four beings watched the sky.

"You should go to the shelters," Daiffidi said.

Modani's beak dipped to him in negation. "We have agreed to leave the space for younger Tha-Li. I feel, one way or another, we are done with this world. Now, tell me. The travels we have made with you, the gardens we have grown together, the troubles we have taken to fend off robbers without killing them," Sani asked. "If we became like you, would we remember all of this?"

"Yes, you will," said Ellen, "and more, much more."

They were silent for a long time, watching the new sun burn. Then Sani's crest raised slowly in a coy humor. "Will I be able to mate again with my Modani?"

Ellen smiled. "For eternity, if you want."

Her crest rose high, her eyes went open and bright. "Then, yes, take us with you."

# STORY NOTES:

The title of this story comes from that Michelangelo painting in the Sistine Chapel where his representation of God reaches down and touches his representation of Man with a single finger. Being immersed in the then-current dreams of nanotechnology, I imagined trillions of nanobots running through the finger into Man to make him more Godlike.

This story was first published in an anthology, *The Age of Reason*, edited by Kurt Roth, at SFF.net in 1999. In addition to making supernova astrophysics an experimental science it touches on some of the "big issues," like "what does it all mean?" and "where are we going?"

I was asked to briefly elaborate on some of the science in the story. Hopefully the following will prove useful, or at least point people in the right direction.

*"A hundred thousand years before Sani's cancer took hold, the great blue disk and ultraviolet arms of the majestic Whirlpool galaxy filled David Martin's field of view."*

The Whirlpool galaxy is about 23 million light years away, south of the tip of the Big Dipper's handle. It is about half the mass of the Milky Way and 70% of its diameter. Assuming David is traveling near the speed of light, he is only a little more distant from the galaxy than the visible spiral is wide. Google "Whirlpool galaxy."

*"Orienting the superconducting loops in every nanocell of his body..."*

David and Ellen's personalities reside in a swarm of trillions of trillions of "nanocells." These are conceived to be roughly the size of biological cells, but made of much sturdier stuff, and not permanently specialized. Linked as a data processing system, they form a supercomputer. As a physical system, the cells can join each other in almost any imaginable configuration. Read Kurzweil's *The Singularity is Near*, and project.

*"...he tacked against the faint plasma breeze of the galaxy's central black hole, gradually bending his path toward his chosen decelerator."*

*"Curious, David and Ellen reconfigured themselves into a great conducting loop and soared in the plasma currents of the cluster..."*

When a charged particle (the "plasma breeze") encounters a magnetic field, it is deflected one way, and, action equaling reaction, the object generating the field is pushed in the other. A current loop creates a magnetic field with a north and south pole, much like a bar magnet's.

*"Most of a billion years of experience was set carefully aside from conscious thought so that they could enjoy real-universe sensation again."*

David and Ellen can turn off their Emulated emotions, when inconvenient. In this case, the fun of experiencing something anew can be lived over and over. Later on, they must turn off the fear of death to finish their mission.

*"As they left the region, they reformed themselves into a thousand telescopes, which they spread into a globular constellation a hundred million kilometers across; a giant's eye..."*

David and Ellen can see Sani's world by forming a large optical synthetic aperture telescope. The wider the telescope, the smaller the objects it can see. For the mathematically inclined,

$$R \approx 1.22 \; L/A$$

where R is the resolution in radians. L is the wavelength of light and A is the telescope aperture. (Be sure to use the same units for L and A if you use this!) To get actual size, rather than the angular size, multiply by the distance to the object. In visible light (a wavelength of 500 nm, or 5 E-7 m), a one-meter-wide telescope would be able to resolve objects 5 E-7 radians apart, for instance, a one-meter spot at 50,000 m. A 100 million-kilometer-wide telescope (1E11 m) might resolve 5 km sources at 100,000 light years. That's ideally — the source must provide enough photons for all the elements of the array to combine, which limits this trick to bright objects.

*"There! An old ruddy, overinflated windbag of a star circled a white dwarf grown heavy from the giant's effluvia. If it grew heavy enough, it would explode as a supernova..."*

The white dwarf would become a "Type Ia" supernova. Wikipedia has a good article.

Very massive stars form ultra-dense iron cores by fusion reactions of lighter elements. The cores collapse when they become more massive than Chandrasekhar's Limit (Google "Chandrasekhar"), about 1.4 solar masses, starting a process that leads to a supernova explosion and a neutron star remnant. The Supernova we saw in the Magellanic cloud in 1987 was this kind of an explosion.

A Type Ia may not go quite that way. A Type Ia supernova starts out as a white dwarf a little less than Chandrasekhar's Limit which then gains mass — generally hydrogen and helium from a nearby companion star that is losing mass in its red giant stage. This forms a layer on top of the carbon and oxygen "ash" from previous fusion reactions. As the white dwarf gets close to Chandrasekhar's Limit, the picture gets unclear. But the fusion reactions that create heavier elements may happen all at once in a thermonuclear explosion that "deflagrates" the star before it can collapse into a neutron star. Since this always happens at about the same mass, and produces supernovae of about the same brightness (about 5 billion times solar luminosity at peak), Type 1a supernovae can be used as "standard candles" to gauge the size of the universe. Google "standard candles."

*...before they had moved out of the Mind of Mars to seek adventure in the real cosmos with nanocell bodies.*

In this future history, the *Mind of Mars* is a supercomputer in the moon Phobos in which billions of human-descended Martians live as computer programs in virtual worlds of their own choosing. They can go back and forth from biological, or other technological bodies, at will. It's mentioned in "Morning on Mars" in *After the Vikings: Tales of Future Mars* (variationspublishing.com).

*Close enough to the orange star for heavy tides, it had a large moon locked in synchronous orbit of about a day and a half. The star's gravity tried to stretch the system, adding orbital energy which the tides in the planet's ocean tried to take away, pounding on its continents — neither, David thought, would win their argument in the lifetime of the orange-tinted star.*

Imagine our moon in a geosynchronous orbit like communications satellites! We wouldn't have the twice daily lunar tides, but we would still have solar tides, which are about half as strong. Modani's world is closer to its dimmer, but not that much less massive, sun. Its solar tides are about as strong as our combined lunar and solar tides.

*Reaching the star, they parachuted through its ionic wind, slowed to a planetary pace, and drank in the light of the star, giving trillions of trillions of tiny flywheels their fill.*

A nanoscale flywheel composed of a single molecule is very strong per unit weight and can store much more energy per unit weight than any conceivable chemical battery.

*We may have to destroy their culture to save their lives.*

When nuclear scientist Enrico Fermi realized that both alien civilizations and interstellar travel were at least physically possible, if not easy, he asked his famous question: "Where are they?" One possible answer is that they are or have been here, but are very careful to avoid disturbing our culture — the way a human scientist might try to not interfere with a colony of chimpanzees. In *Star Trek* lore, this is called "the Prime Directive." As any aliens that might encounter us would be millions, if not billions, of years beyond us technologically, if they don't want to be seen, they won't be.

*"Daiffidi told them how to build shelters that would protect them if the star exploded. They would need to live underground as a separate sun scorched the land for a few weeks."*

To prevent the supernova, David and Ellen must trigger an "ordinary" nova, burning away the hydrogen and helium accumulating on the surface of the white dwarf. The result will be in the top range of ordinary nova luminosity, around a million Suns.

*"...In the worst case, if the star explodes the large way, what will it be like?" ...The first radiation to escape the star will be neutrinos... The temperature of your planet's mantle will increase a degree or so, almost instantly. Magma will start moving.*

Maybe.

The nuclear reactions in the current model of a Type Ia supernova would still produce a lot of neutrinos, though maybe not as much as a core collapse. I've gone a bit beyond what I can show quantitatively here, though we have to allow some new astronomical discoveries to the hundred million years or so between our time and the story's! For instance, what would the axion (a hypothesized dark matter particle) output of a Nova be?

*"...seconds later, a blast of photons will scorch your planet's surface..."*

There should be a gamma ray burst as the shock wave reaches the white dwarf's surface. The "star" rapidly expands and, over the next few weeks, a huge ball of vaporized and highly radioactive nickel and iron will provide most of the energy. Big explosions take big time.

*But no one will be here; In the far reaches of your planetary system, we are preparing a fleet to take you to a new world before that happens. You'll have a badly shocked culture, but better that then none at all."*

Moving an entire planet's population to somewhere in space is not an exercise for those afraid of big numbers. But, when one does the math instead of arguing from personal incredulity, it isn't impossible at all. Look, for instance, at the aircraft and ship production numbers achieved in World War II without even robotics to help! At this point, I'd like to recommend a couple of Arthur C. Clarke stories on this theme, *Rescue Party* and *The Star*.

I'll end with a graph of the luminosity of a supernova versus an ordinary nova versus days since the explosion. The left scale is in absolute magnitude — Google "absolute magnitude" for the Wikipedia article. The right scale is a log scale of luminosity with the sun equal to one.

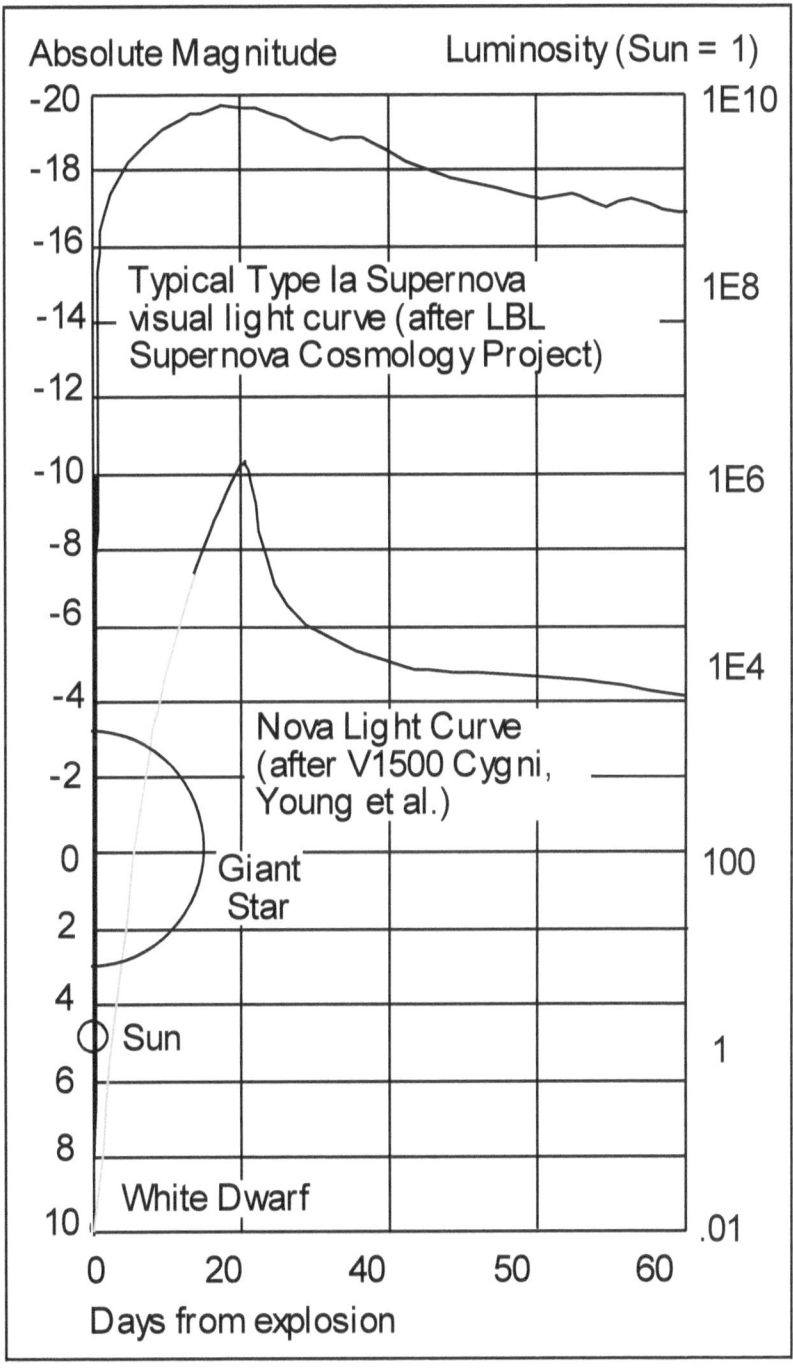

Absolute Magnitude      Luminosity (Sun = 1)

Typical Type Ia Supernova visual light curve (after LBL Supernova Cosmology Project)

Nova Light Curve (after V1500 Cygni, Young et al.)

Giant Star

Sun

White Dwarf

Days from explosion

# WHAT PART OF ETERNITY?

It took Dimitri Cardinal Osarian several seconds to take in the change of his environment, after which he became thoroughly distraught. He had been lying on his death bed, having refused nourishment for forty days and forty nights. The next moment he was here, fully nourished and seemingly unaffected.

He saw an ordinary room around him with a large window overlooking a wooded landscape. He sat on an ordinary chair with soft tan upholstery. It smelled almost unbearably clean. Hospital clean?

His body felt like it had most of his life. Was it material or a simulation? How did one tell? If real, was it flesh and blood? Or was it those accursed nanocells? He momentarily considered biting himself hard enough to draw blood, but realized that experience could be simulated, too.

Dimitri shuddered, asked for forgiveness, then attempted to touch the net.

The net did not respond, but there was a knock on his door

"This is not supposed to happen," he screamed. "Let me rest in peace. Let me be with God!"

"May we come in?" a young woman's voice said.

"As if I have any choice in the matter," he grumbled.

The door slid open revealing a blonde woman and an alien that looked vaguely like a flightless parrot, both wearing white muumuus decorated with flowers he did not recognize. A blindingly white, featureless corridor lay behind them.

"I'm Ellen and this is Sani. Yes, we are all material, not cybernetic, not virtual. It is about eight hundred trillion years since you were last conscious. We're with the reclamation project."

"Reclamation? I don't want to be reclaimed." Then it hit him. "Did you say eight hundred *trillion* years?"

"Yes."

"This isn't heaven, or hell." Dimitri said that as if he were certain, but still in the back of his mind was that his method of leaving what humanity had become might, despite the absolution given by the church, be considered sinful by a higher power.

"This is not a supernatural place," Sani said, not quite answering the question.

"What does God have to say about this?"

Sani's expression was unreadable to him, but Ellen smiled.

"Perhaps *you* will tell *me*, later. Dimitri, we will respect your wishes, but the Whole has decided to let every conscious being whoever was make an informed choice."

Dimitri looked at Sani. She, if it was a she, was not one of the three intelligent species humanity had interacted with up to the time he had finally decided to stop making accommodations and go to God. Resolution faltered in the face of curiosity.

"How many?"

"Approximately ten to the twentieth individuals in ten to the eleventh species, counting hive species as individuals," Sani answered.

"In our gravitational bubble," Ellen added.

Gravitational bubble? Dimitri remembered that cosmologists had speculated that the universe was expanding under the influence of something called dark energy, but that gravity could resist that expansion locally if there was enough matter, enough being something like a cluster of galaxies.

"Isn't everything supposed to die out, use up the hydrogen and everything else and experience a heat death?" But he knew the answer to that one almost as soon as he said it. He was in the hands of beings that did not accept death. Of course. Those who did would be already dead. These would not understand the choice of those who did accept it. He sighed. So much the change, so much the same thing.

"We can draw unlimited energy from the process of expansion itself." Sani said.

"Unlimited?"

Ellen nodded. "Of course, things need to be arranged, balanced and so on. The energy we collect has a mass equivalent, so the gravitational bubble expands. The density is maintained at the right level to avoid a collapse but does constrain the rate of addition of new consciousnesses. Eternity achieved, the Whole are now working on time and the possibility that we may need to create ourselves."

Dimitri started to say "Blasphemy!" but a feeling of great unease came over him. God had never spoken to him, and Dimitri had never known exactly what God was, the way one knows what a bicycle is. He had trusted his feelings, his scriptures, and his authorities — even as he became one himself — believing and loyal but not knowing. He should find a little more humility in himself in these circumstances, and obtain more information. God works in mysterious ways. What they told him seemed entirely too close to prophecy.

"Why the reclamation project now?" Mozart went through his head; Dies Irae.

"Everything had to be worked out, "Sani said. "Before the reclamation projects started, to be sure there would be room. There will be, and the Whole are bringing back as many beings as possible."

The Whole? Now Mussorgsky's music entered Dimitri's mind, with an image of a gigantic demon pulling diaphanous souls from the graveyard to dance for his pleasure. Disney as prophecy?

"What is, uh are, 'the Whole'?"

"Essentially, the consensus of all beings in this gravitational bubble. As you can imagine, with lightspeed delays, it takes a while to come to any conclusion as a Whole, but it delegates."

That process was not totally unfamiliar to Dimitri, though on a much smaller scale. Some people, Unitarians probably, would equate this 'whole' with God. But not Dimitri. Not yet, anyway.

"How... was I, uh, reclaimed?"

"It is, essentially, a fitting process. The project takes all the information available on the subject; its genetics, its writings, the records of others, images and so on, and then creates a model. It runs simulations until the model, essentially, duplicates the behaviors of the original. In your case, the information available was substantial."

"I didn't write everything down." Dimitri crossed himself and tried to remember the first time he had masturbated. While he could recall the unholy feeling of the act, and even who he had been thinking about in his later episodes, he could not remember the first time. "I'm not all there. You have failed. This is a zombie you are talking to. Let it go!"

Sani clucked, not entirely unlike a chicken, Dimitri thought, though more complex. It might have been something in the alien's native language, possibly an expression of exasperation. He was, perhaps, being overbearing, a frequent sin of his, and one that indicated this zombie was not too far off its mark. But surely he could be forgiven some irritation under the circumstances! His final wishes had been denied.

With her feathers back in place, Sani replied. "In time, perhaps. Some memories are, of course, forever lost, but that was true while you were alive as well; for instance, your species sleeps and never has everything when it wakes that it had going into sleep. Does your experience feel any different in that respect? Ellen and I have, perhaps, been through so many changes in form and so many long sleeps, that it seems very simple and natural to us."

"Our memories are well backed up, of course," Ellen added.

Dimitri shook his head. They would never understand. But perhaps there was a higher authority. Not that he, in his zombie form, could have much influence. Or could he? Did the Church still exist? There must be others like him. The only sure way to failure is not to try. "How long has this reclamation project been going on? Can it be stopped?"

While Ellen's smile did not waver, Sani's feathers fluffed momentarily. Was that a sign of the alien's irritation?

"It is almost complete, Cardinal Osarian," Ellen answered evenly. "We saved the hardest cases for last. We'll enable the net for you shortly and you'll be able to learn as much, or little as you feel you need to make your decision."

"I already made it!" Dimitri shouted.

"Uh, your *informed* decision," Ellen said in a way that tried to communicate the weight of hundreds of trillions of years' worth of additional information.

A valid point, Dimitri conceded, to himself.

"But first," Ellen continued. "I would like you to meet our mates and someone who has been asking to see you."

Unholy curiosity got the better of him again, as well as a remembrance of the virtue of forbearance that was expected of his long-ago office.

"Very well." It struck him that zombie him was a conscious being. Whether that being should be called Dimitri Cardinal Osarian was a matter of some question, but, 'I think, therefore I am.' Then he thought about all those simulations that were run to "fit" to him. Would they not have been as conscious? And all simply turned off to try again? Where was the morality in that? Of course, he had turned himself off. He had fought against the technology that had prevented many natural deaths, and then ended up using it himself, after countless people had died believing that they had taken the moral course as a result of his teachings. Others had called him Cardinal Death. He asked forgiveness again.

The door slid open to reveal three beings — a man, another flightless parrot, and... an angel, whose wings brushed the top of the door. He recognized the latter immediately, though she was clothed in a white dress with a bib that tied behind her neck. Ellen kissed the man as the two aliens touched their beaks.

Ellen introduced them. "Dimitri Cardinal Osarian, this is my husband David, Sani's mate, Modani, and someone I believe you know."

He stood up, and immediately recognized that the room was in the gentle lunar gravity that he'd become used to. Fortunately, he caught the arms of the chair to make his rise somewhat less undignified.

"Sister Annette."

"Just Annette now, Dimitri."

"Have you just been... ah, reclaimed?"

She laughed musically. "No, I have been active the entire time, though most of that was in travel stasis." She held out her arms to him and he went to her as though drawn by a force even his iron will could not resist.

"God forgive me," he said, through tears.

She stroked his back, lightly. "God has. I have. Now, you must forgive yourself. You don't want to feel guilty forever."

"Forever?"

She laughed. "Dimitri, what part of 'eternity' do you not understand?"

Visit
briefcandlepress.com
to read about the author,
the science behind some of his stories,
and upcoming publications